The Le

Book 1: Maid for the Billionaire

Book 2: For Love or Legacy

Book 3: Bedding the Billionaire

Book 4: Saving the Sheikh

Book 5: Rise of the Billionaire

Book 6: Breaching the Billionaire

Sign up for the mailing list at RuthCardello.com to be notified as soon as Breaching the Billionaire is available.

Rise of the

Billionaire

By Ruth Cardello

Print cover by Calista Taylor

Author Contact
Website: RuthCardello.com
Email: Minouri@aol.com
Facebook: Author Ruth Cardello
Twitter: RuthieCardello

Dedication:

I am so grateful to everyone who was part of the process of creating Rise of the Billionaire. Thank you to:

Calista Taylor for designing the covers for my series.

My very patient beta readers: Karen Lawson, Heather Bell, Marion Archer, Yeu Kue, and Kathy Dubois—who read multiple versions of the same chapters until I felt they were right.

My editors: Karen Lawson, Janet Hitchcock, and Nina Pearlman.

Melanie Hanna, for helping me organize the business side of publishing.

Brendan Hanna and Tony Archer, for help with Jeremy's computer lingo.

Tory Alyson McCord, for helping me choose a suit style for Jeremy.

My Roadies, whose kindness and support often bring out my sloppily grateful and sometimes tearful side.

And, finally, to my readers: Two years ago, when my teaching job was once again cut because of budget issues, I was afraid. Since then, publishing my romances has not only given me more time with my children, but it has also given me a more stable means to support my family. I cannot thank you enough.

Oh, and last, but not least...

Thank you to my husband, Tony, who listens to the story so many times he dreams about the characters. I love you, hon.

A note to my readers:

Ray Denton is a completely fictional character. His bad behavior in no way represents what an actual first boxing lesson would be like, how a professional trainer would behave, or the author's opinion of boxers.

CHAPTER *One*

SECOND THOUGHTS DON'T belong in a boxing ring.

Jeremy Kater held his ground even as his head snapped back beneath the gloved fist of the man he'd hired to teach him the basics of boxing. What had seemed like an essential component of his transformation was proving to be more painful than he'd anticipated.

He had just raised his gloves to try and block the next hit to his face when his opponent took advantage of the movement and punished his unprotected abdomen with enthusiasm. Ray Denton was a legend in the world of boxing. Not only had he reigned as the world champion heavyweight boxer for several years during his youth, but after his retirement he had gone on to train more than one fighter who had won the same title.

You'd think that a man like that would be happy to give beginner lessons for a generous fee. However, convincing Ray to work with an amateur had been no easy feat. But Jeremy wasn't a quitter. He'd countered every refusal with an offer of more compensation until he'd reached a number that Ray hadn't been able to dismiss.

Years of playing Mighty Punch-Out on his vintage game console hadn't prepared him for the reality of a trained professional. Nor had his one actual fistfight during his senior year of high school given him any skill when it came to breaching the defenses of the man who was currently dancing around him, easily blocking his punches, and landing almost every one of his physical rebuttals.

Another swing, another miss, another failed attempt to block what felt like a sledgehammer to his skull. Jeremy shook his head to clear it. The room spun and tilted. He took a step back to steady himself.

I probably should have waited until after the first lesson to pay him, Jeremy thought. *At least he would have had incentive to make sure I survived it.*

He'd expected his first lesson to include agility work, maybe some shadowboxing. He'd read how boxers used uppercut bags and speed bags to work on resistance. He'd even looked forward to an introductory light sparring match.

This was something entirely different.

The next well-placed hit sent Jeremy to his knees. He sat back on his heels, braced himself, and gasped for air. Ray's face twisted with satisfaction, and Jeremy saw the ugly truth in his eyes.

He wants me to fail.

He thinks I don't belong here.

He's wrong.

Regaining his footing, Jeremy adjusted his headgear, clamped his teeth down on his mouth bit, raised his hands, and swung, a bit wildly, at his opponent. But Ray was too fast for him. Two quick jabs and a cross sent Jeremy stumbling backward against the rope of the ring. Whatever Herculean strength he'd hoped would surface in response to this beating was sadly absent. Even the sting of the blows lessened as they became more severe and his body weakened. His new challenge was no longer his opponent but a growing numbness.

Before he could pull himself off the ropes, a blur of feminine fury flew past him and took a protective stance in front of him.

Jeisa. Barely as tall as the boxer's shoulders and chicly dressed in a sleeveless black jumper, oversized sunglasses, and high heels, his image consultant looked ridiculously out of place in the ring. She flipped her thick, dark mane of hair over one shoulder and waved a hand aggressively at Ray, who seemed momentarily surprised into inaction. Her normally light Brazilian accent thickened as she said, "Stop! He's had enough."

Jeremy pushed himself off the ropes. Although he appreciated her concern, he didn't want her in the ring. This was between Ray and him. Jeisa may have been able to advise him in many other areas of his ongoing transformation, but not in this one.

He didn't expect her to understand why he needed to be here.

He didn't expect anyone to.

Ray looked Jeisa over, whistled in appreciation, and said, "You're one lucky bastard."

Jeisa stepped closer to the boxer and snarled, "And you are a poor example of a trainer."

As Ray's jaw tightened at her evaluation, Jeremy quickly intervened. He put a gloved hand on one of Jeisa's shoulders and turned her around gently. "I told you not to come, Jeisa. This doesn't involve you."

Jeisa spun fully on Jeremy. She gripped his arm and said urgently, "If you want self-defense classes, I can sign you up for karate or something less violent."

In a mocking tone, Ray said, "You should listen to your girlfriend."

"She's not my girlfriend." *This is for Alethea.*

The trainer's eyebrows lifted as he assessed Jeisa for a second time. He winked at her and drawled, "Then maybe she'll be mine."

Something in the man's tone made Jeremy straighten to his full height. A rush of adrenaline seared through him. He met and held Ray's eyes. Without glancing down at Jeisa, Jeremy ordered, "Jeisa, get out of the ring."

"But..." she said.

"Get out."

With obvious reluctance, Jeisa slid between the ropes back to the area around the ring. "Fine," she said, "kill yourself if you want to. You're right—I shouldn't have come. I'm leaving." But she didn't. He knew she wouldn't.

A dark emotion he didn't take the time to identify surged within him, and he went at Ray with renewed force. Ray saw him coming, but he underestimated the momentum his nearly beaten opponent had mustered. Jeremy landed one punishing hit to the boxer's face.

The two men circled each other. Jeremy met the boxer's aggression with his own. Ray might knock him out, but he would not force him to back down. Ray threw a punch at Jeremy's abdomen. Jeremy surprised him by blocking him and then retaliating. His punch connected and set the boxer back a step.

Then everything changed.

Ray's face went red with fury. Trainer turned fighter, and Jeremy prepared himself for what he knew was going to be a very painful rebuttal. Heaving for air, Jeremy planted his feet with determination. There'd been times in the past when he'd allowed the opinions of others to hold him back.

This was not one of those times.

Jeisa Borreto gripped the back of a wooden chair in the dingy South Boston gym to stop herself from hopping back into the ring. The man who called himself a trainer was clearly on a sadistic ego trip, and Jeremy seemed not only to recognize that fact but also to accept it.

Still, the smell of sweat and the sound of fierce exhalations were both incredibly intimidating and disturbingly exciting at the same time. Her own adrenaline was coursing through her, making it impossible for her to look away even when she knew the fight was only going to become more painful to watch.

She jumped when Jeremy's punch connected and Ray's head snapped back. Normally she didn't condone violence, and she was definitely not a fan of this sport in particular, and yet her heart was racing and she felt as if Jeremy's triumph was her own. Was this the high the Romans had sought when they pitted man against beast? Although Jeremy's chance for survival seemed as slim as that of a gladiator, he blocked Ray's next hit and landed another of his own.

Jeisa surprised herself by cheered him on out loud. *What would my father say if he could see me now?* A ghost of a smile flitted across her lips at the thought. *He'd think I've finally lost my mind.* He was already reeling from what he considered her mid-twenties rebellion. She really couldn't blame him. She'd gone to the private schools he'd sent her to without issue. She'd even graduated with a degree in International Relations from the University of São Paulo. She'd been raised to follow the rules, maintain a blemish-free public persona, and blend into the background like a beautiful painting—cherished, but silent.

Was it wrong to want more than the comfortable life he'd given her? If her father had had his way, she'd be married to some wealthy Brazilian businessman, spending the rest of her life being pampered and protected.

Sheltered.

Smothered.

I don't want my only decisions to revolve around who will sit together at the dinner parties I host for some highly successful and equally boring husband.

Life has to be about more than that.

She'd decided to get a job and show her father that she was perfectly capable of supporting herself, but finding employment after the influential Romario Borreto made it known that he didn't want his daughter working wasn't easy. Out of desperation, she'd looked beyond the borders of Brazil and outside of her educational background. No one was willing to take a chance on a foreign unknown—until she found an au pair position through an international classified ad. Not her ideal job, but a way to pay the bills until she found something better.

With her bags packed and with an equal share of enthusiasm and naïveté, she'd flown to Boston, imagining the hardest part of her new life would be acclimating to the cold New England weather. She'd made many American friends at school but had lost touch with most of them when they'd moved back to the States. Still, she'd dreamed of living in America since she was little—Boston in particular. It was as romantic and exotic to her as Paris.

No one would know her. For the first time in her life she could be simply Jeisa. She didn't worry about being alone since she'd be living with an American family.

An ideal way to get to know the culture while hunting for a better job.

Except for one minor detail.

Reese David, the man who'd hired her as a nanny for his family, hadn't mentioned that he wasn't married. *And, oh yes, he didn't have any children.*

Stranded in Boston and unwilling to call home for help, Jeisa had done what many young people do when they apply for their first job. She'd lied.

Lied well, apparently, because she'd landed an entry-level secretarial job at Corisi Enterprises. But even with miles between them, her father left her little room to breathe. He called once a day. So, unwilling to tell him about the nonexistence of her first job, she'd lied once a day—the stories growing like weeds between her and her father until she could no longer see a way around them.

Too late to confess.

I should have spilled the truth before I named the imaginary children.

Definitely before I gave them hobbies and personalities.

If lies were pennies, she'd surely earned her way to hell a few times over already.

I'm no better than Reese. Well, I'm not a sexual predator trying to take advantage of women I lure away from their families with false promises—so perhaps I'm a bit better.

Still, I'm a liar, and there is always a price to pay for being dishonest.

Jeisa winced as Jeremy's brief success enraged the old fighter. Guilt weighed heavily upon her. *It's my fault he's here. A professional wouldn't have allowed him to come. But I'm not a professional—I lied about that, too. If only life were like an*

Etch A Sketch that could be shaken and erased when you drew yourself into a real mess.

I don't want to lie anymore. I don't want to pretend to be someone I'm not. I thought I was better than this, stronger than this.

Did I ever tell you about how my first client died? Yes, he had this ridiculous idea that learning how to box would toughen him up, so he hired a trainer and got himself killed during his first lesson.

Why didn't I stop him?

Well, that's a funny story... one that took Jeisa momentarily back to how she'd gotten what some might call her third job in the United States.

"I don't know anything about being an image consultant," Jeisa remembered clearly telling Mrs. Duhamel. However, denying the matriarch of Corisi Enterprises was as productive as telling the wind not to blow. Always impeccably dressed, she was a maternal force of nature. She knew the names of everyone in the company's Boston building, and they certainly knew her. Everyone stood a little straighter, smiled a little more pleasantly, and typed a little faster when Mrs. Duhamel entered the room.

All that information would have been helpful to know the first week on the job, when Jeisa had stepped into the hallway during a break in what was a particularly harsh, albeit well-deserved, discussion regarding her job performance.

Having typed papers and passed her college courses, Jeisa had figured she could easily handle an office job. And the computer programs they'd asked if she knew how to use? Could a person be blamed for optimistically believing she'd be able to master them before anyone noticed her complete lack of exposure to them?

Really, what was one more little lie when you were bathing in an ocean of them already?

It was a reason for dismissal, at least as far as her supervisor had been concerned. He'd started a conversation that had likely been leading to her termination when he'd been cut off by a phone call, and she'd been sent to the hallway outside his office while he took it.

If only she could go back in time and tell herself not to offer help to the older woman she'd seen carrying a parcel into an elevator. *I should have been fired, called my father with a confession, and worked my way out of this malfeasance.*

Instead, I'm here, watching a good man get a beating because I haven't worked up the nerve to tell him the truth yet.

Why did Mrs. Duhamel—Marie, Jeisa corrected herself mid-thought—*choose me to help Jeremy? Why did I say yes?* The second question was easy to answer. No one refused a request from Marie, not even when the very formidable woman asked to be addressed by her first name. And no one lied to her. With those sharp hazel eyes and a few pointed questions, she'd wrung Jeisa's life story and every last embarrassing truth out of her. Right down to lying about her job qualifications. Instead of firing her, Marie had laid a sympathetic hand on hers and ordered tea, and a friendship was born.

A friendship that had changed everything, even things she hadn't wanted to change.

Her supervisor no longer cared when she couldn't complete a project; instead, he would ask others to input the files he'd assigned her, replacing that work with typing. On one hand it was a relief to be given a job she could do. On the other, it distanced her from her coworkers, whose once-friendly banter evaporated in response to the preferential treatment she now received. They never voiced their resentment outright, however, and Jeisa doubted they ever would. Marie wielded more influence with her friendly visits than most men did when they boomed orders.

Otherwise alone, Jeisa found comfort in Marie's friendship. They started having lunch together whenever she was in town. With Marie's support, Jeisa started to think she'd be able to turn things around. She could make it. She hadn't done anything so awful that it couldn't be repaired. She just needed a little more time.

So when Marie had asked Jeisa for help, refusing hadn't felt like an option. All she had to say was that she was an image consultant. One more small fabrication and she'd have a real shot at being independent. An enormous increase in salary, an opportunity to travel and build a résumé that wasn't based on a fictitious employment history. *Oh yes... and no more typing.*

Until now, Jeisa hadn't felt bad about deceiving Jeremy. She'd felt qualified. Her background had prepared her to teach him how to blend in with the wealthy. And until today she'd been proud of his transformation.

Moments like this were payback for tempting fate with the question—*What could go wrong?*

Sorry, Marie, I broke the first client you sent me—next, please?

Jeisa gripped the back of the chair so tightly that her knuckles whitened. She welcomed the discomfort. *Marie hired me to help him and look at me—just watching instead of doing what I know is right and putting an end to this.*

Jeisa cringed as the trainer stopped toying with her client and his next hit crumpled Jeremy to the ring's padded floor.

"Stay down," the trainer barked, but Jeremy was already pushing himself up off the floor and back onto his knees.

Jeisa nervously chewed her bottom lip. *He's going to get killed. Why won't he just stay down?*

Jeisa held her breath as, with heartbreaking effort, Jeremy struggled to stand. He wobbled. He faltered. Eventually, he straightened and raised his gloved hands in front of him again.

Ray pulled back as if he were about to deliver a final, deadly blow. Jeremy swayed but said nothing. Blood dripped from his nose onto the mat below as the two men stared each other down.

Jeisa took a step toward the ring. An indelicate amount of wrath filled her. *If he hits Jeremy again, that old man had better run, because I'm going kill him.*

"You don't give up," Ray said in recognition and expelled a harsh breath. He lowered his hands and began to remove his gloves.

Jeremy lowered his own and stumbled as his legs gave way a bit beneath him. Relief flooded through Jeisa. She grabbed a clean white towel from a bag near the ring and rushed to Jeremy's side. She slid beneath one of his arms and took his weight on her shoulders, wiping the blood from his chin with the towel. Jeremy took the towel from her and held it to his nose.

Jeisa glared at the trainer. "What were you thinking?"

Ray scowled at her. "He's fine. Nothing a little ice won't fix." He met Jeremy's eyes and said, "Come back next week and I'll train you."

A faint smile stretched Jeremy's swollen and split lips. Jeisa said, "Don't you dare look pleased with yourself. You're lucky if you don't have brain damage from this."

The trainer sized them both up again and asked, "You sure you're not his girlfriend?"

Jeisa said some choice words in rapid Portuguese.

The trainer held one of the ropes up so that Jeisa could maneuver Jeremy out of the ring more easily. He said to Jeremy, "Be here Tuesday morning at eight." Jeremy nodded. "But leave *her* home."

Jeremy chuckled and groaned. "I'll try."

Jeisa glared at him as she helped him remove his gloves and wraps.

Men.

Together they made their way across the gym toward the exit. Jeremy's dark blue eyes were dancing with triumph and a wave of attraction hit her like a sucker punch. When they'd first met, the description that had come to mind had been *earnestly adorable*. Had it really been only a few months since she'd met him? Gone were the old clothes, the unruly mop of brown hair, and the boyish expressions. Even his gray sweats and matching T-shirt were from a modern athletic-wear designer Jeisa had discovered.

Not that fashion had done much to aid Jeremy this day.

He paused and shook his head. Jeisa slid beneath one of his arms again to help steady him. The heat from his body spread like wildfire through her own. Jeremy was all man now, and Jeisa could feel how much he'd changed in every place that their bodies touched. The strong arm draped across her shoulders no longer felt like it belonged to a man who spent his life behind a computer. Boxing was only a small piece of Jeremy's plan to physically transform himself. He'd started running and lifting weights very soon after they'd met. Jeisa hadn't thought it was necessary... *But oh, the results were nice.*

He stumbled as they walked. Her hand flew up to steady him, coming to a rest in the middle of his hard chest, and she felt him catch his breath.

Is he thinking what I'm thinking?

No, no, no, she thought frantically.

Unlike me, Jeremy has always been painfully honest.

Remember that he's doing all of this to win the heart of a woman.

Another woman.

As in, not me.

Her body didn't care. She looked past the swelling and the blood and all she could see were his beautiful, sexy blue eyes. They paused for what seemed an eternity and she couldn't look away.

What would it be like to be loved by a man who is willing to do anything to win your heart?

You could be yourself with such a man.

Love like that doesn't follow the rules.

It is sweaty, and passionate, and the stuff that romances are made of.

An odd expression entered Jeremy's eyes and he straightened away from her, breaking contact. "Jeisa," he said in a gruff voice, "let's go home."

"Yes," she said, and chastised herself for entertaining such thoughts about her employer. She was part of Jeremy's life.

Just not in the way she wanted to be.

CHAPTER *Two*

JEREMY OPENED THE door to his penthouse apartment in uptown Boston. Normally he took a moment to appreciate the ultramodern white furniture and powerful view of the skyline. He liked to think it represented his internal changes. This time, however, he couldn't think past the pain reverberating from a variety of locations on his upper body, and his sight was impeded by the swelling around one of his eyes.

As far as first sessions go, today's had been more painful than expected, but he'd accomplished what he'd set out to do. He now had a boxing trainer, one of the best. Unlike most of Ray's clients, he didn't hope to win any matches—at least not in a ring. What he wanted was much more primal than that. He wanted the look. That almost indescribable quality that makes another man step back and a woman's glance linger.

"You need a doctor," Jeisa said, interrupting his thoughts.

"I need a couch." He touched his swollen eye tenderly as he shuffled through the foyer toward the living room. "And some aspirin."

Jeisa followed him. "You need to have your head examined if you're even considering going back there," she said in a much harsher tone than he was used to hearing from her.

One thing at a time.

He lowered himself gingerly onto his couch, not taking care to protect its pristine surface. He propped his feet up on one side, his head on the other, and said, "I'll double your salary if you stop yelling."

The silence that followed his comment was worse.

He opened his unswollen eye and assessed the woman standing over him. Her arms were folded across her chest and her bright red lips were pursed with irritation. *What is that ridiculous line that men say to women? You're beautiful when you're angry?* He could see—well, he could half see—what they meant. He was pretty sure that when his other eye was fully functioning again it would be in agreement.

Jeisa was a stunning woman on a bad day. She wore her dark hair long—past her shoulders—and untamed. Her feminine flair added a sexiness to even the simplest outfits she wore. The black jumper she'd worn today revealed just enough cleavage to raise a man's blood pressure with merely a glance.

Now, chest heaving with anger and lips pursed as she tried to keep her opinion to herself, she was the stuff of late-night dreams.

Even mine.

I'm only human.

I doubt even married men can look at her and not ask themselves "what if."

Not that she'd appreciate it.

He closed his eye and said, "Say it."

Jeisa asked a bit too innocently, "Say what?"

"Whatever is eating at you."

"You could have been seriously injured today," she gushed, and the depth of emotion in her voice surprised Jeremy into sitting up. He could handle thinking she was angry with him, but he was unprepared for her to be hurt by what he'd done.

I'm an ass, he thought. *Here I am imagining her naked and she's genuinely worried about me. I really have to get this under control. And I will. When I'm with Alethea, I'll be able to look at Jeisa and not imagine those full breasts in my hands, and those delicious lips around my cock. I'll stop wanting to slide the straps of her jumpsuit over her shoulders, drop it to the floor, and savor what would definitely be a slice of heaven on earth.*

He shuddered and turned on his side to conceal how his body was responding to the images of her in the nude his imagination was supplying in abundance. This type of unwelcome and poorly timed arousal would soon be a thing of the past.

Jeisa was the wrong type of distraction at the wrong time. Didn't Marie know any hideous image consultants?

I can't waver now. I am so close to being the man I swore I'd become—so close to having it all. I don't want Jeisa. I want Alethea. Jeisa is here and hot. Of course I'm tempted.

But Jeisa deserves better than that.

She was more than an employee; she was a friend. A friend who was hurting because he'd been foolish enough to let her witness the less savory side of his transformation. Change doesn't come without some pain. He was so used to letting her into every corner of his life that he didn't consider how today might have upset her. "Jeisa, I'm fine. It looks worse than it is." When she didn't look convinced, he tried humor. "Besides, I plan to tell people that you and your Brazilian temper did this."

She almost smiled, but then her beautiful face tightened again. "I'm serious. Don't go back there."

He wanted to ease her worry, but nothing—not even her pleas—would stop him from following through with his training. He'd come too far to turn back now. "Next week won't be like this," he assured her.

"How do you know that?"

"Because we came to an understanding today."

"Really?"

He shared his thoughts openly with Jeisa. "He wanted to prove that I don't belong there."

"You don't. Just like he doesn't belong in your office. God, Jeremy, people send private jets for you. I think you can afford your own security."

She didn't understand, and he didn't expect her to. This wasn't about what he could afford. Money had stopped being an issue as soon as he'd stepped out of the shadows of hacking and offered his services to the highest bidder. He was quickly amassing more money than he'd be able to spend in ten lifetimes, but wealth was only part of what he sought. He still had a long way to go before he commanded the same respect as the men who hired him to work on their software security issues. "You know why this is important to me."

"Alethea," Jeisa said quietly and stood.

There's that look again—she doesn't approve, but she doesn't have to.

No one does.

Jeremy lay back on the couch and closed his eyes. "Yes," he said. An image of the red-haired woman he'd spent so much of his life dreaming of was oddly difficult to conjure. Jeremy didn't let that lessen his resolve. Alethea wasn't just any woman. She was the one who had pulled him through the darkest hours of his teens. She was the goal that had made the years of caring for his father and then mourning his loss bearable.

A goal that had kept him sane when nothing else in his life had made sense.

One that was suddenly now within his reach.

If I don't fuck it up.

"Just go," he said wearily.

He heard the retreating click of Jeisa's high heels on his tile floor. He wanted to chase after her and explain his reasons again, but he fought and won against that impulse. There was nothing to say that he hadn't already said.

A few moments later he heard her return, and then he felt the cold touch of a bag of ice against one side of his face. He covered the bag with one of his hands, feeling miserable in a way that wasn't connected to his physical pain. Having her there made him feel better and worse at the same time, and the conflicting emotions frustrated him. With his eyes still closed, he said, "Thank you. I should be fine by tomorrow. I'll call you in the morning."

Just go.

The sound of Jeisa plopping into one of his armchairs was followed by the soft thud of her discarded shoes. "You could have a concussion. I don't think you're supposed to sleep."

Please tell me she's not going to stay.

"The Internet says that's a myth."

She let out a long sigh. "If I leave now, I am going to spend the rest of the day wondering if you're okay."

If you stay, I'm going to spend the rest of the night suffering, and it won't be for the reasons you think. He growled, "So you're just going to sit there and stare at me while I sleep?"

"Yes."

He hated how his blood pounded at the thought of her taking care of him. Hovering beside him.

Close.

Tempting.

Torture.

Jeremy wondered what she'd say if he put the ice on his lower region, where he apparently needed it more. *She'd probably kick my ass.*

On the outside, Jeisa was calm and sophisticated, but he'd glimpsed her inner fire. The image of her standing between him and the boxing trainer, like some protective lioness, filled him with an emotion he couldn't define.

She's beautiful.

Fierce.

The kind of woman a man marries.

Another man, he corrected himself.

Just before Jeremy drifted off to sleep, he felt the comforting warmth of a blanket being draped over him and he smiled again. *Jeisa.*

Jeisa soaked in the quiet of Jeremy's apartment and the soothing rhythm of his light snore. *Idiot*, she thought. *No one is worth what you're doing to yourself.* Calling him a name in her mind provided her only the briefest comfort, before a real sadness settled over her.

Unless you love them enough that you're willing to do just about anything. Even stay when they told you to leave and blame it on a concussion. Then, I guess, all the rules are off. Jeisa tucked her legs beneath her and watched Jeremy try to escape his pain via a fitful sleep. She relived the fear that had filled her when she'd seen Ray cock his hand back for one final blow.

For about the millionth time, she regretted not keeping their working relationship purely professional, but where he was concerned she'd thrown all common sense aside.

She thought back to the first time they'd met. He'd arrived on her doorstep in a suit that had clearly belonged to someone else—about twenty years ago—and shyly presented her with a surround-sound system for her television. Although she'd refused the present, he'd quickly shed his jacket and was halfway through installing it before he'd stopped, put down the wires he was in the process of organizing, and said, "Did you say you *didn't* want it?"

She'd nodded.

He'd sat back on his heels and smiled sheepishly at her. "I'm sorry. I guess I'm nervous."

Right then and there she'd known she was in trouble. She hadn't been sure what to expect from Marie's description: a socially awkward computer genius poised to earn a substantial amount of money. She certainly hadn't considered that he could have eyes as blue and warm as the first day of summer, and a smile so disarmingly sexy that his general state of disarray didn't matter.

"No, I'm sorry," she'd said and joined him on the floor, tucking the hem of her sundress under her knees. "What a generous gift. And I didn't even ask if you needed help."

His grin had widened. "Possibly because you'd said no."

She'd grinned right back at him. "Possibly, but it looks amazing."

"Marie told me to bring you something. Since you haven't been here long, I figured you wouldn't have one of these." His face had reddened a bit as he said, "It was easier than flowers." Suddenly serious, he'd looked directly into her eyes and said, "I really want this to work, and I'll do whatever it takes." And he had. He'd tolerated a spa day, several fittings, and even etiquette lessons on which fork to use with which course in a fine restaurant. In the spirit of change, he'd included her in his travels, his social events, and almost every aspect of his transformation—until now.

She'd expressed her opinion before, during, and after his boxing lesson, but her feelings on the matter hadn't swayed his decision. She hadn't realized until just now how much he'd already changed. Soon he wouldn't need her at all. No matter how close she felt to him, at the end of the day, she worked for him.

This is a job.

Just a job.

Someday Jeremy will be nothing more than a name on my résumé.

The thought brought a heavy weight to Jeisa's heart. *The only idiot in this room is me. He knows what he wants, and nothing is going to stop him from getting it. What would my life be like if I had the same courage?*

Jeremy groaned and rolled over onto his side, covering his bruised face with one arm.

I'm going to miss him.

I'll miss the private smile he gives me when we mingle at a party and only I know that he practiced everything he is going to say.

I'll miss the midnight phone calls when something goes particularly well for him at a meeting and he wants to share the wonder of how quickly his life has changed.

How can I continue to help him become the man he thinks he wants to be when I'm already in love with the man he has always been?

CHAPTER *Three*

"I HAVE PLENTY of security on my payroll if you need to borrow some," Dominic Corisi said with some humor when Jeremy entered the infamous computer tycoon's office. Dominic's joke lacked the warmth that would qualify it as friendly ribbing. Instead, it was another reminder that Jeremy provided work for Dominic's company and operated within his realm because he was useful, not because he was an equal or a friend.

Jeremy said, "About the server in the Demor Republic, you were right to send me out there. No one had accessed it yet, but it would've been easy had anyone wanted to."

Dominic studied Jeremy, tapping one finger thoughtfully on his desk. He sat back and nodded.

Jeremy said, "I am juggling a few projects right now so if there's nothing crucial you need me for, I'll be in and out of the country for the next couple weeks."

"That's fine," Dominic said. Then he shook his head as if finding humor in his own thoughts. "You look like you lost a fight in a back alley. I have to know—was it a bookie? Did you get caught in bed with someone's wife?"

Jeremy met the older man's eyes and said, "It's none of your business."

A slow smile spread across Dominic's face. "I should accept that, but I am going to need a hint or this is going to bother me all day. I don't like mysteries."

Instead of giving Dominic what he wanted, Jeremy countered with a question of his own. "If our roles were reversed, would you tell me?"

An eyebrow rose in concession. “No.”

You have to give him credit for being honest—even brutally so. “Then about the next three weeks. You can reach me via email if anything comes up. I’m not sure my cell phone will work everywhere I’m going.”

“Where wouldn’t your cell phone work?”

He didn’t need to know, so Jeremy didn’t share his plans. “Jake has my contact information. I’d appreciate it if you use it for emergencies only.”

If Dominic wanted to ask another question, he kept his thoughts to himself.

Jeremy turned and was preparing to leave the office when Dominic’s business partner, Jake Walton, entered and saw Jeremy’s face. “What the hell happened to you?” He looked quickly at Dominic for an explanation.

The last thing Jeremy needed was for Jake to get involved. With a bit of strategy, Dominic was easy enough to maneuver around, but Jake was different. And neither of them needed to know about his foreign projects. Jeremy was quickly gaining clients who were willing to pay him any price to do what he’d always done for fun.

Dominic stood. “Hey, don’t look at me. I had nothing to do with this.”

Jake didn’t look entirely convinced. “Are you in some kind of trouble, Jeremy?”

Jeremy shook his head.

Jake persisted. “Dominic will send you into the most dangerous situations without hesitation, but you can say no.”

“Dominic had nothing to do with this,” Jeremy replied blandly.

A look of genuine concern filled Jake’s face. “Since you are technically not an employee, Dominic cannot actually fire you. You don’t have to be afraid of him.”

“I’m not afraid of him.”

Dominic walked over and slapped Jeremy on the back. Jeremy winced, still feeling a body hangover from his boxing lesson the day before. Dominic's support held the sting of payback. He smiled at Jake and said, "Oddly, he isn't. I must be getting soft."

Jeremy's comeback was interrupted by the arrival of Dominic's assistant, Marie. She rushed into the mix, and when she saw Jeremy's face she turned, hands on hips, and glared at both Dominic and Jake.

Jake was the first to state his innocence. "Marie, I found them like this."

Marie turned to Dominic and raised one eyebrow in question.

Dominic suddenly looked more like a guilty boy caught with his hand in the cookie jar than the notorious billionaire he was reputed to be. "I had nothing to do..."

Giving in to temptation, Jeremy slumped his shoulders and said in a weak voice, "He didn't mean for it to happen, Marie. Don't worry, I'm okay."

Dominic spun on his heel and reached for Jeremy, who knew him well enough to have taken a step back out of his reach. "You little shit."

Jake's laugh boomed.

Too wise to be used as a pawn, Marie chastised the group. "You boys are enough to give me heart palpitations. One of you needs to tell me what happened to Jeremy."

After a brief and awkward pause, Jeremy muttered, "I'm taking boxing lessons."

Dominic barked out a laugh, once again proving what he thought of Jeremy. "Boxing?"

Jeremy said, "I'm sure you've been in your share of fights, Dominic."

Dominic nodded. "Even had my ass kicked a few times."

Marie jumped in. "Dominic..."

Dominic said, "Sorry, Marie. I just can't believe anyone would pay someone to do that."

Jake added his two cents with humor, "That's because with you, so many people will gladly do it for free."

Dominic turned to his grinning partner and growled, "I let you hit me one time and now you think you're a badass, Jake."

Jake shrugged. "If I remember correctly, you didn't *let* me do anything, and it was a whole lot more than one hit."

Jeremy interjected, "Do you two need to be alone?"

Dominic's eyes narrowed as he said, "Your wit must be the reason for your trainer's enthusiasm."

Marie addressed Jeremy, "Jeisa told me that you would be in and out of the country in November."

Jeremy nodded.

Marie asked, "Will you spend Thanksgiving with your family?"

Jeremy shrugged. "My mother has worked almost every Thanksgiving that I can remember. She's probably working this one."

"Your mother still works?" Jake asked in surprise.

"She doesn't believe that what I'm doing is a reliable source of income."

Dominic asked, "And what exactly do you do? When you're not working for us, that is."

Jeremy said, "You know my skills."

Dominic said, "A man could get killed doing that for the wrong person."

"Or he could make a fast fortune," Jeremy countered.

Jake said, "I have to agree with Dom on this one. I don't think you know how quickly it can get dangerous." His eyes narrowed slightly. "Or do you? Is this still about Lil's friend?"

Marie cut in. "Jeremy, we're celebrating Thanksgiving with the Andrades this year. I'm sure Jake's parents will be there and would love to see you. If your mother can't come, at least bring Jeisa. It'll be her first Thanksgiving in the United States and she shouldn't spend it alone."

"I'll see…" Jeremy hedged.

Marie continued, "We'd all like you to come. Wouldn't we, Dominic?" When Dominic said nothing, Marie put a hand on one of her hips and stared pointedly at him. "Jeremy has done more for us than we will ever be able to repay."

Dominic gritted his teeth and said, "You can come."

Jake joked, "That's as good as his invitations get, Jeremy."

When Jeremy didn't speak, Marie touched his sleeve and said, "It would mean a lot to me if you came."

A velvet steamroller. She might look soft on the outside, but *no* was not a word she recognized.

Jeremy avoided the eyes of the other two men in the room and said, "I'll see what I can do."

With that, a carefree smile returned to Marie's face and she linked arms with Jake. "Now, Jake, what is going on with your wedding plans with Lil? I thought you'd be married by now."

"We want to keep it small. We thought January would be good," Jake said as he walked out of the office with Marie.

Dominic returned to his seat behind his desk, propped up his feet and said, "Marie seems to like you."

"Is that a problem?"

"Not unless you disappoint her."

"Are you threatening me if I don't come to Thanksgiving with you?"

"I don't make threats." *I make promises,* his tone implied.

Jeremy couldn't contain his response. He grinned and said, "That is awesome! I have to say that to someone someday in exactly that tone. I love it. You sound like a modern mafia godfather."

Dominic shook his head. "You are one crazy bastard."

Jeremy grinned again, turned to leave, and said over his shoulder, "From you, that's a compliment."

He heard Dominic growl a curse at him as he left. Not too many people stood up to Dominic. He carried with him not only his reputation but that of his unscrupulous father. People feared him, and rightfully so.

Which made mocking him that much more fun.

As Jeremy walked through the hallway, he replayed the office scene in his head.

Yes, he was choosing a dangerous path. Any number of the connections he was presently cultivating could turn deadly if they went sour, but the alternative was unacceptable.

If this gets me killed, it's better than spending another day as the man I was.

So, threaten away, Dominic, you don't scare me.

I've got nothing to lose.

Dominic Corisi stripped to his boxers and joined his wife beneath the thick silk comforter of their bed. She rolled onto her back and smiled up at him, greeting him with a warm kiss that would normally have had him stripping down further. Instead, he found comfort in her kiss, then settled himself next to her, tucked her into his side, and laid a hand across the small bump of her stomach.

Abby raised one hand and laid it on his cheek. "What's wrong?"

Dominic shook his head and forced a small smile. Everything since the moment he'd met Abby had been better than he'd ever imagined his life could be. "Nothing."

"Then why are you scowling at me?"

A tender smile spread across his face, the kind only she inspired. She knew him so well. "You know I don't like to bring work issues home."

Abby ran a hand lovingly down his neck, down his arm, and settled on top of the hand on her stomach. "We're a team, Dom. You don't have to protect me. You're allowed to have bad days. It's not going to ruin the happiness we've found. In fact, it'll make what we have even stronger."

Dominic absently rubbed her stomach as he mulled her words. He was still getting used to sharing himself with someone, but Abby didn't settle for less than everything. Still, uncomfortable as it sometimes was, she had a way of looking into the darkest corners of his heart and easing pains he'd long tried to deny.

"It's Jeremy," he said with a disgusted shake of his head.

Abby cocked her head to one side in question. "Jeremy Kater? Lil's friend? The hacker? I thought you said he was doing great things for Corisi Enterprises."

"I don't like him."

Propping herself up on one elbow, Abby said, "He seems like a nice enough guy. Every time I've met him, he's been polite. Marie says that he has really come out of his shell since he's been working with that image consultant she hired for him."

Dominic growled.

Abby smiled gently and kissed her husband's tight jaw. "Oh, I see. Marie took him on as a project, and you don't like to share her."

"That's not it at all," Dominic denied brusquely. "She doesn't see him for what he is." When his wife didn't say anything, he added, "And she invited him to Thanksgiving, for God's sake."

"Thanksgiving, huh? Well, there will certainly be enough food at the Andrades'. So, what is he? Tell me."

He shouldn't have brought it up. Trying to tell Abby about someone's faults was like trying to tell a passing rain shower not to make a rainbow at the slightest hint of sun. She saw good in everyone. Normally it was something he admired about her, but right now he simply wanted her to agree with him. "He's a cocky ass, that's what he is. He has no respect for authority. He won't sign a contract because he says he doesn't work for anyone but himself. I don't trust him. No one knows what he's capable of. If he wasn't so good at what he does, I'd cut him loose, but my instincts tell me that it's better to have him working for us rather than against us."

Abby chuckled, which only irritated Dominic more.

"It's not funny. He's unpredictable, and that's dangerous. He's charging full speed into international alliances, many of which he won't disclose, with no regard for the danger it could bring him and anyone associated with him."

"He reminds me," said Abby, as she stopped laughing to lay a hand on her husband's shoulder, "of someone else I know."

"He's nothing like me. He thinks just because he has never lost in the virtual world that he's invincible in real life. That kind of arrogance can get a man killed."

Abby countered gently, "Then it sounds like he could use a mentor."

"No."

Abby simply gazed patiently up at him.

Dominic admitted another uncomfortable truth. "He mocks me to my face. If it wasn't for Marie, I'd give him the smackdown he's begging for."

Abby waited a moment, then said, "Marie took his mother out a few times. I know why Marie wants to see Jeremy succeed."

Dominic scowled down at his wife. "There is nothing you could say that would make me like that kid."

She gave him that stubborn look he'd fallen in love with their first week together. "I think you're wrong, Dom. He grew up in a two-parent home, but his father was bedridden for most of his life. Jeremy took care of him from a young age—too young, so his mother could work. They had nurses, but nothing full-time. Jeremy was homeschooled so his father would never be alone. His mother said Jeremy was her rock. As the medical bills piled up, Jeremy used that online world to help pay for his father's medical bills. His father passed away at the beginning of what would have been his final year of high school. Can you imagine what his life was like? If he's angry with the world, doesn't he have the right to be? You know what anger can do to a young man."

"Stop. I hate it when you do this." He felt an unwelcome twinge of compassion for Jeremy and his stolen childhood.

His wife sensed the crack in his armor and went in for the kill. "I'm serious, Dom. From everything I've heard about him, he's a good man. With your help, he could become a great one.

Marie looked past your reputation and saw who you really were. Maybe you should trust her instincts with Jeremy."

He was beginning to agree with his wife, but he wasn't yet ready to admit it.

Abby said, "There must be something you like about him."

Dominic conceded, "Sometimes he makes me laugh. He's such a shit, it's funny."

Abby smiled and nodded with approval. "See. You have something in common."

Returning his wife's smile, Dominic admitted, "He's taking boxing lessons with someone whom he's paying to beat him senseless. It's pretty amusing."

Quickly concerned, Abby said, "Is he okay? Why would he do that?"

Dominic shrugged. "I guess he wants to toughen up."

Abby kissed her husband lightly on the lips and said, "You think he has no respect for you, but I'll bet he admires you."

Dominic gave his wife a cocky smile. "What's not to admire? I'm handsome, rich, and married to the most incredible woman on the planet."

That earned him a second chance at the warm welcome she'd offered him earlier. She pulled his head down to meet her lips again. "And humble..." she laughed between kisses.

He raised his head, looking serious for a moment, and corrected her. "Grateful."

Their eyes met and held. Abby said, "We both have so much to be thankful for. Would it hurt you to help Jeremy find his way?"

He ran a thoughtful thumb lightly over his wife's pink lips, which at that moment were turned up into a knowing smile. "Will I ever be able to say no to you?"

"Not when you know I'm right." She sat up and slid her satin nightgown over her head, revealing her amazing breasts, which were growing even larger as her body changed with pregnancy. "Like right now, I think you're wearing too much clothing."

Dominic quickly discarded his boxers and rolled onto his back, pulling his naked wife with him so that she straddled him. He ran an appreciative thumb in a slow circle around one of her erect nipples. "Tell me what you want, wife."

She smiled down at him, her eyes brimming with love, and said, "You, Dom. Tonight. Tomorrow. Forever."

His erection swelled against her moist center. "Let's work on tonight first. I didn't think you could get more beautiful or sexier, but knowing that all of this also has given us," he laid his hand gently on her stomach again, "a family. I don't have the words to tell you what it means to me."

Abby leaned down, kissed her husband, and said against his lips, "Then show me."

And he did.

Tenderly.

Joyfully.

Reverently.

All night.

And then again the next morning as they showered together.

CHAPTER *Four*

TWO WEEKS LATER, Jeisa's phone rang in the middle of the night. She rolled over and hid her head under her pillow, but the phone kept ringing. Eventually, she gave in and answered it, her voice thick with sleep. "Alô?"

"English, Jeisa," Jeremy said cheerfully. Way too cheerfully for—she opened her heavy eyes and groaned when she saw the time—three o'clock. "Sorry to wake you, but I have to ask you something."

Jeisa fell back into her pillows and resigned herself to the conversation. It wasn't the first time he'd called her from another time zone. For a man with such a high IQ, he had a hard time understanding that just because he was awake, it didn't mean the rest of the world shared that state. "What?"

"I need your opinion. Should I lease a plane or a jet?"

"Are you kidding me?"

"No, I'm serious. The planes are huge. You should see some of the ones they are showing me over here. Some of them have two floors and a theater. A fucking movie theater on a plane. Can you believe that?"

"Jeremy, I'm going back to sleep now."

"Wait, I have to make the decision this morning. The jets are equally amazing. You can get anywhere in about half the time. Which one do you think makes me look more… dangerous?"

"Have you considered a fighter plane?" she joked.

Too seriously, Jeremy answered, "They don't let civilians have those."

Jeisa groaned. "I know. Can we look at your options when you get back?"

"No, I need it for this trip. Plane or jet. Which one would you rather fly in?"

Resigning herself to the conversation, Jeisa said, "Tell me about the plane again."

"They have one that used to be owned by some old guy before the economy took a dive. It has three bedrooms and an office. They suggest you hire a cleaning and wait staff for it if you buy it."

"Sounds amazing."

"But the jet is exactly like what you see in the movies. It's a small six-seater—sleek, powerful, fast. It might be more impressive."

"To whom?" When Jeremy didn't answer, Jeisa sat straight up in bed. "Are you going to see Alethea on this trip?"

"I invited her to join me in the Tenin Republic. With their government fending off highly sophisticated rebel attacks, they want their network to be as secure as possible."

Sounds dangerous, Jeisa thought, but she knew that was the point. From everything she'd heard about Alethea, she'd be drawn to the area like a moth to a flame. Jeisa tried to remain neutral. *This is what he's worked so hard for.* "So they want their own hacker."

"Exactly. There have been breaches at one of their military bases that may have been a hack-guided air strike. I can make sure that doesn't happen again. It may have been an inside job, though, so it actually makes sense to bring Alethea in on this one."

She wanted to yell, *"No! It's too dangerous. Too soon. I'm not ready to lose you yet."* But she stopped herself. *Lose him? He's already gone.* She forced herself to sound supportive. "Sounds like the opportunity you've been waiting for."

"It is," he said, but he didn't sound as excited as he should have.

She took a guess at why and asked, "But you're not sure you're ready?" When he said nothing, she pushed past her own feelings on the matter and told him what he needed to hear.

"You are. I have no doubt that you'll win her heart. Do you know why? Because I've watched you reach every goal you gave yourself over the last few months. You set your mind to something, and you made it happen. There aren't many men who can say that. She'll be impressed—no matter which aircraft you arrive in."

"Thanks, Jeisa. I don't know what I'd do without you."

Now there's a real kick in the pants. A man finally says what I've always longed to hear, and it's only because I'm helping him win the heart of another woman.

"Good night, Jeremy."

"Oh, before I forget. Marie invited us to Thanksgiving at the Andrades' house. The Waltons will probably be there. I'd like to go."

"So, go."

"I want you there with me."

No, no, no. "I don't think that's a good idea." *It's time to put some distance between us before I make a fool of myself.*

"You know how I am in social situations like that. I need you there."

"Thanksgiving is two weeks away. You could be with Alethea by then. Trust me, you won't need me."

"Rushing is not part of my plan with this trip. This week will be all about business—and letting her see the new me."

"There was nothing wrong with the old you, Jeremy."

"You know what I mean. She hasn't seen me since Dominic's engagement party. Things are different now."

They sure are.

She heard the smile in his voice as he joked, "It will take her time to soak in my new awesomeness."

Despite the heaviness of her heart, Jeisa couldn't help but chuckle with him. "She may not recognize you now that your head has gotten so big."

"Lucky for me, I have you around to keep my ego in check."

Not for long.

Not once Alethea realizes how wonderful you are.

"Come with me to the Andrades' for Thanksgiving, Jeisa. I need you."

His words brought unexpected tears to her eyes. She brushed them away impatiently and said, "I'm tired, Jeremy. Let's talk about it when you get home."

"I should be back Friday morning. I'll bring you those chocolate truffle things you love."

"Brigadeiros?" she asked, her mouth watering. "You are now forgiven for waking me up."

His deep laugh sent a shiver of pleasure down her back. "I'll come straight to your place when I fly back in a couple days and tell you how the trip went."

Like a bucket of water to the face, his words shifted her focus back to the reality of what his trip would mean to them. "Sure," she said with much less enthusiasm. *Why not? Nothing a woman loves more than hearing a man talk about another woman.* "See you Friday morning. And get the jet, Jeremy. Alethea will love it," she said and hung up.

She should have wished him good luck, but the words had caught in her throat. Rolling onto her side, she hugged a pillow to her chest and fought back a confusing swirl of emotions.

Alethea Niarchos stepped out of the limo Jeremy Kater had sent for her and onto the tarmac of the Tenin Republic's private government airfield. The heat rising off the runway made Alethea momentarily wish she'd waited within the vehicle's cooled interior, but patience had never been one of her virtues. She'd agreed to meet Jeremy partly because working with a foreign government would take her career to a whole new level, and partly because his involvement here intrigued her. On paper, it was a parliamentary democratic country, but in practice it was essentially a dictatorship. Prime Minister Akia Alvo had started his reign as a hero, being voted in after a government coup fifteen years earlier. Some said that the power had gone to his head. He'd filled his cabinet with those loyal to him, and although both he and his loyalists had been reelected, the press had cried foul on the process before he'd silenced them internally and banned foreign press.

The Jeremy she'd known since early high school would never have put himself or his skills on the market so publicly. Revealing himself would likely prove as dangerous for him as it was obviously financially lucrative.

What are you really doing here, Jeremy?

If money was all he sought, he could have found that merely by extending his association with Corisi Enterprises. His work in Najriad for the royal family had given him international recognition that he could have parlayed into any number of big contracts—and for a hefty fee. *Why Tenin? Why get involved in a teetering government?*

The answer came to her while she waited for the hatch door of the jet to open. *Because money is no object when one's survival is on the line. A government in crisis is as rich as it is volatile.*

We could get killed here.

Or make a fast fortune.

Both possibilities were equally exciting. Lately she'd found the routine of what she did somewhat depressing. If she had to sit in on one more corporate-performance appraisal meeting where they focused more on damage control than prevention, she'd gnaw off her manicured nails. Eventually they would sell themselves on the importance of tightened security without giving her a tedious overview of their company first. More than once she'd been tempted to stab a CEO with one of her stilettos just to see if she could—and then make it out of the building alive.

Kill me, just don't bore me.

Thanks to her recent affiliation with Dominic Corisi, the challenge of finding new jobs had disappeared—along with any enjoyment she found in testing building security systems. She had more potential clients than she had time to work with, but how much fun is breaking into a building if you're asked to?

The hatch of the jet opened, and it took Alethea a moment to recognize Jeremy. Where was the pasty white man who had looked exactly like what he'd been: a computer geek who lived in his mother's basement? His slightly rounded cheeks were now cut in strong lines, accenting his sharp blue eyes. His charcoal pinstriped Alexander Amosu suit was tailor-made to his new muscular frame. As he stopped to talk to the pilot before descending the stairs, Alethea's jaw dropped in surprise. The modern cut of his thick brown hair was short, but edgy. It spoke of youthful power. *Move over, Dad, your son is taking over the company.*

Not that Jeremy necessarily had a company—or even a father, for that matter.

Honestly, Alethea had no idea what he had. She'd never paid much attention to his personal life. He'd always been her hacker friend—a reliable source of information one couldn't obtain legally.

She shook her head in wonder. *People don't change that dramatically, do they? You don't spend your life in a basement and then suddenly transform into a male model with an aircraft that screams, "Put me on the front page of Forbes."*

He started down the stairs, saw her, and smiled.

She surprised herself by smiling back.

Jeremy, huh? I never would have believed it.

She expected him to approach her awkwardly, as he always had, with that look that said he longed to hug her in greeting. Instead, he strode confidently to her and held out a hand as if she were a business associate of his. "Alethea," he said smoothly, "I'm glad you made it on time. Our meeting is in twenty minutes at Alvo's compound."

His strong hand closed over hers, and she forgot what she was going to say.

Jeremy?

This can't be Jeremy.

He was the one who broke contact and motioned to the armed jeep detail that surrounded the limo he had sent for her.

"I know you like to keep a low profile, but with the recent uprisings, these are necessary."

Alethea nodded, slid back into the limo, and gathered her thoughts. A hundred questions swirled through her head, but none of them sounded flattering, so she held them in and waited for her filter to surface. "Nice jet," she said and mentally kicked herself. *Since when don't I know what to say to a man?*

His smile turned to a pleased grin that spread across his face, and for just a moment she glimpsed the boy she'd known for so long. He used to smile like that when he'd successfully hacked into a site someone had told him was impossible to access. "I'm glad you like it," he said in a deep voice that was both familiar and completely foreign to her.

He sat across from her and opened a briefcase on his lap. "I brought you a hard copy of the layout of the compound we'll be in today, as well as that of the base that was attacked."

"Whatever happened to breaking in first and getting hired later?" she joked.

One of his eyebrows arched in subtle recognition of her humor. "You can try that, but in Tenin they tend to kill more than they imprison. This is the big time, Alethea. You get in with this government and you can set your price with countries instead of companies."

Damn, Jeremy. I want to take whatever vitamins you're on.

"I appreciate you bringing me in on this," Alethea said, and she did. This was exactly the kind of adventure her life had been lacking. She took the papers from him.

He shrugged. "You were a natural choice. We've known each other a long time."

Not true, Jeremy, Alethea thought. *If this is you, I never knew you at all.* Putting down the papers, she studied him again and shook her head in bemusement. *Were you always this good looking and I didn't notice?* Or was it that, for the first time since she'd met him, he didn't look the least bit interested in her? She sat back, crossed her legs, and watched his reaction from beneath her long lashes.

She'd chosen a blue-and-black color-blocked tank dress. She was fully aware of how the material molded to her body like a second skin, and she'd never been above using her natural assets as leverage. Men were easier to handle when they were slightly off balance—something she'd always found disappointingly easy to do. Jeremy's eyes drifted to her legs, back to the view in the window behind her, then returned to her face. Casually, dismissing her flirtatious move.

A zing of excitement coursed through Alethea. *Jeremy, you can pretend, but I know you're into me. You've always been into me.* She graced him with the sexiest smile she had in her arsenal. Heat flooded her cheeks when he looked amused instead of flustered.

In a perfectly calm, surprisingly disinterested voice, Jeremy said, "If you have any questions about the plans, we only have about ten more minutes before we arrive." He pulled out a tablet from his briefcase and began to read over a document.

Oh, I have questions, but not about the plans.

What the hell happened to you, Jeremy, and why do I suddenly want prove to you that I am much more interesting than anything you can pull out of that briefcase?

Jeremy listened to the prime minister drone on about the political climate of his country and was tempted to check his watch. He didn't want to hear justifications or propaganda. He wanted to get his hands on their computer network to see for himself if it had been breached.

The careful expression of interest on Alethea's face suggested that she was equally impatient but was wisely keeping her thoughts to herself. She caught him looking at her and sat a little straighter in her seat.

When Jeremy had run through this scenario in his head, he'd been pretty sure it would fall short of his fantasy. But it didn't. Not judging by the sultry smile she snuck him when the prime minister looked away. She'd never met his eyes for so long when they spoke nor chose to sit so close to him when given a chance to do otherwise.

If he were a fisherman, he would have said she was circling the bait.

When the prime minister walked out of the room for a moment to take a phone call, Alethea said, "We make quite a team, Jeremy. He's drooling over us."

Jeremy deliberately kept his voice cool. "He seems to be."

"Do you have any other countries lined up?" she asked, excitement evident in her voice and the dancing light in her eyes. He'd known this project would interest her, especially since her recent work had seemed routine by comparison.

Everything was coming together exactly as he'd planned. He'd even anticipated this question and practiced his response in front of a mirror many times. He hoped it sounded natural when he drawled, "Let's see how this one goes first."

Bam.

There it was—the spark of real interest in her eyes.

She's never been able to pass up a challenge, and I just made myself into one.

I can't wait to tell Jeisa that it worked.

CHAPTER *Five*

I'M NOT HERE because Jeremy is with Alethea.

I'm here because it's the right thing to do.

Jeisa followed Marie through the foyer of her Beacon Hill luxury condo. It was full of a tasteful mix of American and European antiques, the collecting of which was a well-known hobby of Marie's. If Jeisa remembered correctly, she owned a home near each of Corisi's headquarters and loved filling them with furniture she found in nearby shops. Dominic's wife, Abby, had once joked about Marie's passion for finding priceless pieces in small, unknown shops most people would have dismissed.

Today had been Jeisa's first invitation to Marie's home, and she wished she hadn't agreed to it. This was a conversation she would have preferred to have at Marie's office. In Marie's home, her prepared speech felt like she was reneging on something personal.

But I'm not.

I didn't let her down.

This is more of a mission-accomplished visit.

Marie waved to the space around her and said, "Don't mind how small the place is. I used to own a big home. I sold it when my husband passed away."

"I'm sorry to hear that," Jeisa murmured.

"Don't be," Marie continued. "It's going on eight years now. I still miss Stan every day, but the pain has grown bearable. Time does that. I've found happiness again, but my perspective has changed. Material things don't matter much to me anymore. My home is wherever my boys are."

"Jake and Dominic?" Jeisa asked, feeling suddenly unsure if she should have referred to them as informally as she had.

Marie turned and smiled. "Yes, those boys. I don't know what I'd do without them."

From what little Jeisa knew of them, she felt confident when she said, "I'm sure they feel the same way about you."

"It is such a relief to see them settling down with good women." Marie met Jeisa's eyes with meaning. "Men get lost if left out there on their own. Women ground them."

The world according to Mrs. Duhamel.

"It's beautiful how you've all gotten so close. Do you have children of your own?" Jeisa asked. She knew the basics of the older woman's life, but as open as they had been, the topic of Marie's past had yet to come up.

Marie's eyes suddenly lost a bit of their twinkle. "I had a son once. He passed away in his crib before he turned one. The doctors never found the cause. He was simply with us one day and gone the next. My husband was a strong man, but he never recovered from that. A piece of him died along with our son and it never did come back."

No words of comfort seemed adequate, so Jeisa merely nodded.

Marie sniffed, then seemed to shake off the memories. "Kevin would be Dominic's age now had he lived. You never replace those you've loved and lost, but if you're lucky and you keep your heart open, sometimes you get a second chance at a family."

"What a beautiful way to look at life."

"There are many things we cannot change, Jeisa, but we can choose how they affect us and our decisions. Life is too precious and short. Fill it with all the love you can and savor every damn moment of it." She tamed the one errant lock in her otherwise perfectly groomed blonde layered bob. "Well, enough of that. I'm sure you didn't come here to listen to me prattle on about the past. Let's go sit down so we can talk."

As if on cue, a muscular middle-aged woman, her brown hair pulled back in a severe bun that accentuated her square jaw, came out of the kitchen in a blue housekeeper's uniform. She asked if they would like to be served tea in a deep voice that had Jeisa checking to see if she had an Adam's apple.

"We would love some, Alice," Marie said warmly. When the housekeeper left the room, Marie whispered, "Don't let the outfit fool you—she carries a gun in that apron and I'm pretty sure she's some sort of martial arts expert." Her voice grew even softer. "Her tea is horrendous, but I wouldn't mention it."

Jeisa's eyebrows shot up and her eyes flew to the kitchen door.

Marie chuckled and waved away Jeisa's concern as she led her to two walnut cushioned Bernhardt tub chairs settled near an unlit fireplace in her sitting room. "Dominic worries about me. I've assured him that I'm not going anywhere, but he feels safer with someone guarding me." A twinkle returned to her eye. "If he would hire a beefcake bodyguard for me I wouldn't care about the poor cooking. I suppose I should be grateful. I stay trim with Miss Brown because I never want seconds."

Beefcake? Jeisa did a double take at her friend's description of her preferred bodyguard type. Marie acted so matronly that it was easy to forget she was only in her early sixties. Looking past the overly modest neckline of her blouse and the straight lines of her long skirt, Jeisa realized that Marie was actually quite fit for her age. Unlike the Brazilian women Jeisa was accustomed to, Marie had chosen to conceal rather than accentuate her natural beauty. "That's awful," Jeisa said, referencing both Miss Brown's cooking and a growing suspicion that the woman who guided so many people may be in need of a bit of help herself. *If only I weren't here to say good-bye.*

Reading Jeisa's comment as referring only to the topic at hand, Marie chuckled and whispered, "Would you like to try her biscuits so you can see what I mean?"

Jeisa shook her head with a smile. "My father taught me to never tease an armed housekeeper."

Marie nodded. "Wise man, your father. Is he still in Brazil? He must miss you very much."

"I guess. We talk every day." *Whether I want to or not.*

"What does he think of you working with Jeremy?"

Jeisa shrugged.

"You still haven't told him?"

"To tell him about Jeremy, I'd have to tell him about Reese, and that story would have him on the first plane here to get me."

"So, he thinks you're still an au pair?" Jeisa nodded. "Oh, hon, when he finds out that you've been lying to him it'll only be worse."

"I'm going to tell him. I just haven't come across the right time to do it."

"There is no wrong time for the truth."

"You don't understand. This was my chance to show him that he's wrong about me—that I do know what I'm doing. Telling him that I came here for a job that never existed will just prove everything he thinks about me is right."

"How old are you, Jeisa?"

"Twenty-four."

"Jeisa, parents love their children. They may not love them the way the child wishes she was loved. They may have faults. They may disappoint their children again and again. But I have never met a parent who did not love his child. You are not the first person to feel misunderstood, or to fear that your father won't be proud of the real you. But he'll never have the chance to prove how much he loves you if you're not honest with him."

She made it sound so easy.

Marie lightened the mood again with a smile. "And there's another topic I'm sure you didn't come here to discuss. What did you want to speak to me about, Jeisa?"

Jeisa gratefully accepted a cup of tea from the housekeeper, even though she normally preferred coffee. The saucer and cup would occupy her hands and give her something to look at while she broke the news to the older woman. "Mrs. Duhamel," Jeisa began.

"Since when don't you call me Marie? Mrs. Duhamel makes me sound so stuffy," she added with a warm smile.

"Marie," Jeisa started again, "it's about my current position."

Marie put her own cup to the side and folded her hands on her lap, her body language the polar opposite of what Jeisa knew about her. She might wait patiently for an explanation, but that didn't mean she would accept it. However, this time it was important that she did.

Jeisa hesitated.

I hate to disappoint her.

But I'm not. This is for the best, and she'll see that.

Jeisa mentally reviewed what she'd planned to say one final time before speaking.

"Has something happened?" Marie asked, leaning forward with concern.

Yes.

No.

That's half the problem.

"No," Jeisa said hastily. "It's just time for me to move on to another client."

Marie's eyes widened. "Do you already have one lined up?"

"No," Jeisa admitted.

"Are you finding it difficult to live on your present pay?"

"The salary has been more than generous," Jeisa rushed to explain.

"So, it's that you don't enjoy the work?"

"No, these past few months have been amazing." Jeisa sighed. None of this was coming out as eloquently as she'd planned. "Jeremy doesn't need me anymore."

"Oh," Marie sat back and folded her hands on her lap once more. "I see."

"You hired me to help him with his image. No one would think that he's anything but a wealthy businessman. He can mingle at events without a problem. He is networking now with very powerful people, and his success will continue."

"Did Jeremy suggest that you were no longer necessary?" Marie asked.

"No, we haven't talked about any of this. I wanted to speak to you first. This was an incredible opportunity for me and I don't want you to think for a moment that I don't appreciate it. I do."

"So, you'd like to leave the position, even though you don't have another one lined up?" Marie asked. She spoke softly, yet Jeisa still felt like she was at an inquisition.

"Yes?" Jeisa responded lamely, wanting to kick herself. *No wavering. I came here to tell her that I'm quitting. There is no clause in my contract about giving notice. Jeremy doesn't need me anymore. It's that simple. Why am I having trouble saying that I'm done and I don't want to work with Jeremy anymore?*

Because it's nearly impossible to look into those kind, wise eyes and lie—even if it's a lie that I've half-convinced myself is true.

"Did Jeremy make an unwelcome pass at you?" Marie asked.

Jeisa laughed a bit in a self-depreciative way. *I wish.* "Jeremy's not like that. He's a gentleman."

Marie tapped her index fingers together as she mulled Jeisa's response. "Did he invite you to Thanksgiving with us?"

"Yes."

"Good," Marie said.

"But I'm not going," Jeisa added in a rush. "Please understand that normally I would love to join you. You, Abby, Lil, the Andrades… everyone has been so kind to me. I would love to say yes, but I don't belong there."

Marie merely met her eyes and waited.

Waited for the truth.

When Jeisa could hold it back no longer, she blurted, "Jeremy is meeting up with Alethea on this business trip. He's going to show her the new him and I can't imagine that she'll turn him down. He's brilliant, handsome, funny, loyal to a fault..." Jeisa stopped when she realized how much of her own feelings she was revealing in her description.

"Sounds like a man any woman could fall in love with," Marie added.

"No woman with any sense," Jeisa grumbled to herself. "He has his heart set on Alethea."

Marie asked, "Tell me, do you think she's a good choice for Jeremy?"

If you can't say something nice, it's best to say something vague. Jeisa hedged, "It's not my place to say."

Marie stood and said, "Well, then let it be mine." She crossed to stand over Jeisa. "Alethea is a self-centered, self-absorbed, adrenaline-seeking junky who prioritizes her addiction to excitement over the safety of the friends she claims to care for."

Well, Marie, how do you really feel about Alethea? Jeisa choked back a surprised laugh. "I haven't met her," Jeisa said.

Marie turned away and settled herself back in her chair. "I have," she said with a tone of contempt. "She has been using Jeremy since they were in their teens. She came from money but had been thrown out of every private school of any standing. So she attended public school and did her best to make a mockery of her time there as well. When Jeremy needed her most, she did nothing for him. She'd be the first one to tell you he's an easy mark to manipulate. Do you really want him to end up with someone like her?"

"It's his choice to make, not mine."

"Are you certain about that? I've seen you and Jeremy together. He obviously cares for you. With a little encouragement, he might just forget about his ridiculous childhood obsession."

Or he could break my heart.

"I came to the United States to find myself, not a man."

"Find yourself?" Marie gave a delicate snort. "No one ever found themselves by running away from what they want. It's when you decide to fight for something you believe in that you discover what you're really made of. What do *you* believe in, Jeisa?"

The directness of the question brought a spontaneous confession out of Jeisa. *Besides Jeremy?* "I've always wanted to work on the next generation of toilet design and distribution."

"Excuse me?" Marie's eyebrows pinched into a small line of confusion on her forehead.

"Back when I was at university, I read an article about an American billionaire who was hosting global contests for designing the perfect waste-disposal system. He saw it as a way to bring safe water, possibly even an energy source, to isolated areas in third world countries. It was such a basic goal that I couldn't stop thinking about it. How is it that in this day and age there are still people who cannot access clean water or sanitary means of disposing of waste? We talk about diseases, but we don't like to talk about what contributes to them. I'd like to be part of a movement to change that."

Here it comes. In the silence that followed, Jeisa had just enough time to regret her decision to share that particular aspiration. *Just like my father, she's not going to see past the unpopularity of the topic to the seriousness of the need.*

Jeisa remembered the one and only other time she'd made this admission aloud. Her father's response had been, "You are not linking your name publicly with waste disposal. Not while you're my daughter." She still wasn't entirely sure what that meant, but she'd been wise enough not to push the issue further with him.

When Marie spoke, Jeisa almost dropped her cup and saucer. "Jeisa, I like you more every time we speak. I can see why you don't want to spend the rest of your life as an image consultant. You have more important projects waiting for you." Another woman might have said those words in a snarky tone, but Marie meant them. "Now, my only question is: What is stopping you from doing it?"

Normally I would have said, "Father," but she's right. He dismissed it as a silly idea, but how would he know how important it is to me when I haven't done anything toward that goal? I've been so busy thinking about the ways he disappointed me that I didn't consider that I may have let myself down. I need to stop focusing on why I can't do something, and start making things happen.

Like Jeremy does.

Suddenly the boxing trainer made sense to Jeisa.

Just like me—he needs to prove something to himself.

"Wait," Jeisa said, "I thought you were trying to talk me into going after Jeremy."

"One should never be exclusive of the other. If you have to choose between your dreams or your man… always choose your dreams. The right man will love your strength and your passion. He'll join your cause or cheer you from the sidelines. The man who leaves would have probably left you anyway—he just would have picked another reason."

Fear shot through her as she considered Jeremy as a serious possibility. It was one thing to moon over a man you know you'll never have. It was an entirely different thing to decide to go after him.

No. He's already made his choice.

And it's not me.

Jeisa put down her cup, sighed, and stood. "I appreciate your advice, Marie. I really do. It doesn't change what I know I have to do, but thank you for understanding."

Marie stood and nodded. "Follow your heart, Jeisa. Things tend to work out for the best when you do."

Jeisa turned to leave, then stopped. Somewhere during their conversation she had changed her mind. No, it wouldn't be easy, but she didn't want to lose Marie as well as Jeremy. "I won't be working for Corisi Enterprises anymore after today, but I'd like to come back to see you now and then, if that's okay."

Marie smiled. "I'd be hurt if you didn't." Jeisa was about to step out of the room when Marie said, "I'll ask around and see if I have connections to that water project you're interested in."

Jeisa opened her mouth to say it wasn't necessary but was cut off by a *tsk, tsk* from the older woman.

She said, "Make an old woman happy and let me do this for you."

Jeisa smiled. "You play dirty."

Marie's smile brightened. "Sometimes."

The housekeeper met Jeisa at the door, her enormous shoulders practically filling it. Jeisa smiled sweetly at her and was rewarded with a steady stare. The woman turned and Jeisa followed her out. Just before she stepped out of the room, Jeisa paused and said, "Thank you, Marie. For everything."

Marie nodded and waved good-bye, once again looking every bit the unassuming sweet lady she pretended to be. *You can't fool me anymore,* Jeisa thought, and chuckled to herself. Marie would be far too gracious to ever turn down a gift, and Jeisa decided to use that fact to her advantage. *They don't call me an image consultant for nothing.*

The next morning, Jeremy greeted the doorman as he entered Jeisa's apartment building at seven thirty. "Morning, Tim. How are Carol and the kids?"

The smile of the older man, whom Jeremy guessed was in his late thirties, was easy and open. "Good, thank you. How was your trip?"

Jeremy thought over the last few days and said, "Successful. I accomplished what I set out to do. Did you get that science project done for your youngest?"

Tim chuckled. "I did. I think the teacher suspects that I helped her, though. Maybe I shouldn't have soldered the pieces together."

Jeremy laughed, "Hindsight is crystal clear, huh? Have your wife send her a gift card for coffee or something. She might let it slide."

Shaking his head, Tim said, "You don't know Mrs. Dubois. She runs a tight third-grade ship. I'll be lucky if I get off with a warning."

Remembering something, Jeremy reached into the interior breast pocket of his suit and pulled out an envelope. "I almost forgot. Someone gave me season tickets to the Boston Celtics. I'm not a big sports fan. You want them?"

"Are you serious? I mean… I couldn't accept them."

"Consider it a tip for all the times you've given me advice on the fly."

Jeremy opened the envelope and held out the tickets. "There are four here. You could take your whole family." When Tim hesitated, Jeremy said, "Hey, if I keep them they'll end up unused and forgotten. If you don't want them, at least take them and find them a new home. It's a shame to see them go to waste."

Tim pocketed them reluctantly. "Thank you."

Jeremy nodded and started walking toward the elevator, then decided to take the stairs. The more he worked out, the more alive he felt, and today he was riding high on his latest success—with the Tenin government, and with Alethea.

Life is good!

"Sounds great. Okay, I'm heading up. It's early, so Jeisa is going to be grumpy, but I brought a peace offering." He held up a bag of Brazilian brigadeiros from her favorite bakery.

He took the stairs two at a time up the four flights to Jeisa's apartment.

After a few moments of increasingly louder knocking, she answered and half-leaned against the door she held open for him, dressed in pink shorts and a plain white T-shirt. It was obvious from her sleep-heavy eyes that he had woken her, and it was equally obvious from the nipples he could clearly see through the thin material of her shirt that she'd rolled straight out of bed to answer the door.

The image hit him like a sucker punch. He fought an impulse to bury a hand into that long, wild tangle of dark hair and haul her to him for a morning kiss. *Not now,* he mentally addressed his errant loins. *Not Jeisa.*

Her scent sent a pulsing rush of blood southward. He stood just in front of her, glad that his jacket was long enough to conceal the effects of his momentarily haywire libido.

What is wrong with me?

I didn't feel like this when I was with Alethea.

She motioned for him to enter, and although his feet didn't move, a part of his lower region certainly did—with surprising enthusiasm.

Shit, I didn't feel like this at all with Alethea.

Jeisa pushed a lock of hair behind one of her delicious ears and said, "Are you coming in or not?" Her voice sent unexpected shivers of pleasure down his spine.

You know you're in a bad place when just the word "coming" is enough to clear your head of all coherent thought. He took a second look at how she was dressed. No woman should look that good straight out of bed.

Her eyes met his and she blushed slightly, but she didn't look away. Was it possible that whatever insanity had overcome him was something she felt too?

He leaned in until their lips almost touched and breathed in the scent of her. His heart pounded in his chest. In an attempt to regain some control, he raised the bag he held in one hand and said, "I brought..."

She took the bag from him, quickly turned, and re-entered the apartment. He followed, releasing a shaky breath.

Holy shit.

She led the way to the small kitchen and busied herself making coffee for both of them. Jeremy sat on a barstool at the counter, grateful for how it hid the evidence of his arousal.

"Was your trip successful?" she asked without looking back at him.

He tried to answer but got momentarily lost in the long expanse of tanned legs that her shorts revealed and the tight little ass they just barely covered. "I got the contract," he said, his mouth suddenly dry.

"That's great," Jeisa said, still not turning from the coffee machine. "Did you see Alethea?"

His enthusiastic retelling of his trip died before it he uttered a word of it. Was it his imagination or was Jeisa upset? A myriad of emotions swirled within Jeremy. He strove to get things back to normal between them. "Yes, and she loved the jet. You were right about that."

"I'm glad," Jeisa said and turned, leaning back onto her hands, which gripped the edge of the counter on the opposite side of the small kitchen. The pose lifted her breasts and pressed them even more tightly against the material of her thin T-shirt.

Jeremy swallowed hard.

Seeing Alethea should have lessened his attraction to Jeisa. Instead, it had done the opposite, and he was struggling to understand what that meant.

"What did she think of the new you?" Jeisa asked.

The triumph he'd felt about finally gaining the interest of Alethea felt out of place with Jeisa. Still, he wasn't about to lie to her. He tried to lighten the mood with a joke. "I rocked her world."

Jeisa spilled the coffee as her hand jerked. She swore in Portuguese as she mopped the hot liquid off her bare legs. When she looked up, her eyes were full of hurt that had nothing to do with the spill.

No, Jeisa doesn't feel that way about me... does she?

"Did you kiss her?" Jeisa asked as if the question were torn from her.

"No," Jeremy said. He could have. She'd given him the opportunity when he'd dropped her off at her plane. His reluctance hadn't made sense to him until just now. "That wasn't part of the plan."

Nor was this.

"But now the two of you will be working closely on this project, won't you?" she asked.

"Yes," he answered and hated that he felt guilty. She knew this was what he'd been working toward. None of it was a surprise. The only unexpected part was how empty his success now felt.

"I'm happy for you," she said, her voice thick with emotion. "You did it, Jeremy. You fought for what you wanted and you got it."

Did I?

Jeisa continued, "I guess now is as good a time as any to tell you that I won't be going to Thanksgiving with you. In fact, I've already resigned my position, effective immediately."

Whatever Jeisa had expected, it wasn't for Jeremy to surge out of his seat and corner her against the counter. He said, "What are you talking about? You can't quit."

His nearness had an instant effect on her ability to concentrate. She tried to slide away, but he blocked her retreat by placing a hand on the counter beside her. She licked her suddenly dry lips. "I already did. Marie understands my reasons."

"Well, I don't," he boomed with an emotion she hadn't seen from him before, "and you work for me."

Jeisa shook her head. "Technically I work for—or rather I did work for—Corisi Enterprises."

He ran a frustrated hand through his hair. "You can't quit. I need you."

Oh, how I wish that were true.

Just as her heart started to soften a bit, opening ever so slightly to allow a ray of hope in, Jeremy said, "You said you would come with me to Thanksgiving next week. I can't go to the Andrades' alone."

Of course, he needs me to choose his suits, prepare him with topics for light discussion. What next, pick up the condoms in case Alethea joins them? No way. I'm done. "I never agreed to go with you."

His frown deepened. “Why are you doing this Jeisa? I don’t get it.”

Something in her snapped. She raised herself onto her tiptoes, yanked his head down and settled her lips on his, using a kiss to tell him what she couldn’t yet put into words.

Like a match to dry kindling, heat burst from the kiss on both sides. His hands were instantly on her waist, pulling her against his bulging erection. His mouth welcomed her as if this were their hundredth kiss instead of their first. She rubbed herself boldly against him and was rewarded by feeling him shudder with pleasure against her.

Easily, he lifted her onto the counter behind her and she leaned back, making no effort to stop one of his hands from sliding beneath the hem of her shirt and settling on her breast. Gently, almost reverently, teasing and exploring her excited tips. Standing between her open legs, he eased his other hand inside the loose material of her shorts, sliding it beneath her silk panties and claiming one side of her bottom, rubbing it deliciously and easing her forward on the counter until his hardness was straining against her moistness.

Her head fell back with the pleasure of it, and his lips began to worship her neck. His hot breath tickled her ear. He tasted her as if she were an addiction he’d long fought to deny but had finally given in to.

With one hand, he lifted her shirt; when his mouth claimed one of her breasts she was lost to the intensity of it. For just a moment, it didn’t matter that his heart belonged to another woman. Time and reason fell away, leaving only a raging need within both of them.

His phone rang in the pocket of his jacket, jarring Jeisa back to reality.

What am I doing?

She placed a hand on Jeremy’s shoulder and pushed against it. He raised his head, those blue eyes burning with the same desire she still felt pulsing within her. Still, sanity was creeping in. “Stop, Jeremy. We can’t do this.”

His hands stilled, not yet withdrawing. His ragged breathing was testament enough to how mutual the encounter had been. Yet, he stopped when she asked. Many men would have been resentful or angry. Jeremy was neither. He rested his forehead on her shoulder and took a calming breath. His hands returned to her waist, maintaining a contact but easing the intimacy of their embrace.

The ringing stopped as his phone likely went to voice mail.

A question nagged at her. She had to ask. "Who called?"

His head straightened. "Who cares?"

She didn't want to, but she did. "I do."

He stepped away from her and checked his phone. He didn't have to say who had called. She knew. When he said nothing, Jeisa hopped off the counter, straightened her clothing, and said, "You should go, Jeremy."

Before I make an even bigger fool of myself.

His face flushed and suddenly he looked a bit defensive. "I didn't know until just now that you liked me. You never said anything."

"Some men aren't as oblivious as you are," Jeisa said, knowing she was really angry at herself.

Jaw tight with anger, he said, "You should have said something."

His words cut through her like a dull knife ripping her heart into frayed pieces. "Why? You've made your choice abundantly clear," her voice broke a bit as she spoke.

Jeisa watched his face as confusion replaced his anger. He raised a hand to touch her, but she moved away from him and toward the door. He followed her. At the door he said, "I never meant to hurt you. I care about you."

Care about—not love.

"Please go, Jeremy." She opened the door for him.

He took a step through it, but stopped just in front of her. "I want to tell you that she means nothing to me, but I won't lie to you."

Marie's theory on honesty doesn't hold water when tested.

There is definitely a wrong time for the truth.

"Good-bye, Jeremy."

He didn't move. He opened and closed his mouth several times as if he'd started to say something and then decided against it. Finally he said, "Come to Thanksgiving with me."

Jeisa shook her head. "I can't."

He added, "We need time to figure this out."

"What am I supposed to do, spend a week with you and hope that at the end of it you choose me?" *Give you more of a chance to break my heart if you don't?*

Jeremy leaned down and claimed her lips with his as if testing something. She swayed against him. There was no denying the instant heat that rocked them both. When he broke off the kiss, he whispered, "One week, starting Monday."

Her stomach flipped as she asked, "Why Monday?"

He didn't answer; instead he took a step back and said, "I'll send a car for you. Have an overnight bag packed."

She shook her head. "I am not going to sleep with you to help you figure this out."

With a confident smile that was a blend of the man he'd always been and the man he was becoming, Jeremy winked at her. She caught her breath. "Who said anything about sleeping?"

Jeremy's phone rang again, but this time when he checked it he looked relieved. "That's the gym reminding me that I have a session with Ray this morning. I'm in a lot less pain the next day if I don't make him wait." With one final quick kiss, he said, "I'll see you Monday."

He was already inside the elevator and out of earshot by the time Jeisa mustered a response. "I didn't say yes."

Oh, who am I kidding?

What kind of woman agrees to give a man a week to choose between her and someone he spent the last decade lusting over?

Only a woman in love would be that stupid.

Marie, what if you're wrong?

Jeisa closed the door of her apartment and leaned against it.

Or what if while fighting for what you want, you discover that you don't like who you are? I've spent too much time avoiding confrontation and wondering why I never get what I want. I run. I hide. I make excuses for my weakness.

But I can change.

When has anything wonderful come to those unwilling to risk something for it?

The road back to respecting myself starts here. I'm going to give Jeremy that week he asked for because if I don't I will always wonder what might have been. This isn't something I'm giving him, it's something I'm giving myself.

And if he breaks my heart?

I'll survive, because that is what strong women do. They pick themselves back up and move on.

An image of Marie flitted through Jeisa's mind like a gentle reminder of something else she needed to address.

I should call my father and tell him everything.

Jeisa picked up the phone and just as quickly replaced it. He was not going to be happy.

I'll tell him after Thanksgiving.

CHAPTER *Six*

LATER THAT MORNING, after an hour-long boxing lesson with Ray and an extended run, Jeremy headed into Corisi headquarters in Boston. His custom-fit navy-blue Caffrey suit was comfortable yet bold. He wished he could say the same for his mental state. Neither the extra miles he'd added to his morning run nor the long, hot shower he had indulged in afterward had slowed his racing thoughts. *Jeisa. Alethea.* And a kiss that rocked everything he thought he knew. Jeremy sought out the one man he knew could help him and breezed by the secretary who would normally have stopped him.

Dominic Corisi was on the phone when Jeremy entered his office. Jeremy walked up to his desk and plopped into one of the chairs just in front of it.

"I'll call you back," Dominic said into the phone and hung up. Jeremy didn't take offense to the glare the other man gave him. That was Dominic.

Jeremy cut right to the reason he was there. "I need your help."

One dark eyebrow rose in doubt, but Dominic remained silent.

Never having been good at niceties, Jeremy strove to find the right lead-in to the conversation he wanted to have. "We're sort of friends, aren't we, Dominic?"

"No, not really," Dominic said in a somewhat dry tone.

Jeremy shrugged. "I might deserve that. I do enjoy trying to piss you off."

Dominic expelled a harsh breath. "Is there a point to this?"

"Is it possible to be in love with someone while you lust after someone else? Or as soon as you realize that you lust after someone else, does that mean you were never in love?"

Not a muscle moved on Dominic's face, and his silence continued to the point of awkwardness. Eventually Dominic said, "Get the fuck out of my office."

Jeremy didn't budge. He'd never gotten anything from backing down. "I'm serious. I respect your opinion. What do you think?"

"I think you picked the wrong person to give you the birds-and-bees speech."

Shaking his head, Jeremy persisted. "I don't think so. You've been linked to countless women in the press. I assume they were all women you wanted to be with sexually. How did you know that Abby was the right woman for you?"

Jeremy thought that Dominic was going to tell him to leave again—or perhaps even call security—but Dominic's expression softened at the mention of his wife. "I realized that when I was with her I was a better man." A small smile stretched his lips and he added, "For example, she's the reason you're still alive."

Jeremy nodded as he mulled Dominic's answer.

If he based his decision on which woman made him want to be a better man, Jeisa won hands down. She was patient and supportive. She didn't judge his weaknesses, and therefore he had never hidden them from her. They shared an honesty he couldn't imagine ever achieving with someone like Alethea.

I want Jeisa, and if I don't do something fast, I'm going to lose her.

Dominic leaned forward onto one elbow and said, "Now get out."

Despite the harshness of Dominic's command, Jeremy stood and smiled. He'd gotten the answer he'd come for. "Thanks, Dom. I know what to do now."

As he was leaving, he said over his shoulder, "See you Thursday at the Andrades'."

He heard Dominic swearing as he closed the door and chuckled.

I'm growing on him, Jeremy thought as he sauntered down the hallway.

A million things to do that day, but first—and most important—Jeremy had a date to plan.

Where do you take someone when you can afford to take her anywhere?

A few hours later, Jeremy was sitting in his office in the Corisi building, being far from productive. He listened to voice messages from two senators, a handful of headhunters, and a reporter he had no intention of calling back. He even listened to a message from Alethea. She was heading back to Tenin to double-check something and she wanted to know if he could join her. She suggested they celebrate Thanksgiving abroad while looking into something she didn't want to discuss on the phone.

There was a time when he would have given anything for such a message from Alethea. Today, it left him cold. All he could think about was Jeisa and how he wanted to spend the week getting to know her better.

Bold plans for a man who had no experience in such things.

Why the hell did I say I'd pick her up on Monday? I should have given myself more time to come up with something amazing. Still seated at his desk, he was staring out the window of his office when Marie knocked lightly on the door and entered. He stood to greet her.

Marie studied his face. "I'm glad to see you're sporting fewer bruises these days."

Jeremy smiled. Marie's visit felt like sunshine after a storm: welcome, warm, and an uncomplicated joy. "Good to see you, Marie." He held out a chair for her and sat across from her. "What brings you here?"

"Have you seen Jeisa since you returned?"

He felt his face redden. “Yes.”

“So, you know she’s quitting?”

“I talked her into staying for one more week. She and I will be at the Andrades’ house with you for Thanksgiving.”

“That’s wonderful! How did you convince her?”

His face warmed even more.

A huge smile lit Marie’s face. “You don’t know how happy this makes me.”

Jeremy cleared his throat and cautioned, “Marie, don’t make it more than it is. We haven’t even had our first date yet.”

“Well, what are you waiting for?”

He leaned back in his chair and covered his face with one hand. “I told her I’d pick her up on Monday morning and to have an overnight bag ready.”

“You did that?” Marie asked with happy surprise.

Jeremy grinned, unable to conceal the pride he felt in his confident order. “I did.” Then he sobered. “Now I have to figure out where to take her. Where did Dominic take Abby on their first date?”

Suddenly serious, Marie leaned over and placed a hand on Jeremy’s. “It doesn’t matter where they went. This journey is all about you and Jeisa.”

Jeremy shrugged, uncomfortable with her correction. “I don’t want to disappoint her.”

Marie lightly squeezed his hand. “When a man plans something special for a woman he cares about, there’s no room for disappointment. Choose something you know she enjoys doing.”

Feeling a weight settle on his chest, Jeremy admitted, “That’s a problem, then, because we’ve spent most of our time together talking about my goals and what I want. I don’t really know what she likes.”

Marie smiled again. “She likes you. Even I know that. A smart man like you will figure the rest out.”

Jeremy stood, sudden inspiration hitting him. “I’ve got it.” He returned to his desk and started typing on his laptop.

"You're a genius, Marie. I know how to find out what she likes."

Marie went to stand behind him. "Jeremy." She stretched out his name as a warning.

Jeremy was too excited by what he was uncovering to let her concern slow him down. "She doesn't even use numbers or symbols in her passwords. That was the easiest code to break. I'll have to talk to her about that."

Marie put a hand on his shoulder. "This wasn't what I meant, Jeremy."

Jeremy pointed to his screen and said, "Marie, you said that I need to know what she likes. Well, what better way to do that than to check out her recent searches online?" He tapped the screen when a local florist came up. "She has a standing order for a weekly delivery of a bouquet of flowers native to Brazil, but she states that she wants it to be different each week." He took a moment to digest what it meant. "So, she misses Brazil and likes surprises." He continued to scroll through the information, his fingers furiously taking him from link to link. He paused on one page and said, "Hey, she searched for information about me while I was gone." He smiled back at Marie, who simply shook her head at him.

His lightheartedness fell away as his searches revealed more. He covered the page with his hand when he stumbled upon a personal purchase. Heat filled his face. He said, "I love that she has one, but you shouldn't see this, Marie."

Marie stepped away from the computer and cautioned Jeremy, "Just because it's easy for you to do, Jeremy, doesn't make it right."

Jeremy reassured her. "I won't read more than I need. I promise. As soon as I find something that makes for a perfect date, I'll stop."

Marie leaned over and closed the laptop on his fingers. "Take her to California. There is a university out there that is working on a prototype for a toilet they say will improve the living conditions in third world countries. Jeisa is very interested in that research. Interested enough to consider moving out there to be part of the project."

Jeremy eased his fingers out of his laptop. His own mother had never tried to rein him in, perhaps because she'd always felt guilty for how much she'd asked of him. Marie had no such qualms. He had a greater respect for her and her relationship with Dominic now that he'd seen this side of her.

Toilets?

Marie was never wrong, but Jeisa hadn't given any indication of being interested in them.

Toilets, huh? He couldn't suppress his smile. *Is it possible that beneath her sexy façade there beats the heart of a geek?*

While cautiously watching Marie out of the corner of his eye, he slowly reopened his laptop and did a quick search for the project she'd mentioned. After reading the university's article on the subject, he said, "These prototypes are amazing! And solar powered. That is so cool. The site talks about saving the world and I can see how they could. Just amazing."

He closed the laptop and looked across at Marie dubiously. "Can I really build a romantic trip around visiting a waste-disposal facility?"

Marie smiled, her good mood returning. "Normally, I would say no, but it's a passion of Jeisa's. You know how they say that the way to a man's heart is through his stomach? The way to a woman's heart is through appreciating whatever she loves. Let me make a few phone calls. I'll set everything up. All you have to do is get in the limo I send for you."

Jeremy crossed the room and hugged Marie. She protested lightly and brushed him away, but she was smiling as she did so.

"I don't know what I'd do without you, Marie."

Her smile was kind when she said, "I get that a lot."

Jeremy stared absently out the window long after Marie had left his office. His phone rang several times, but he didn't answer it. His body might still have been in the office, but his heart and mind were already imagining California with Jeisa.

On Monday morning, poised on the edge of her couch, Jeisa started to text Jeremy but then deleted the partially written message. Instead, she reread the earlier text he'd sent her.

"See you at eight."

Not, "I love you."

Not, "I can't stop thinking about you."

Just, "See you at eight."

Oh, my God, what if he didn't really mean it about the overnight bag? Or he might have changed his mind. What if he met up with Alethea over the weekend?

I'm not sixteen. I know the rules.

Rule number one in the book of how to protect your heart: Do not go away with a man who loves another woman. It only leads to heartache.

Rule number two: Do not spend the weekend shopping and having your hair done for a date you are not going on. If you forget why, refer to rule number one.

Rule number three: Do not sit on your couch, dressed to impress, for an hour before said date with an overnight bag by the door and then overthink the situation. If you've decided to throw caution to the wind and do something you know is wrong, at least try to enjoy yourself.

Jeisa jumped off the couch at the first knock. She smoothed the skirt of her dress and answered the door. Her breath caught in her throat when she saw Jeremy.

Dressed in one of the designer suits she'd chosen for him, he held out a bouquet of red begonias. Jeisa took the flowers. *Beautiful and odd at the same time. Only Jeremy.* She said, "I should probably put these in water."

Neither of them moved.

Jeremy said, "You look amazing."

Jeisa smiled and said, "So do you."

Which earned her a smile in return.

Jeremy took her by the hand and said, "Don't worry about the flowers. Let's just grab your bag and go."

Before we both change our minds. He didn't have to say it.

Jeisa looked into those deep blue eyes and made a decision.

I want Jeremy.

For tonight, if that's all we can have.

Screw playing it safe.

With that she threw the bouquet of flowers over her shoulder and into her apartment with abandon.

Jeremy laughed in surprise and pulled her to him for a crushing kiss, one that cleared her head of any lingering second thoughts and replaced them with a hum of need. The kiss deepened as his arms enfolded her and she sank into the bliss of his embrace.

When they were both shaking with need, Jeremy broke off the kiss, rested his forehead on hers, and said, "We'd better go."

"Where?" she whispered.

He straightened and took her hand in one of his and her bag in the other. "It's a surprise, but I think you're really going to love it."

Her heart tightened in her chest. *I already do. That was never the problem.*

Jeremy followed Jeisa into the back of the Hummer limo that Mrs. Duhamel had arranged for the date. Soft, romantic music filled the dimly lit interior. Jeisa looked uncertain where to sit and finally chose the back corner. Jeremy chose the seat next to her, but left a space between them.

She was nervous, and he felt ridiculous.

Get a grip.

We've ridden in dozens of limos together.

This time was different and they both knew it. As they pulled out into traffic his phone rang. *Dammit, I should have turned it off.* He decided to ignore it.

Jeisa looked across at him. "Aren't you going to answer it?"

"No."

It stopped ringing for a moment, then started up again.

Jeisa said, "Someone really wants to speak to you."

With a sigh of resignation, Jeremy took out his phone and checked the caller ID. He groaned. "It's my mother."

Jeisa relaxed a bit and waved her hand. "She's only going to worry if you don't answer."

"You're right," he said and swiped the phone's screen with his thumb. *Way to kill a mood.* "Hi, Mom. Can I call you back tomorrow? I'm kind of busy right now."

"You're always busy lately," his mother said with no intention of hanging up. "I miss you."

Jeremy looked out the window and spoke softly, hoping his words were not audible to Jeisa. "I miss you, too."

"Well, all I wanted to tell you is I changed my work schedule around so now I will be able to spend Thanksgiving with you and your friends."

Oh, boy.

"Will Jeisa be there?" his mother asked.

"Yes," Jeremy said and instantly regretted sharing that information. By the pleased expression on Jeisa's face, he guessed she'd heard his mother's question.

"Fantastic! Next time you see her, tell her I asked about her. She is so sweet. That's the kind of woman I'd like you to marry one day."

Oh, the universe has a sense of humor.

"Mom, I have to go."

"I mean it, Jeremy. You've wasted enough time on that crazy redhead. You need a nice girl. You two would make the most beautiful children."

Is it any wonder I'm still a virgin?

"Bye, Mom. I'll call you when I get back."

"Back from where? Where are you going?"

"I'll call you tomorrow," he repeated and hung up.

A hint of self-doubt began to creep in and sour Jeremy's mood. *It doesn't matter what suit I wear or how much money I make. Am I fooling myself to think I belong here? To think that someone as cultured and beautiful as Jeisa could really want a man like me?*

The warmth of Jeisa's hand on one of his thighs jolted him. He swung around and found that she had closed the distance between them and was smiling sweetly up at him.

"I think it's beautiful that you're close to your mother," she said and gave his thigh a supportive squeeze.

He laid his hand over hers on his leg and said, "I'm sorry. This isn't how I imagined the beginning of our first date would go."

A look came into Jeisa's eyes that he hadn't seen before, and the intensity of it shook him to the core. She said, "I don't want to go on a date with the man you think you need to be to impress me. I love the man you are."

"Love?" Jeremy gulped hard.

Jeisa nodded.

When he said nothing, a hurt darkened her eyes. She said, "I know you're not in the same place I am, but I thought you should know." Her voice was thick with emotion.

Love.

Shit.

The words took root in his heart and a warmth spread through him. *Jeisa loves me.*

Then panic stole his breath. *Jeisa loves me.* None of the etiquette lessons she'd given him had prepared him for what to say when he couldn't sincerely parrot the words back. Do you thank someone for their honesty? Do you pretend you didn't hear it?

Oh, look at her face.

She really wants me to say it back.

A thousand wild emotions rushed through him.

Last week I still thought I wanted to be with Alethea.

I'm not ready for love.

I care about Jeisa.

I want to be with her tonight.

That's not love.

I can't say something I don't mean just to get in her pants. She deserves better than that.

She deserves honesty.

He cleared his throat awkwardly and said, "I don't know what I feel, Jeisa, or where this is going. If you want me to drop you off back at your apartment, I can do that."

Those brown eyes of hers darkened further as she asked, "Is that what you want?"

He squeezed her hand beneath his and said, "No. I want to spend this week with you." As he said the words, his confidence in what he wanted from her grew. Yes, he would love to explore her incredible body and discover what it's like to sink into the hot, welcoming center of a woman, but he wanted something else even more. "We don't have to have sex. I want to get to know you. I want to know what you like, and what you hate. The past few months have been about me. I want this week to be about you."

She met his eyes and seemed to be debating something. "I'll give you one week. But if you don't know how you feel by Thanksgiving, I'm leaving and I won't want to see you again. Promise me that you'll respect that."

Jeremy considered her beautiful face, her kind eyes, and pulled her closer. He hugged her into his chest and tucked her head beneath his chin. He tried to lighten the mood with a joke. "It's going to be embarrassing if I have to return the value pack of condoms to the pharmacy."

She sat back, some of her sadness dissipating, and swatted at him. "Value pack?"

He pulled her back into his side and said, "One didn't seem like enough—we do have a whole week."

She chuckled into his chest. "You're an ass."

He hugged her tighter.

I am, but hopefully it's a temporary condition.

CHAPTER *Seven*

WHEN THE LIMOUSINE pulled onto a private airfield just outside Boston and stopped alongside a 757 jumbo jet, the light conversation Jeisa and Jeremy had maintained for the last twenty minutes came to an abrupt end as her jaw dropped. She looked from the jet across to Jeremy, and then back to the supersized aircraft. “Oh, my God!”

Jeremy guided her out of the limo and up the stairs to the jet. The attendants stood back, present and welcoming but unobtrusive. The room just inside the aircraft was furnished with cream-colored leather chairs and couches which surrounded a dark wooden table. The walls were covered with silk and accented with gold.

“Would you like a tour?” a woman in a formal tan suit asked. She then led them through the plane, describing the contents of each opulent room as they passed through it.

Jeremy took Jeisa’s hand in his and flushed a bit. “Is this where I confess that Marie helped me plan out the details of the trip? The jet I rented was about a quarter of this size.”

A wave of relief flooded Jeisa. *This isn’t the one he rented for Alethea.*

Jeisa had grown up in the comfort of an upper-middle-class Brazilian family, but this kind of wealth was beyond anything she was used to. The jet made a statement, and it was a bold one.

She and Jeremy followed the attendant through a dining area, past the guest bedroom, and into a master suite that was another exercise in luxurious excess. Gold-plated fixtures in the master bath. Mohair furniture embroidered with emblems that were repeated on the accent pillows throughout the room. A king-sized bed was the focal point of the suite.

Hand in hand, Jeisa and Jeremy stood at the foot of it. The attendant said, "We leave in about ten minutes. Make yourselves comfortable. You'll have absolute privacy unless you'd like something, in which case just press the button on this screen. We have a fully stocked kitchen and bar."

Jeremy was the first to speak after the attendant left. He said, "I bet this is one of Dominic's."

Jeisa nodded. *It made sense.*

"That makes this his bed," he said with a light laugh in his voice. He ran a hand over his face. "Even if you throw yourself at me, we can't use this room."

Jeisa looked up at Jeremy from beneath long lashes. "What makes you think I'm going to throw myself at you?"

Jeremy turned her toward him and put his hands on her hips. "A man can hope, can't he?" And he lowered his mouth to hers. Between kisses he said, "We don't have to take it further, but I can't help myself. I've thought about kissing you all day."

Reason retreated as passion flared between them. His tongue hungrily sought hers, and she was helpless in the face of her body's response. When he touched her, nothing else mattered. She wrapped her arms around his neck, holding him to her, rubbing herself wantonly against him in a way she'd never offered herself to another man.

He was right to be optimistic.

There was no denying that she wanted him.

The pilot's voice came over the intercom. "You may want to secure yourselves. We are about to take off."

Jeremy reluctantly ended the kiss, but he didn't set her back from him. He smiled down at her. "Do you think Marie put us on this jet because she thought it would deter us?"

Jeisa took a shaky breath and smiled up at the man who fluctuated between friend and potential lover with ease. The dry humor he used when he shared his thoughts with her was one of the many qualities that had made her fall in love with him. Most men hid themselves behind some macho persona—the same persona Jeremy was trying to present to the rest of the world. But when he was with her, he was simply Jeremy. He didn't protect himself or mislead her.

Sometimes she wished he would.

If he breaks my heart, I'll have no one to blame but myself.

She knew that all she had to do was tell Jeremy that she was uncomfortable and he would stop. Stop the date. Stop their week together. Stop those fabulous kisses that rocked her to the core.

And what?

I let this become another dream I wasn't brave enough to try for?

No, I'm not going to live half of a life anymore.

My change starts here.

Jeremy pulled her closer and whispered in her ear, "The more you look at me like that, the less I care who owns this jet."

The floor shifted beneath them as the jet started down the runway. Jeremy braced himself against the edge of the bed and eventually sat, pulling Jeisa down to sit sideways across his lap.

For a long moment, the only sound in the room was the soft hum of the jet's engine as the plane accelerated down the runway. When it left the ground, Jeisa and Jeremy were pushed back to recline on the bed side by side. Every place their bodies touched pulsed with hot need.

She looked up at him and said the first words that came to her mind. "There's always the guest room."

He shuddered against her. One hand came up to cup her chin, lifting it until she was forced to look directly into his eyes. "Are you sure?" he asked huskily.

Maybe he didn't love her.

Maybe he never would.

But the man who looked down at her with such tenderness and concern for her feelings was one that she wanted to share herself with.

She nodded and whispered, "Yes."

The plane leveled off. Jeisa could have eased herself off Jeremy, but she didn't. She'd made her decision and now waited for his.

He stood up, swung her up into his arms, and carried her down the hallway to the guest bedroom. He placed her in the middle of the silk comforter as if she were the most delicate of treasures.

Never breaking eye contact, he slid out of his suit jacket and shoes and joined her. She expected a frenzied rush, and so she wasn't sure what to think when he didn't immediately kiss her.

Instead, he propped himself up with one elbow and looked down at her while his free hand traced the neckline of her dress. The back of his fingers brushed the curve of her breast through the material of her dress, then continued down her waist and hip. He tucked a curl behind her ear and, with one finger, traced the line of her chin before lightly caressing her lips.

Jeisa couldn't breathe. Her body melted beneath his touch. She moistened and clenched at the thought of where his adoring hands would go next. He traced the line of her shoulder and she closed her eyes, arching her back instinctively, offering him access to more.

The heat of his breath fanned her neck lightly, teasing her with warmth as he withheld the touch of his tongue.

"Take off your dress for me," he commanded softly, and her eyes flew open.

She sat up, lifted her dress over her head, and dropped it on the floor beside the bed. Shifting forward onto her knees, she slid a finger beneath both sides of her silk panties and eased them off along with her shoes. She turned fully toward him, naked and unashamed, knowing that what they were about to share would have meaning for both of them.

He rolled onto his back, pulling her with him so that she was straddling his still-clothed waist. His erection strained against the material of his suit pants, ready for her even while still being restrained. She rubbed herself against his excitement and threw her head back.

Both of Jeremy's hands went behind her, cupping her buttocks and encouraging her to continue her intimate caress. His strong hands moved up her back, pulling her downward until her lips hovered just above his. "I want you, Jeisa. I've never wanted anyone as much as I want you right now."

His words gave Jeisa a confidence she'd never felt during sex. The few men in her sexual history had taken more than they'd given. She hadn't realized until just then how little control she'd felt with the others. Even now, even as she was naked against his obvious need, he was giving her the power to set the pace.

She claimed his lips with all the passion building within her. Her tongue teased and invaded his mouth, inviting him to deepen their connection. She arched herself back, not breaking the kiss, to allow room to undo his belt and unbutton his trousers. She pulled his shirt free and unbuttoned it from bottom to top, hungrily running her hands over the chest she had exposed.

He slid out from beneath her, quickly shedding his clothing before rejoining her. This time they lay side by side, each exploring the other's body while they kissed. He eased her onto her back and slowly, excruciatingly slowly, caressed every inch of her.

Nothing escaped his worshiping touch. His lips traced the curve of her waist, the bend in her arm. He tasted the small of her back with a hot enthusiasm that few men exhibited even during a more intimate connection. Systematically, he was learning where she was most sensitive to his touch, and when he found those spots, he lingered there—moaning with desire each time she shuddered from the sheer pleasure that rocked through her.

He brought her to the brink of ecstasy and then paused. Jeisa took her cue from him and ran her hands over every one of his hard muscles she could reach. She thought she'd had good sex before, but by comparison those experiences felt rushed. Jeremy not only wanted to get to know her, he wanted her to know him.

In her own exploration, she learned as much about what pleased her as what excited him. There was a new exhilaration that came from licking just the right spot and watching his eyes close from the pleasure of it. She gave him more of herself because she knew that in just a moment the dance would shift again and she would be the one quivering helplessly beneath his attention.

Jeisa gasped when one of his hands sought more intimacy. His first caress was an open palm cupping and rubbing her mound. Then his thumb delved between her labia and claimed her clitoris. He broke off the kiss and studied her expression while he began a gentle rub, increasing the pressure and rhythm until she was writhing beneath his hand.

He slid another finger between her folds and buried it deep inside her, seeking and finding a spot that had her clutching the silk bedding around her. As his fingers worked her from the inside, Jeisa couldn't contain her moans of pleasure. She bit her lip in pure passion as heat began to build and spread through her. It started where his fingers played and washed over her until she was gasping and crying out his name as she climaxed.

She was still shuddering as ripple after ripple rocked her when she heard the soft rip of a condom package being opened. Their eyes met and held while he positioned himself between the thighs she spread wide for him.

He sank into her, closing his eyes for a moment with a look of sheer ecstasy on his face. Then, holding himself above her with his well-muscled arms, he watched her expression as he began to move within her. Slowly at first and then with more power. She clung to his back and met his thrusts with her own, loving how he filled her.

He leaned down, kissing her lips again as he rocked inside her. His hot mouth moved on to worship her neck and the curve of her shoulder. She felt a wave of rapture begin to build again. Each thrust brought her closer to what she thought was impossible for her—a second orgasm.

His body tightened as hers soared and they came together with her almost sobbing from the intensity of it. With one final kiss, he slid out of her and rolled onto his side for a moment. In seconds, he was back, lifting her naked and spent body back into his arms, tossing back the comforter and tucking her beneath it before joining her and wrapping his arms around her from behind.

He whispered into her ear, "I hope you enjoyed that as much as I did. It was my first time, but I've done a lot of reading on the subject so I feel like I nailed it."

Jeisa spun in his arms and almost shrieked, "You were a virgin?"

He looked pleased with himself. "If you couldn't tell, then all those Internet articles were right. I know a couple of other moves that I didn't use this time because I figured we could leave something for next time."

Oh, my God. He was a virgin.

He was probably saving himself for Alethea.

I'm going to Hell.

"There won't be a next time." She pulled away from him, covering herself with the blanket and folding her arms over it. "You're twenty-five," she said in what sounded like an accusation.

His good mood faded a bit as he said, "Does it matter? Because I don't care if you weren't a virgin. You weren't, were you?"

A question every woman loves to answer.

"No," she said through gritted teeth. "I wasn't."

He shook his head in confusion. "Then what's the problem?"

Jeisa threw back the comforter and grabbed her dress from the floor, feeling less vulnerable as she layered her clothing back on. "The problem is that when Marie hired me to teach you everything you needed to know so you could get Alethea, I didn't expect the lessons to include this."

She knew her anger was misdirected.

It wasn't Jeremy's fault she suddenly felt dirty and cheap.

That's what happens when you throw caution to the wind. You crash on the rocks.

"I don't understand," he said slowly as he sat up in bed, the sheet falling onto his lap.

Jeisa didn't either, but she couldn't stop herself from retreating and throwing harsh words at him as she went. "This whole thing was a mistake. You. Me. This date. I never should have said yes."

She opened the door, realizing as she did that there really wasn't anywhere she could run on a flight to God knows where.

"Can you at least tell me if it was any good?" he asked in his classic dry style.

Her answer was the slamming of the door behind her as she retreated to another part of the jet.

Jeremy fought and won against the impulse to chase her. Instead, he fell back onto the pillows, linked his hands behind his head, and stared at the ceiling. He needed time to process what had just happened. His knee-jerk reversion to humor had done nothing to alleviate Jeisa's angst. Without anything to compare it to, he had to face the real possibility that it might not have been as good for her as it had been for him.

She'd looked like she was enjoying it and, unless he was totally wrong, he could have sworn she'd had two orgasms. Maybe she was used to more. Some women were—at least according to the sites he'd read.

He replayed the scenario in his head. He'd assumed that the phrases she'd cried out in Portuguese were indicative of climaxing, but now he wasn't so sure. *I should have taken more time. What an idiot I am—saving what might have been the best for her for another time. I may never get another time with her. Not if our first was a complete wash.*

He thought about how beautiful she'd been standing in the doorway of the bedroom, her hair tousled from sex and her cheeks pink with emotion. *I should have told her to come back to bed. I shouldn't have joked when I knew she was upset.*

I'm too comfortable with her. They had a friendship unlike any he'd known before. He hadn't expected her to be angry when he'd shared the truth about his limited sexual experience.

It didn't make sense to him. Why wouldn't she want to be his first? He wished he could have been hers.

But I have better—I'll be her last.

The thought startled him into sitting up.

I don't want another man to ever touch her.

A devil of a thought challenged his inner declaration.

That would mean that Jeisa would be the only woman I'd ever sleep with. Am I ready for that?

He flopped back onto the bed. An image of her rolling over and greeting him with a kiss each morning tickled his imagination. He closed his eyes to savor the sensual collage his mind was conjuring. Jeisa laughing with him as he practiced greeting dignitaries. The light scent of her perfume when she leaned in to adjust his tie. Jeisa's voice husky from sleep. He hardened as the images became less innocent. Jeisa's tongue meeting his with enthusiasm. The taste of her skin. The feel of her wet center welcoming his fingers, making him suddenly wish he had gone the step further to taste her.

Yes.

He was fully erect and throbbing with a desire to lose himself in Jeisa's arms again when she opened the door. He rolled onto his side and quickly bunched the sheet in a way he hoped concealed his erection.

Her knuckles were white on the hand that clutched the door handle beside her, the only sign that she was more upset than she wanted to let him see. She said, "Most men would have followed me and apologized."

He met her eyes and told her the truth. "I'm not sorry."

She inhaled an angry breath.

He added, "It was amazing. You were amazing."

Her face reddened. "That wasn't what I was talking about."

"You want me to apologize for not having slept with a hundred other women?"

She looked angrily at the ceiling and then back at him. "That's not what I'm saying."

"Then I have no idea what I'm supposed to be sorry for."

Her face crumpled and in resignation she said, "You're right. I don't know what I want. Maybe there is nothing you can say."

Except those three words you need to hear.

He wanted more than anything to say them, but when he tried to they hung unsaid on his lips. He wasn't a player and Jeisa wasn't just some woman. His feelings were still too fresh to trust. He didn't want to say anything until he knew he could offer her forever.

He left the bed and took her into his arms. She stood rigid within his naked embrace. "Come back to bed, Jeisa."

She looked up into his eyes and whispered, "I thought I could do this, but now I don't know."

His heart thudded in his chest. He put her back a step, maintaining contact by holding her hands, and took a calming breath. There was no way to conceal how his body was responding to being so close to her, and he didn't try. She was risking everything to be with him; he wouldn't hide his own vulnerability. "So, what do you want to do?"

Her big brown eyes searched his and she shrugged a shoulder helplessly.

Jeremy turned, slid into his boxers and then trousers. He wanted her badly, but more than that, he wanted to comfort her. He kissed her softly on the lips and took her hand, leading her out of the bedroom and into the main area of the jet. "Let's go see what Dominic has for a movie selection."

Jeisa joined him on a couch, and he tucked her into his side as he navigated the high-tech television remote. His penis was still half-cocked and pulsing merely from her nearness, but Jeremy didn't mind. Jeisa laid her head on his shoulder and he kissed the top of her head. He would have her again, of that he was sure. For now, it was pure heaven just to hold her.

Action movie.
War movie.
Mafia movie.
Thriller.

It didn't really matter what they chose to watch—Jeremy doubted either of them would be able to concentrate on it. He ran a hand lightly up her bare arm and felt her shiver against him. He was just starting to reconsider his decision to bring her out of the bedroom when she asked, "Were you really homeschooled your entire life so you could take care of your father?"

His hand stilled. "Yes."

As she sensed his mood darkening, she quickly said, "I'm sorry. If you don't want to talk about it, I understand."

He hugged her tighter and surprised himself by wanting to share another first experience with her. He never talked about his past, but this was Jeisa, and he wanted her to know him. "You can ask me anything."

"Tell me what Alethea did to help you during that time. Tell me why you spent so many years loving her."

Her request punched the air straight out of his lungs. He closed his eyes and chose his words with care. "She was my escape."

Jeisa leaned back a bit so she could see his face and gently prodded, "Tell me."

Suddenly he wanted to. He looked her in the eyes as he said, "When I was very young and my father could still get around a bit, I loved being with him. He was a good man, but his body slowly betrayed him. At first all I had to do was be around in case he had a bad day, but as he grew weaker, he needed more extensive care. His mind was still there even when he could no longer speak or control his bodily functions. I don't think there is a better definition of hell on earth than being trapped within yourself. I did what I could to make it easier for him. He was ashamed of his weakness in front of nurses, but not with me, so I did what needed to be done most of the time."

"You were so young," Jeisa said softly.

Jeremy shrugged. "Responsibility doesn't wait until you're old enough to handle it. My mother's friends said we should put him in a care facility, but by the time he was at his worst I was already in my teens, and Mom and I decided to let him have the dignity of dying at home."

Jeisa wiped away tears that started streaming down her cheeks.

Once Jeremy started talking, the story came out of him like water over a dam that had held back too much for too long. "He passed away during what would have been my last year of high school."

"And?"

"And I discovered that high school wasn't all I'd dreamed it would be. I attended for about a week before it was painfully obvious that I didn't fit in."

"Oh, Jeremy," Jeisa said, her voice thick with emotion.

He didn't look away. He didn't have to. This was Jeisa, his best friend. "We are what we know. I had weird little habits I wasn't even aware of at the time. Some of them I've eradicated, some still crop up now and then. Hoarding food is one of them. My mother worked two jobs to pay for the nurses and medication my father needed. Sometimes we didn't have money for groceries. I used to steal food from anywhere we visited. Sometimes I still catch myself filling my pockets if I'm somewhere I don't feel comfortable."

Jeisa nodded with understanding. "That's very common in children who were neglected."

Jeremy's head whipped back and hot anger surfaced. "I was not neglected. My mother is one of the strongest women I know. She could have left him when things got hard, but she didn't."

The touch of Jeisa's hand on Jeremy's cheek calmed him. He hadn't realized until just then how raw his emotions still were on some topics.

She said, "No, but you paid a hefty price for that decision."

He didn't agree, or was it that he had never allowed himself to consider it? "When you love someone, you do what you have to do, not what's easy. We made it work. Who knows who I would be today had she chosen another path? I used that time at home to learn about computers and to hone a skill that is more marketable than any college degree would have been."

"And Alethea?"

He didn't want to discuss her, not now, not with Jeisa, but he did because he knew she needed to understand. "I met her online when I was fifteen and we've kept in contact since then." He thought back to the first time he'd met Alethea in person, tall and lean with a riot of sophisticated red hair and a dangerous gleam in her eyes. "She was everything I wasn't. She was popular, rich, and crazy enough to do just about anything for the bragging rights of saying she did it. I used to tell myself if it weren't for my father, I would have been the same."

"But you never dated?"

Jeremy shook his head. "You saw the way I was. I was so far out of her league it's amazing she used to visit me at all."

Jeisa hugged his chest. "No, it isn't."

Jeremy's heart warmed at Jeisa's words. With fresh eyes he looked back at the times he'd spent with Alethea. He realized that the memories he had of her were tied more to his desire to feel worthy of her than to actually wanting to be with her physically. He'd never seen their relationship in that way before, but when he compared how he felt about Jeisa to his feelings for Alethea—there was no comparison.

Alethea was a boyhood dream.

Jeisa is the woman I love.

Every muscle in Jeremy's body tightened as the realization hit him hard.

I love Jeisa. She is the first person I want to share good news with, and the only one I feel truly comfortable sharing my shortcomings with. I'm a better person because she came into my life. He looked down into her upturned face and smiled. *And she loves me.*

Why the hell are we pretending to watch this movie?

He had to tell her. "Jeisa—"

She put a finger on his lips and silenced his words with hers, saying, "I'm tired of talking about Alethea."

Me, too, Jeremy thought and pulled Jeisa onto his lap.

The ability to speak left him when she lifted her dress over her head, filling his vision with her beautiful, full breasts. There would be plenty of time to tell her about his revelations.

Later.

For the moment, all he could think about was how he was going to employ every technique he'd read about until she was screaming his name as she came over and over again. And then, when she was quivering and almost spent, he was going to sink into her and claim her as he brought her to yet another orgasm.

He wasn't sure how many times a woman could climax in one session, but he'd always liked to push the limits of what was considered possible. It was how he'd become so good at hacking. You don't ask yourself if something can be done. You choose your path and do whatever it takes.

Again and again.

All day long.

As often and as creatively as necessary.

Back in the guestroom of the jet, Jeisa woke slowly without opening her eyes. Every muscle in her body was relaxed, every inch of her sated. A satisfied smile curled the corners of her mouth as she remembered how she and Jeremy had spent the last several hours.

Holy shit.

The way he'd explored her—worshipped every corner of her with his tongue and hands—was gloriously insane. She'd thought she knew the difference between good sex and bad sex… or at least mediocre sex. She had no idea her body was capable of reaching multiple orgasms again and again. Like fad diets that promised crazy results, she'd always assumed those how-to articles were all sensation and very little reality.

Until Jeremy.

What he lacked in experience he more than made up for in enthusiasm and attention to detail. *I don't really care where he takes me. I may never have the energy to move again.*

As if sensing her thoughts, he shifted against her back. His strong arm pulled her tighter against him, but he didn't wake. Their spree had apparently left him just as spent.

This is what I get for not telling him that he was amazing the first time. Jeremy sees failure as a challenge. I'd better give him some good news about his performance after this or it'll be like this every time.

Jeisa smiled at the thought.

Which might not be such a bad thing, she thought and chuckled.

"Are you okay?" a deep male voice asked in her ear before he nuzzled it and relaxed again.

Outside of the emotional roller coaster I'm on?

Sure.

Jeisa rolled over in his arms and tucked one of hers beneath her head. Nothing in her experience had prepared her for Jeremy, and she didn't mean his sexual talent. The thought of losing him now was unimaginably heartbreaking, and she wasn't one who normally mourned the end of a relationship.

Because I've never been in love before. What she'd thought was love now seemed so shallow and juvenile to her. A part of her was terrified of how their week together would end. *He couldn't share all of this with me and then choose her.*

He cares about me. Please let that be enough.

She touched his cheek with one hand. "I'm more than okay."

She felt his smile before she saw it.

Their eyes met and held for a long, suspenseful moment. He wiggled his eyebrows suggestively and with a chuckle she admitted, "You're incredible. Is that what you want to hear?"

His smile dimmed a bit and his eyes revealed the seriousness of his answer. "Only if it's true."

"Because you want to be better than anyone else?"

He laid his hand over hers on his face. "When it comes to you, yes."

The way he was looking at her had her almost believing he could be in—

No, don't do that to yourself.

Reading more into what he's saying or trying to rush him will only lead to heartache. Give him his week and just try to enjoy this while it lasts.

In case it doesn't.

He was still watching her.

Still waiting.

Post-sex commentary wasn't comfortable for her. She looked at his chest as she spoke. "It's never been like this for me before. I've had good sex, but until you, I never had great sex."

He lifted her chin and smiled into her eyes. "I was afraid I might have gotten a little carried away, but after the first time I wanted to make sure."

God bless his dedication to mastery.

He rolled onto his back, pulling her with him so she was half-draped across his chest as it rumbled with humor beneath her. He stared up at the ceiling while absently running a finger down her bare back. "Jeisa, we need to talk . . ."

The pilot's voice came over the intercom. "We have about twenty minutes before we begin our descent. You will want to secure yourself for landing at that time."

Jeremy nodded and kissed Jeisa's forehead, easing away from her and throwing the comforter back. Jeisa felt the physical separation like a loss. She sat up without thinking of covering herself.

She had to ask. "Jeremy, what were you going to say?"

He was already pulling his trousers up over his boxers. After he picked his shirt off the floor, he leaned down and gave her lips a quick kiss. "It can wait. Right now I am going to take the world's fastest shower in the other room. I'd invite you to join me, but then we'd never make it to our appointment on time, and I can't wait to see what you think."

What I think?

We both know what I think.

You're the wild card here.

He gathered his socks and shoes and bolted from the room. The plane banked, and Jeisa caught a glimpse of herself in the mirror across the room and shot out of bed.

Thankfully the plane had two showers. It was one thing to engage in a marathon of steamy sex and quite another thing to go out into public looking like you did.

Beneath the hot spray of water, Jeisa closed her eyes—at peace with the universe and completely sated. The plane dipped beneath her feet, shocking her into action.

Okay, okay.

She rushed through the rest of her shower and threw on a form-fitting orange dress in record time. The lightest touches of makeup, a quick brush of her hair, and she made it to the seat beside Jeremy with very little time to spare. He handed her a seat belt and then secured himself.

Landing was a reminder that not everything lasts forever. Not their flight. Maybe not their time together.

"You look..." Jeremy's voice trailed away as the words eluded him.

"I hope the word you're searching for is 'beautiful,' " Jeisa joked, but the heat in his eyes replaced her humor with an emotion so poignant that Jeisa suddenly felt uncertain. "Where are we going?"

With some relief, Jeremy regained his composure. "I told you, it's a surprise. You'll have to wait and see."

Jeisa looked out the window as the jet touched down with a few light bumps and decided that surprises were overrated. One moment she had felt a joy unlike any she'd imagined possible, then her mood had flipped and she wanted to run back to Boston. Try as she might, she didn't feel there was much chance that she was going to enjoy this surprise, considering that her nerves were already beginning to fray.

When the plane came to a stop, Jeremy linked his fingers through Jeisa's, and she turned back to meet his eyes. With his free hand, he undid his buckle and then hers, and pulled her out of her chair into his arms. "Trust me," he said, misunderstanding her mood as anxiety related to their outing.

"I do," she whispered and meant it, meeting his kiss halfway.

I just don't know how I'll survive if you tell me this isn't what you want.

CHAPTER *Eight*

STEPPING OUT OF the limo and into the faculty parking lot of the Watts Institute of Technology, Jeisa was overcome with emotion. Not only was it one of the country's most prestigious schools, but it was also the home of the Global Water Project—the same grant-funded initiative she'd told Marie it was her dream to work for. She was familiar with the building they were about to enter because it was featured in almost every documentary she'd watched on the project. Of all the places Jeremy could have taken her on their first date, bringing her to the doorstep of her life's ambition felt a bit surreal and took their excursion to a whole new level. She clung to his hand, too overwhelmed to speak.

Looking a bit uncomfortable, Jeremy confessed, "I guess I can tell you now. Marie told me you were interested in a certain project to help third world countries. We looked into who was working on it and Marie took care of the rest. I thought you would want to see a demonstration and meet the team."

"You set up a tour of the Global Water Project?" Hers was a rhetorical, wonder-filled request for confirmation rather than an actual question.

He raised her hand to his lips and kissed her fingers before answering with humor. "Unless you're harboring another waste-disposal fascination that you didn't tell Marie about?"

Her eyes filled with instant tears, probably smearing some of her newly applied mascara. Jeisa wiped it away even as she looked up at Jeremy in awe. She was so happy she started to cry again. "I can't believe you did this."

He went pale and asked, “You’re saying that because you’re glad we’re here, right?”

She threw her arms around him and buried her wet face in his neck as she hugged him. “I love it! I absolutely love it!”

After only the slightest of hesitations, he wrapped his arms around her waist and held her shaking body to him. He murmured into her hair, “I just wanted to make sure.”

She tilted her head back and pulled his down so she could express in a kiss exactly how much the surprise had pleased her. With a teasing flick of the tongue, she deepened the kiss and reveled in how his tongue met hers with a hunger their earlier time together should have alleviated but hadn’t. Had they been somewhere private, she would have ripped his clothing from him and thanked him in a way he would not soon forget.

A young man’s voice spoke beside them, softly at first and then with increasing volume until neither she nor Jeremy could ignore the interruption. Jeremy broke off the kiss, but instead of instantly addressing the other man, he looked down into Jeisa’s eyes, and the fire she saw burning there tempted her to say they should forget about the tour and spend the rest of the day on the plane.

The man cleared his throat loudly and, in a tone that revealed his immense discomfort with the scene he’d just witnessed, said, “Excuse me, Mr. Kater?”

With a shake of his head, Jeremy turned and put out a hand to greet the man, even as he pulled Jeisa close to his side. Jeisa couldn’t help herself—she wrapped both arms around Jeremy’s waist and hugged him tight, then wiped a stray tear from one of her cheeks.

Jeremy laughed at the man’s expression. “She really likes toilets.”

The man had brown hair, was of average build, and looked to be in his mid-twenties. His honey-colored round-rimmed glasses made him appear a bit bug-eyed, and his plaid shirt and argyle sweater gave him a geeky look. He smiled at Jeremy’s comment. “No one here would consider that odd. It’s one of our obsessions. My name is Henry. I'm one of the post-grad students working on the project and Dr. Wheaton asked me to be your tour guide today."

Jeisa pried herself from Jeremy's clutch and also shook the man's hand. "Thank you for letting us visit your facility. My name is Jeisa. You have no idea how much this means to me."

Henry shook her hand and grew more flustered the longer she looked at him. He quickly broke off contact with her and returned his attention to Jeremy. "We were told that one of you might be interested in joining us on the post-production side."

Jeremy nodded toward Jeisa. "That would be Jeisa."

Jeisa breathed out a dreamy sigh. "I'd love to help in any way I could."

Jeremy looked down at her and asked, "You believe in the project that much?"

What she might have protected from another man, she didn't feel she needed to hide from Jeremy. He'd said that he wanted to know her and he was honest to a fault. She nodded slowly. "Yes, I do."

He took her hand in his and gave it a supportive squeeze. "Then so do I. Let's go see what makes these toilets so amazing."

During the tour that followed, Jeisa was sure that Jeremy would lose interest, but he didn't. And she herself was absolutely engrossed. Periodically she would realize that she was asking question after question without really giving Henry time to answer. She pondered the team's decision to keep the prototype simple and inexpensive instead of using more cutting-edge technology. Yes, the units needed to be easy to maintain and had to be cost-effective, but some of the more expensive materials might survive extreme outdoor conditions longer. She inquired if their decisions had been influenced by budgetary concerns, and of course they partially had been.

I could change that. The thought echoed through her.

Too soon, Henry concluded the tour in the department's office area. Jeremy assessed the variety of computers being used—everything from desktops to razor-thin tablets were scattered on the five desks that shared one large room. Without asking, Jeremy took a seat at one of the desks and turned the computer on. "Do you ever worry that someone may tamper with your records or steal your ideas?"

Henry rushed over to where Jeremy was seated. His voice went up a few octaves. "Most of what we do here is pretty transparent, since we hope the technology we're designing is going to be utilized by many countries in the future. But we do have some sensitive information on our server that we safeguard."

"What do you use? A closed network?" Jeremy typed something in even as Henry protested.

Suddenly sweaty, Henry said, "I don't really know. Our IT guy sets it up for us."

Jeremy kept typing. "Do you want to test how secure it is?"

Henry paled a bit and croaked, "No. I'm not authorized to okay that."

Jeremy continued, regardless of Henry's lack of permission. "Get your IT guy on the phone. I'll ask him."

Jeisa put her hand on Jeremy's arm in caution. "Jeremy, what are you doing?"

Jeremy paused for a second. "This project is important to you. That makes it important to me. Do you know how much data the Waltons had stolen from them because they didn't properly protect it? One day you're designing a humanitarian Global Water Project, the next you see your invention powering drone missiles. Is that what you want?"

"No," Jeisa admitted reluctantly.

Henry picked up a cordless phone and said, "Ted, can you come to GWP's office? There's someone here who'd like to meet you."

"Give me the phone," Jeremy instructed. He wedged it between his ear and his shoulder and started typing again. "Ted? You don't know me, but I want to show you something." His fingers flew as he navigated the university's system with ease.

"I just locked you out of the system, Ted. By the time you get here, I could have everyone else locked out too, and have uploaded the data to Cypress's Viber before wiping this one clean. You need a better firewall."

Jeremy hung up. Jeisa and Henry stared at him—open-mouthed. As if he were doing something routine, he said casually, "He said he'd be right down."

I bet he will, Jeisa thought. *Hopefully not with the police.*

Ted arrived within minutes and he wasn't alone, but his entourage looked more like a star-struck geek squad than security.

An androgynously dressed woman with short, spiked blonde hair and retro square black glasses stepped forward, offered her hand in greeting. "I've read about you on some blogs about who to watch in software design," she said. "Is it true that you worked side by side with the Waltons?"

Jeremy stood and shook her hand. His wide smile revealed his own hero worship of the older couple. "I did, and they were everything you'd imagine they would be. The shit they are working on right now is so far beyond what anyone else thinks is possible, it's mind-blowing."

The woman practically melted at his feet in open adoration.

Oh, please, Jeisa thought.

The woman continued to gush. "I'm sure they felt the same about working with you. Your avatar is a legend in the Lindar gaming community as well as in cyberspace in general. The way you used it as a signature stamp whenever you blocked Sliver was genius. When he tried to shut down Rycom and you closed him out just for the fun of it, you became an icon. He must hate you, but the rest of us loved watching you beat him. You're practically an online superhero."

Oh, for cripes' sake. What is she going to do next, whip open her shirt and ask him to sign her Superwoman lingerie?

Of course, Jeremy was eating it up, and Jeisa wanted to kick him in the leg. But she refrained—barely. Thankfully, Ted redirected the conversation to the issue at hand. "About the server..."

Jeremy was instantly serious. "If I can gain control this quickly, you're vulnerable to many people."

Ted shook his head in sad agreement. "I've been warning them about that for years, but we don't have the funding to update it. When it comes to creating, the sponsors are willing to write big checks. I can't convince them that protecting the infrastructure is just as vital."

Jeremy returned to the seat behind the computer he'd used as an access point and motioned for the small group of men and women to gather behind him. He said, "I'll add some block codes that you can change and encrypt after I'm gone and at least you know you'll block anyone from gaining remote access to your system. I can also build in the equivalent to roadblocks so if anyone did break your code, they would only gain access to a limited area before encountering another encryption. That would at least buy you time to stop them."

Ted sought the agreement of a tall, thin man in the back and then nodded. "Do it."

There was a beauty to the ease with which Jeremy closed out the distraction of his audience and performed the complex task. Jeisa had always known that Jeremy was intelligent, but here he was, surrounded by some of the greatest minds in the country, and they were in awe of him.

He wrote down a few codes on a piece of scrap paper he found beside the computer and handed them to Ted. "These will allow you to update the others. Change them as soon as I'm gone. I made them so tight that I shouldn't be able to break them if you do it right."

The man in the back walked forward, then gave him a wide smile. "If you ever need a job, you can have Ted's."

Ted didn't seem bothered by the threat. He countered with, "If you decided to come work here, Jeremy, I'm sure they'd also offer you his job."

The tall man's smile dimmed. He seemed about to say something more, but the woman who'd been gushing over Jeremy chimed in, "Or you could start your own university. I'd transfer for you."

Jeisa rolled her eyes. *I may throw up.*

Jeremy stood and walked over to put his arm around Jeisa. "I have more on my plate than I can handle already, but I appreciate the offer."

Jeisa looked up at him, not quite sure if he was referring to the employment or the blatant flirtatious offer from the blonde woman.

More than he can handle?

He'd better be referring to me and only me.

He winked at her and Jeisa relaxed, leaned into his embrace, and for a moment forgot they weren't alone. He'd asked her for a week so he could sort out his feelings. One week was beginning to feel like forever. She raised herself up on her tiptoes and kissed him with all the pent-up emotion coursing through her. He lost himself in the kiss, seemingly as oblivious to those around them as she was.

One of the men said, "He is the luckiest bastard on the planet," and the mood was broken.

"I'd say she is," the adoring post-grad student countered with a sigh.

Another man veered off on a tangent. "I don't believe in luck. It implies a randomness that is disproved as patterns of behavior eradicate unknowns."

Excited by the impromptu debate, another man added, "Unknowns can never be fully eradicated, so some randomness will always exist, and therefore so will luck."

Jeremy ended the kiss with a chuckle and whispered in Jeisa's ear, "I think we should go before they decide to keep us for observation." He pulled back, still holding Jeisa's hand in his, and said, "Thank you for the tour and for letting me play a bit with your server." He handed the tall man his card. "Call me if you have issues."

They made a hasty escape, hand in hand, not slowing until they reached the outer door, where the driver met them. They fell into the limo, laughing against each other.

Jeisa said, "I thought they were going to ask you for your autograph."

Jeremy sat back, satisfied, and held her to his chest, admitting, "It was fun to be the cool guy for once."

Jeisa traced his chin with her forefinger. "Is that what you want, Jeremy?"

He took her hand in his, holding it to her chest. "I used to think it was all I wanted."

Jeisa held her breath. "And what about now?"

Jeremy's mouth closed on hers and instant heat flooded her. When they touched, the questions that plagued her were washed away by the urgency of her desire. He slid her sideways onto his lap, settling her on the evidence of his need for her. "Now I want you."

Oh, God.

His words shot through her, erasing the last of her coherent thoughts and replacing them with a need so intense she followed her impulse and sank to the floor between his feet. On her knees, she pushed his legs apart and kissed him while unbuckling his belt. Her hands greedily sought and freed his erection.

She sat back on her heels and met his eyes, loving how they burned for her. She felt herself pulsing and moistening with excitement, and suddenly she understood how pleasing someone else could be just as exciting as being pleased.

She leaned down, took him into her mouth, and lavished him with the same amount of attention he had shown her earlier. She licked him, cupped him, welcomed him deeply into her mouth. When he was moaning with pleasure, she stood, dropped her panties to the floor, sheathed him in the condom she'd felt in his pocket earlier, turned around and lowered herself onto him. In this half-seated position, she found the ecstasy of control. His hands slid up her dress and cupped her bare ass. She sat back and his hands came around to her front and cupped her breasts as she raised and lowered herself again and again onto him. She swung her head wildly to one side, baring her neck to him and loving how he plundered it with his hot tongue.

When she thought it couldn't get better, he eased her forward and put a hand on her back to steady her. They joined together again and again in a rhythm they created.

Withdrawing from her for just long enough to change his position, he turned her so she could brace herself on the bar on the opposite wall of the limo. Steadying himself by placing one hand next to hers, he held her still with his other and thrust inside of her again—sending a flood of heat through her. Bent over as they were, his breath was hot on her back as the intensity of his thrusts increased and sent her over the edge into a sobbing state of bliss.

He paused, then slowly began to move again, deeper and more powerfully than before. She'd barely recovered, and the sensation was almost too much to bear. She looked up and caught his eyes, hot with desire, in the mirror in front of her and couldn't look away. This time he was in control, rolling his hips and reaching the spot that sent shivers of pleasure through her.

God, let the airport be further away than I remember. I don't want to stop.

I don't want this to ever end.

He reached around her and sought her clit with those talented fingers of his. He claimed her nub with his fingers, rubbing with an ever-increasing speed as he took her from behind. She gasped for air, cried out his name, and they came together with one final, shuddering thrust.

The limo came to a gentle stop at the entrance of the airport. She and Jeremy quickly replaced their discarded clothing and disposed of the evidence of their coupling. Jeisa smoothed her hair, hoping she didn't look as wantonly wild as she felt.

Neither moved even as they saw the jet through the window—a reminder that even life's most amazing days come to an end. Tucked into his side, Jeisa peered up at Jeremy and said, "Thank you."

Jeremy kissed her forehead. "I think you already thanked me."

She playfully slapped his thigh. "I mean it. This was wonderful."

Jeremy raised her chin with his hand and said, "It'll only get better, I promise you."

The very savvy limo driver parked in front of the jet but made no move to interrupt them.

Jeisa laid her head on Jeremy's shoulder and tried to simply savor their closeness, but her mind raced on mercilessly. *Hold onto a little piece of your heart*, she warned herself, but she knew it was too late for that.

He has to love me—he just has to.

Back on the jet after takeoff, Jeremy hugged Jeisa to his side on the main area couch. Although liftoff had only taken moments, the physical pain of sitting separately in their own chairs had made it feel like an eternity and he'd taken her eagerly back into his arms as soon as it was safe. The intensity of their connection was more than a little unsettling.

He worked up his courage by mentally rehearsing what he was going to say.

Jeisa, I should have said this before, but I had to make sure I didn't really love Alethea.

No, don't mention her.

Jeisa, I'm an idiot because I love you.

I mean, I've been an idiot—I do love you.

He rubbed his chin in her hair and breathed in the scent of her shampoo, marveling that he'd never smelled anything so wonderful. *I should leave the word "idiot" off.*

His phone vibrating in his breast pocket was an unwelcome interruption. He shifted Jeisa slightly to one side and checked the caller ID.

Alethea.

He turned off his phone and slid it back into his pocket. Jeisa tensed in his arms.

"You could have answered it," she said slowly, straightening away from him.

"It wasn't important," he said, watching Jeisa's expression tighten with emotion.

"Was it Alethea?"

He didn't bother to deny it. "Yes."

"Is there a reason you feel that you can't talk to her in front of me?" Jeisa turned on the couch and hugged her legs to her chest.

Only about a million. "I thought now was a bad time."

"I know you still work with her. I'm not a fool. I know that means you have to talk to her. Ignoring her phone call doesn't make her go away."

Jeremy reached for Jeisa's hand but she scooted back, away from him. "I can call her back if you want."

Jeisa stood and turned her back to him. "No, I don't want you to call her back."

Jeremy went to stand behind her. "Then I'm confused."

She spun around, hands on her hips, and said, "And how do you think I feel?" She closed her eyes and took a deep breath. "I can't do this. I thought I could do this, but I can't. I'm losing my mind."

He reached out for her but she stepped back. "Jeisa..."

"No, don't touch me. When you touch me I forget how much the rest of this hurts."

He pocketed his hands and rolled back on his heels. The last thing he wanted to do was hurt her. He'd thought they were having the kind of first date people shared a secret smile about together on their fiftieth anniversary. Had he misread the situation that badly? "I don't understand."

She covered her eyes with one hand, hugging herself with her other arm. "I can't have sex with you anymore. Not like this."

What did she mean *like this?* “I thought you said it was wonderful.”

She lowered her hand, her eyes now shiny with tears. “It was wonderful. Too wonderful. I came here because I love you. Today was amazing—all of it. You showed me how good it could be between us. I can’t help falling deeper in love with you, and it terrifies me.”

“Because you think I don’t love you?” he asked with relief. That was easy enough to rectify. “Jeisa, I do.”

He wasn’t prepared for her angry denial of his admission. “Don’t. Don’t say it now. Not when I just told you that I’m not having sex with you anymore if you don’t. How am I going to believe you? I’ll always wonder if you only said it because I forced you to.”

“But I do love you.”

“See, I don’t believe you. You’re only saying it because I cornered you into it.”

Man, women are a puzzle. Jeremy sought clarification before deciding how to proceed. “So, let me get this straight. You slept with me because you love me. It was so good that it made you love me more, but you don’t want to sleep with me again. Ever?”

Jeisa’s face flushed with anger. “I didn’t say ever. Don’t twist this all up.”

I’m trying to untwist it, he thought. “Okay, so the problem is that you don’t think I love you.”

“No, the problem is that I let myself get tangled up in a situation that was wrong for me from the start. I shouldn’t have taken that job at Corisi Enterprises. I should have never lied about my typing skills. I should have called my father and told him the truth. Then I wouldn’t have met Mrs. Duhamel and started working with you.” She waved an angry hand in his direction. “I came here because I wanted to be a strong, independent woman. And look at me. I’m lying like a teenager and practically begging some man to love me while I try to quit yet another job that I’m not qualified for anyway.”

Jeremy grasped onto the only part of her tirade that made sense to him. "What are you lying about?"

"You. Me. Everything. My father thinks I'm an au pair."

Amusement made the sides of Jeremy's mouth twitch as he suppressed a smile. "You told him you're babysitting me?"

"No," she sighed angrily. "It's a long story and one that I don't want to get into right now."

"Are you sure it wouldn't help if I told you again that I love you?" He instantly regretted defaulting to humor in the midst of a confrontation. She glared at him and began cursing in Portuguese.

She took a deep breath and calmed herself. "Fine. Joke about it. I should be grateful to you for making the decision easier."

Jeremy ran a hand through his hair. "What decision? Jeisa, I didn't mean..."

With her lips pressed in an angry line, she announced, "I won't be going to Thanksgiving with you. I don't need to wait until then to know that we can't work this out."

Jeremy paced in front of her, hating how his inexperience with women was likely the reason the situation was going from bad to finished. WWDD: What would Dominic do? Asking himself that question had successfully guided him through the rest of his transformation. Perhaps he'd been wrong not to apply it to his relationship with Jeisa.

Women don't respect weak men.

Be bold.

"You will come to Thanksgiving with me." He felt a rush of pride when his tone held just a hint of a warning.

Jeisa cocked her head in surprise. "Are you threatening me?"

"I don't make threats," he mimicked what he'd once heard Dominic say.

She tossed her hair over one shoulder and advanced on him. Still angry, but undeniably also excited by what he'd said. "After today, I'm not going anywhere with you."

Dominic really knows what he's doing. I can't believe this shit works.

"We'll see about that," Jeremy said vaguely, trying his best to look intimidating.

Jeisa turned with a huff and moved to the other side of the cabin. She sat in a chair, clicked on the television and turned her back to him.

Jeremy almost laughed.

She was adorable over there, making a production of giving him the silent treatment.

He knew enough not to say that to her. He relaxed into the couch and propped his feet up on the table in front of him. This particular puzzle was going to require some strategizing.

How do you get a woman who already loves you to start talking to you again long enough to convince her that you're meant to spend the rest of your lives together?

How do you get her to believe that you love her?

You propose!

Now that he had the solution, he was less worried about her present mood. Jeremy folded his arms over his chest and smiled.

And I know just when to do it!

The only thing worse than ignoring a man for a six-hour flight and half of a limo ride home was periodically checking to see if your silence was bothering him and being slapped with the harsh reality that it was not. Even now, Jeremy looked perfectly content to read his emails on his tablet and make phone calls as if he were alone.

Proving rather clearly that my instincts are correct and he doesn't have feelings for me. He is probably counting the minutes until he boots me out of this limo and drives off—probably never to see me again.

Which is fine.

At least then I have my answer and I can go back to focusing on the real reason I came to the United States in the first place. For me.

I don't need a man to make me happy or successful. I may not be a good office clerk, but I'll find my way.

Her dream job at WIT was now interwoven with too many memories of Jeremy. *But it's not the only university working on a humanitarian grant. I'm good with politicians and mingling with corporate giants. I could be a professional fund-raiser anywhere.*

There are a lot of things I can do.

I haven't given myself enough time to find where I belong.

She studied Jeremy's profile as he read over another document on his tablet.

Just where I don't.

The limo pulled up at the front of her apartment building and the driver opened the door for her. She hesitated. *This may be the last thing I ever say to Jeremy. I don't want it to end on this sour note.*

He put down his tablet. "I'll pick you up around ten on Thursday morning. The Andrades have requested everyone be there by two."

Jeisa's eyes flew to his, trying to read him but finding nothing there but cold determination. "I told you that I'm not going."

"And I told you that you are."

"It's not like you can threaten to fire me. I already quit. I'm not working under contract, so legally you can't force me to go."

"Be ready at ten."

"Or what?" Jeisa asked, confused with how she could be both angry and excited by his refusal to accept her answer.

He leaned over, slid a hand beneath her hair, and pulled her face to his. He tasted her hungrily, pulling her out of her seat, and Jeisa lost the battle against her own restraint. She was kneeling between his legs, drowning in the heat of his kiss, trying to remember all the reasons she didn't belong there. He kissed her jaw and whispered into her ear, "Or I will close that door and make love to you right here until you say yes."

Jeisa could barely hear him over her own ragged breathing. *He means it.*

And I want it.

She shook herself mentally.

Saying yes would only prolong the pain of uncertainty.

Saying no would gain her an immediate pleasure that wouldn't prove anything more than what she already knew—she was hopelessly, helplessly in love with him.

She sat back on her heels and implored, "Just let me go, Jeremy."

His jaw tightened and his eyes darkened with emotion. "No. You promised me you would go with me and you will, even if I have to track you down and drag you there." He ran a thumb over her lips. "Although we may both enjoy that option, too."

Jeisa stood on shaky legs and stepped out of the limo, temporarily too stunned to reply.

"See you Thursday," Jeremy said and joined her on the curb, taking her overnight bag away from the driver and handing it to her doorman himself.

Jeisa grabbed her bag from the doorman. "I no longer work for Mr. Kater, Tim. I'd appreciate it if you don't let him in anymore."

"Yes, ma'am," Tim said.

In a steel tone, Jeremy said, "No one will stop me from taking you with me on Thursday."

"There is nothing attractive about a domineering man," Jeisa snapped.

He leaned down and whispered in her ear, "Then why do you look like you'd love to invite me upstairs?"

Her head jerked back in denial. "I do not."

He traced her jaw with his thumb, moving on to part her eager lips. Her breath came in short, excited breaths against his hand. "Yes, you do."

She slapped his hand away. "A man with more experience would understand the difference between anger and desire."

The corners of his eyes wrinkled with humor. "Then it sounds like I need more experience."

With a stream of choice Portuguese phrases, Jeisa turned away from him and headed into her apartment building.

Tim beat her to the door and opened it for her, then returned to Jeremy's side and asked, "Tough trip?"

"Best of my life," Jeremy answered with a smile, then whistled as he reentered the limo.

CHAPTER *Nine*

THE NEXT DAY, Jeremy did answer Alethea's phone call. "Jeremy, thank God. I started to worry when you weren't picking up."

Jeremy sat back in his office chair at the Corisi building and propped his feet on his desk. "I was busy."

"Well, get *un*busy and back to Tenin because we have a problem."

"What is it?"

"You know how I get feelings about stuff, right? Well, my instincts tell me that something is seriously wrong here."

Was it possible that she'd heard about Jeisa and was jealous?

The answer mattered as little to Jeremy as the project out there did.

"I'm not going anywhere. Not this week, anyway."

"Didn't you hear what I said?"

"I heard you. Did you hear me?"

Alethea sighed angrily. "What the hell is wrong with you, Jeremy? This is your project. Don't you care if it falls apart?"

Not when he was fighting for something much more important. "Call me if you find something concrete. Otherwise, I'll fly over next week and check everything out myself. Deal?"

"No, that's not acceptable. What if—"

"Bye, Alethea. We'll talk next week."

"Do not hang up on me, Jeremy."

He did. Alethea thrived on drama. In the past he would have let her drag him into whatever crazy scheme she was hatching—

one to combat a crisis that, chances were, didn't actually exist. *Not this time.*

He finally had something to lose.

And he was damned if he was going to.

He picked up the office phone and called the downstairs desk at Jeisa's apartment building. "Tim, do you have a minute to talk?"

"Mr. Kater?"

"Yes, it's me, Tim. I need some help and you're the only person I can think of to ask. Can I send a car to pick you up?"

"I'm working, Mr. Kater."

"When does your shift end?"

After a short pause, Tim answered, "Two hours."

"Great. I'll send my driver then."

"Mr. Kater, I have a wife and kids. I can't do anything illegal."

That stopped Jeremy short. "Tim, I want to go pick out a ring for Jeisa and I need a second opinion. What did you think I was asking you to do?"

Tim laughed with apparent relief. "I don't know."

Jeremy continued, "I just figured that you're married so you chose correctly once. I can pay you for the time if you want."

Tim answered in a slightly offended tone. "You don't have to pay me."

Jeremy dropped the arrogant tone he caught himself using more now. "Tim, I'm sorry. Let me start over. I really want to pick the right ring for Jeisa and I value your opinion. Do you mind meeting me when you get off work? I want to buy the ring today. And don't call me, Mr. Kater. I'm Jeremy."

"Okay, Jeremy. I'll go, but I don't know about rings. My wife picked her own."

Hmm. "Do you think she'd come with us?"

Tim laughed. "Are you serious?"

"Never more so."

Tim said slowly, "We'd have to get a babysitter."

Money might not solve all problems, but it certainly made many easier to deal with. "I can pay for that. It's the least I could do. Hey, and after we pick a ring I'll lend you the limo and driver for the night. You could take your wife out for a nice dinner or something."

"She'd love that," Tim said, and then added with more enthusiasm, "She'd probably love everything about this." He laughed. "I'll call her and have her meet me here. She can have her sister watch the kids."

Inspiration hit Jeremy. "Better than that, I'll have a limo pick her up and bring her to get you. You can both meet me at the jeweler's." He smiled into the phone and added, "I'll have my secretary book a room for you at the Ritz-Carlton in case she really loves it. Don't worry about paying. This is on me."

"You sure?"

"Yes, unless you don't want me to."

Without hesitation Tim said, "No, I'm in. I can't remember the last date I had with my wife. If I'm lucky I'll have to call in sick tomorrow."

Jeremy shook his head. Tim was honest and funny, and beginning to feel like something his years of isolation had cheated him of—a friend.

"Here's hoping you do, Tim. See you in two hours."

"Thanks, Jeremy. And, uh, sorry I thought you were asking me to assist in a kidnapping."

Jeremy chuckled. *I bet Dominic gets those comments all the time. This is so awesome.*

He forced himself to sound serious. "No problem. See you at the jeweler's."

"Yes," Tim said, "see you then."

Jeremy was still chuckling ten minutes later when he walked into Dominic's office to drop off a report. Dominic looked up from his desk and scowled at Jeremy. "What the hell is so funny?"

Jeremy shook his head and bit back a laugh. "You wouldn't get it."

Which only deepened the scowl. Jeremy burst out laughing. He knew he should stop, but he couldn't help himself. He retreated from the room before Dominic lost his temper and jumped his desk to get him.

Someday they might be in a place where he could tell Dominic the whole story, but they weren't there yet.

Two days later, Jeisa still hadn't left her house. She didn't bother to change out of the shorts and T-shirt she'd worn to bed the first night, since she didn't have a job to report to. She threw her hair back in a ponytail, grabbed an aptly named carton of *Chocolate Therapy* ice cream and a cup of black coffee, and dragged a thick blanket from the closet to make a comforting nest on her couch.

Day two of the pity party.

She opened the carton and flipped on the TV.

News? No, too depressing.

Daytime talk show? Too happy.

Documentary? Too much trouble to find a good one.

She considered calling her friends in Santo Amaro, but they hadn't understood her desire to move to the United States in the first place. Why work when you don't have to? Why leave a life where everything is given to you? *Because I'm tired of the rules. Be good. Be quiet. Be beautiful. Just don't be yourself.*

She chose a station that played soft music without words. The last thing she needed was to hear someone singing about loving and losing. She put the half-eaten ice cream on the coffee table in front of her couch and tucked herself beneath the blanket.

What am I doing?

Hiding.

Wallowing.

Hating myself for caring that Jeremy hasn't called me.

It didn't matter that she'd rehearsed exactly what to say when he did call, or that each version included telling him it was over. *Over almost as soon as it began.* Memories of the two of them, enjoying each other intimately and wondrously, kept sneaking in and threatening what was otherwise an anti-Jeremy self-pep talk. *Okay, I'm awful at relationships. I panic and run. Does admitting it bring me closer to recovery?*

A light rap on her door echoed through her apartment. She flipped off the music channel. She threw back the blanket and thought, *I'm not ready to see anyone.* Usually Tim called upstairs for guests. The only one he'd ever let through unannounced was Jeremy. *Used to let through,* she stressed to herself. *I told Tim not to admit him.*

Jeisa rushed to the mirror and groaned. *Oh, my God, I look awful.* She wasn't wearing any makeup, and the shadows beneath her eyes were prominent. And her hair was taking the elastic as a suggestion rather than a restraint, defiantly sticking out here and there. She looked hastily around the room. There was still a pile of tissues on the kitchen counter left from when she'd broken into tears while looking for a midnight snack. Two days of dirty dishes were stacked on the counter.

I guess I don't have to look good when I tell him for the final time that I don't want to see him again.

Jeisa opened the door slowly and almost slammed it again when she saw who was there.

Marie, in all her perfectly groomed glory, smiled politely at her as if she were meeting Jeisa for their weekly lunch rather than visiting her apartment for the first time. "Jeisa! I'm so glad you're home. I tried to call you but you weren't answering your phone, so I thought I'd drop by and check to make sure you're okay. I hope you don't mind."

Which reminded Jeisa that she'd turned her phone off during the tour of the university. *Shit! How could I have forgotten to turn it back on?*

Because you had other things on your mind, she mocked herself.

Maybe Jeremy did call.

I don't care, she declared to herself.

"May I come in?" Marie inquired.

Jeisa shook her head to clear it. "Of course, Marie. I'm sorry. Come in." She stepped back to allow the older woman entry.

Marie walked past her, looked around, then turned her attention back to Jeisa, who was squirming with embarrassment. Jeisa rushed to put some dishes in the sink. "Don't mind the mess." She took the blanket off the couch and threw it in the bedroom, closing the door quickly behind her. "Would you like to sit?" Jeisa asked, then groaned when Marie picked the spot next to the melting carton of ice cream.

"Are you ill? I have a fabulous doctor who actually does house calls. No one does that anymore, but I'm old-fashioned like that," Marie said with concern.

Jeisa sat across from her on a chair and hugged a pillow to her stomach. "No. No. I'm fine. Would you like something to drink?"

Marie took another quick look around the room and shook her head. "Jeisa, I came to apologize."

Jeisa's grip on the pillow tightened as she waited.

"I shouldn't have encouraged Jeremy to take you to San Francisco. I shouldn't have pushed, but from the moment I met you, I thought you'd be perfect for him. You're sophisticated, well educated, and kind—exactly what Jeremy needed. And, to some extent, I was right. The difference between him before he met you and now is indescribable. You didn't just give him a makeover, you gave him confidence."

I gave him more than that, Jeisa thought wryly.

"Thank you," Jeisa said thickly, her mouth dry from nerves.

"He's a good man."

"I know he is."

"But he hasn't had a lot of experience with dating."

I'm intimately aware of that also, Jeisa thought, but said nothing.

"A man like that may not know how to express himself well. He may be shy about things that another man wouldn't be."

Any less shy and I wouldn't have been able to walk off the plane, Jeisa thought and stifled a giggle that stemmed more from nervousness than real humor.

Marie continued, "I thought for sure the two of you would come back from your trip as a couple. You can tell me that it's none of my business, but was it awful?"

Jeisa laid her hands over both of her flushed cheeks and said, "It was wonderful. He was wonderful." She closed her eyes for a moment, gathering her strength. When she opened them, Marie was looking at her with so much sympathy that Jeisa nearly broke down into tears.

"Then why do you look so miserable, dear?"

One tear escaped down Jeisa's cheek and she hastily wiped it away. "It's over."

"Because it's easier to end it now than risk losing him to Alethea?"

She hated that Marie knew exactly what she'd spent the last two days trying to deny to herself. Jeisa nodded and another tear spilled forth. "Does that make me weak?"

"No, sweetie, it makes you human. Love is terrifying sometimes. To experience it fully, you have to give yourself to it and trust that it won't trample your offering. Did you take my advice and give him a little encouragement?"

Jeisa blushed. *More than a little.* "Yes."

"And?"

Hugging the pillow to her again, Jeisa confessed, "He said he loves me."

"But you don't believe him."

"No."

"You've put him in an interesting position—one in which a man either decides to prove himself or walk away."

With her throat thick with emotion, Jeisa asked, "Did he talk to you about the trip?"

"He wouldn't say a word about it so I knew something went wrong. What did he do?"

"It wasn't him, it was me," Jeisa admitted. "I panicked. I told him that I don't want to see him again and that I won't go to Thanksgiving."

"And what did he have to say about that?"

Jeisa smiled at the memory. "He said he'd drag me there if necessary."

Marie looked pleased with Jeremy's threat. "Good for him. It's nice to see him going after what he wants."

Jeisa blushed a deeper red. Her mouth opened to say something and then snapped shut when nothing came to mind. Finally she said, "It's not that simple, Marie." Taking a shaky breath, Jeisa asked, "How do I compete with someone he has spent his whole life wanting?"

"You don't. You trust him to make the right decision, and you go with him to Thanksgiving. What's the alternative? Sitting here and finishing that carton alone?"

Jeisa imagined the weekend gathering: the Andrades, the Corisis, possibly even Jeremy's mother. "I don't know if I can do it. I don't have a great track record with men. I tend to believe them even when evidence for why I shouldn't piles up, and then I end up in a worse situation. How many times do I have to be wrong before I learn to trust my head instead of my heart?"

Marie stood. "I hope you never learn that. I certainly haven't."

"Marie—" Jeisa stood and started to say something but Marie interrupted her.

"No, I'm sorry. I came here to apologize for interfering and there I go, butting into your business again. Lil says I'm as bad as Abby, and I'm not entirely sure that's a compliment."

Jeisa took one of Marie's hands in hers and said, "I don't know how I got lucky enough to get on the list of people you care about, Marie, but I am grateful that I did. Even when I don't agree with what you're saying."

Marie squeezed Jeisa's hand lightly, then picked up her purse from the couch. "Would you do me a favor?"

Jeisa doubted there was a person on the planet who could refuse Mrs. Duhamel when she put on her sweet old-lady expression and used that unassuming tone. "I'll try."

"Go outside for a walk today. The answers you're looking for won't be found on your couch."

"They're on the trail behind my house?" Jeisa joked.

Marie went to the door, then stopped. "No, but sunshine is. All that fresh air will hopefully remind you that you're young and healthy with a world of opportunities before you. Whether it works out with Jeremy or not, life is too short and too precious to waste. It's just a shame that we often don't realize that until it's too late."

Jeisa rushed forward. "Marie, are you okay?"

Marie adjusted the purse on her shoulder. "I'm fine, dear. Sometimes I just miss what I used to have. I try not to think about it, but even I get lonely." When Jeisa would have said more, Marie said, "It's not a topic I want to discuss further. Just remember that nothing is forever. Not the confusion you feel today, not your time on this planet. Don't make excuses for not living the life you want. If you want to make a difference by getting involved in a movement, don't wait for a perfect time or the perfect situation, just do it. Love like you're on borrowed time. If you wait for the perfect family, friend, or relationship—you'll spend your life waiting instead of living. I spoke to the president of WIT and he said he'd find a spot for you on the water project whenever you're ready. But, before you do that, call your father. Oh, and when Jeremy comes to pick you up—get in that limo."

Jeisa threw her arms around Marie and let the hug say what she couldn't express. Mrs. Duhamel returned the hug and then said, "Okay, enough of that. I need to get back to the office. Dominic and Jake left for New York last night. I like to peek in now and then to make sure everything is going smoothly in their absence."

I'm sure you do. Jeisa smiled at the thought.

While Jeisa showered and changed into a jogging outfit, she thought about what Marie had said. Jeisa didn't often think about her own mortality or that of others, but Marie was right. Life was fragile. Her own mother had passed away unexpectedly, suffering from a fatal illness that claimed her life within days.

No wonder Dad worries so much.

He has loved and lost.

Just like Marie said, some men never come back from that.

I have to call him.

No more putting it off. He deserves to know the truth.

When he didn't answer her first ring, Jeisa called his house and spoke to the maid. Sonia had been with her family for as long as she could remember and was a very good judge of her father's moods. If anyone knew where her father was and if this was the best time to talk to him, it would be her.

Sonia answered, "Jeisa, where have you been? Your father has been trying to call you for days. He flew out last night to go find you in Boston."

Oh, my God. "Dad's coming here?"

In rapid Portuguese, Sonia said, "If 'here' is the home of Reese David, then yes. He should already be there."

Please. Please. Please. Do not let him find Reese before I do. "I have to go, Sonia. I'll call him right now."

Barely breathing, she dialed her father's phone and paced while it rang. *Pick up. Pick up.*

"Jeisa?" her father's voice boomed through the phone.

"Dad! Where are you?" Jeisa asked in Portuguese.

Romario's answer boomed through the phone in their native language. "Where am I? Where are you? I'm at some imbecile's house and he's trying to tell me that he doesn't know you. He says he doesn't have a wife or children and that I must be confused about where you work."

Jeisa sat down on a chair as her legs gave way beneath her. It didn't matter that her father dressed in the finest clothing and spoke multiple languages, he'd fought his way to the top of the

Brazilian government and would fight just as ruthlessly for his daughter's honor. "Can you put him on the phone for a minute?"

Of course he wouldn't. He'd never done a single thing she'd asked him to. *You'd have to value your daughter's opinion for that.*

"Where are you?" her father demanded.

"I'm safe, Dad. I don't work for Reese and I never have. I don't live there. I have a great apartment in uptown Boston. Just let me talk to him for two seconds to remind him how he knows me. I can clear this misunderstanding up."

With a bit of a growl, her father handed the phone over to Reese. Jeisa didn't waste time with a greeting. In English she said hastily, "You need to tell my father that it was a big misunderstanding and that you are sorry. I would start groveling now. You might even want to cry. Trust me."

"I am not going to apologize to a man who just broke my door down. I'm calling the police."

They'd never get there in time. "I have two words for you to consider before you do that—political immunity. He's going to get off, even if he kills you. And if you live, do you want the news to find out why he came after you? Because I'll gladly tell them." She let her threat sink in.

After a moment, Reese swore under his breath and started to apologize to Romario. Her father took the phone back. "Tell me you didn't date this man. He's a sniveling idiot."

Although Reese deserved the punishment her father likely wanted to give him, Jeisa couldn't let that happen. She knew what bad press could cost her father's career. Having a reputation for being tough on issues is not the same thing as being arrested for breaking into a man's home and beating him to death. The American newspapers would have a field day with the story if she didn't do something fast. "Dad, I never even went to his house. I've been working in an office building as an image consultant since my second week here. Honestly, I talked to that guy once on the phone when I first arrived and decided not to work for him. I wouldn't even recognize him in a lineup."

Her father was quiet for several long moments. From what Jeisa heard in the background, it sounded like he'd left Reese's house and had gotten back into a car. "So you've been lying to me for months?" The calm in his voice revealed the depth of his anger.

"Yes," Jeisa said lamely, knowing that she'd waited too long to tell the truth. "I didn't want to disappoint you."

"And this isn't disappointing? Pack your bags, you're coming home."

Jeisa took a deep breath. *Not this time*. "No, Dad. I'm not."

"You don't have a choice," he grated.

For the first time Jeisa saw that she did. She really did. Marie was right—how was her father ever going to see her as an adult if she continued to act like a child? It was time to take a stand, not against her father, but for herself. "Dad, I'm sorry I worried you. I'm sorry that I lied to you, but I'm not going home." She gave him her address. "I have a life here now and if you'll listen to me, I'll tell you about it."

For the next thirty minutes, over the sound of the GPS directing her father closer and closer to her home, Jeisa told her father about the job she had taken at Corisi Enterprises and how that had led to working with Jeremy as his image consultant. She left off the part where she was quitting and they had dated. There would be time to explain that part once he'd calmed down.

Her father didn't sound happy, but he didn't interrupt her as she'd worried he would. He must have heard something in her voice when she mentioned Jeremy, because he said, "Just tell me that this Jeremy is nothing like the whimpering American I just met."

Jeisa remembered how Jeremy had stood up to the professional boxer during what he still called his first lesson. *Jeremy didn't whimper*. "No, I think you'd actually like him."

"I'll tell you what I think after I meet him."

"Meet him?" Jeisa asked, her voice going up an octave in distress.

"I want to see this life you've made for yourself and I'm going to. Is there anything else you want to tell me about this Jeremy?"

"No," Jeisa hedged, as she often had in the past. She instantly regretted doing so, but old habits were hard to break. *With her father, the less she said the better.*

"Then first we are going to sit down and talk about the importance of honesty in a family. After that, you are going to introduce me to this man you say you work for."

He doesn't believe me, and really I can't blame him. "Dad, this isn't a good time for that. Tomorrow is an American holiday, Thanksgiving. We were going down to New York to celebrate it with some coworkers and friends, but I'll tell him I can't go."

"No, don't. I'll go with you. Sounds like the perfect way for me to get to know the people in this new life you say you have made for yourself."

Yes, perfect.

That's what Thanksgiving was becoming—a perfect disaster.

CHAPTER *Ten*

JEREMY ABSENTLY CHECKED the pocket of his black tuxedo for the ring boxes as the limo navigated the busy streets of Boston. Rings. Check. He'd purchased his own private helicopter, which was now fueled and waiting for them at the Corisi building, a much closer option than the airport. Transportation. Check.

Normally he wouldn't have made his mother, Therese, travel alone, but he had special plans for this short trip—plans he'd confessed to his mother when she'd sounded hurt that he wanted to travel alone with Jeisa. "Mom, we need privacy because I'm going to ask her to marry me."

After praising the powers above, she'd exclaimed, "You plan to propose on a helicopter? Jeremy, a girl hopefully only gets one proposal. That doesn't sound very romantic. How are you going to get down on one knee if you're strapped in with headphones?"

He explained his choice. "Don't worry, this is a luxury copter. It's as nice and soundproof on the inside as any vehicle. It'll be filled with roses. I even ordered champagne so we can celebrate. Trust me, it'll be perfect."

His mother let out a joyful laugh. "I'm going to have grandchildren!"

"Easy, Mom. She has to say yes first."

"What sane woman would say no to you, Jeremy?"

More than you'd think, he thought, but only one mattered.

His mother gushed, "I should come over and take a picture of you and Jeisa that morning. You never went to a prom. I don't have any pictures like that."

"Mom, stop."

As quickly as she had started laughing, she started crying. "You gave up so much for me and your dad. I want you to be happy."

The weight of her sorrow tore at him, as it always had. He reassured her just as he'd done a thousand times before when they'd talked themselves into an uncomfortable place. "I am happy, Mom. And you are going to make the world's best grandmother."

Sniffing, Therese said, "No matter what Jeisa says, I want you to know how proud I am of you. You are an amazing man and I hope she sees that."

It had been a relief to end that phone call, even though her words had warmed his heart. "Bye, Mom. I'll see you at the Andrades'. Try not to cry all over Jeisa when we make our announcement."

"I can't promise anything," his mother had said, laughing.

Stepping out of the limo in front of Jeisa's building, Jeremy looked up to the floor her apartment was on. He took a deep, fortifying breath and stepped toward the entrance. Tim opened it for him.

"Good morning, Mr. Kater," Tim said in a rush.

"Jeremy," he corrected him.

Tim nodded and followed him inside. "Jeremy, before you go upstairs there is something I have to tell you."

Jeremy stopped just inside the foyer. "Did she instruct you to call the police or something if I showed up?"

Shaking his head, Tim said, "Worse. Her father is upstairs."

That wiped the smile off Jeremy's face. "Her father?" Why would Jeisa call her father? *Because she meant it when she said she didn't want to see me again?*

No, she's upset with me, but she loves me. Why wouldn't she tell me her father was here?

Maybe she would have if I had called her.

Damn, I knew I shouldn't have left our last words hang between us until now. I wanted to play it cool like Dominic would have, but I should have put my pride aside and called her.

Jeremy sought some answers from Tim. "What is he like?"

Tim whistled. "Huge. Dressed like he lives in suits. And not happy."

"You should buzz her apartment this time."

Jeisa answered her intercom.

Tim said, "Mr. Kater is here to see you."

"Send him up," she said breathlessly.

"Yes, ma'am," Tim said and clicked the intercom off. "Good luck."

Jeremy straightened his shoulders and braced himself. "How bad could he be?"

Tim gave him a pat on the shoulder and said, "Dads are tricky, Jeremy. They are programmed to not like the man their daughter chooses. It'll be like walking through a minefield with two people watching to see if you can navigate it. They know where the explosives are, but they won't tell you. When dealing with potential in-laws, all you can do is step lightly and pray. Trust me, the less you say the better."

Jeremy nodded. "Thanks, Tim. I'll keep that in mind. She did say I could go up, though, so I'm feeling optimistic about this. She might have had time to rethink her last words to me. Hell, maybe her father is here because he wants to meet the man who has made his daughter so happy."

"I love your sense of humor, Jeremy."

Jeremy headed for the stairs grumbling to himself. *I wasn't joking.*

When Jeisa saw Jeremy's formal attire she was glad she'd chosen a floor-length gown and encouraged her father to wear a tuxedo. The Andrades were casual in their manner with each other, but they loved to dress to impress and Thanksgiving would likely be no different. Although their event began in the afternoon, they would dress for the late hours the party would stretch into. Jeremy waited at the door to be invited in, and Jeisa was thankful for his uncommon discomfort.

This may work. All I have to do to avert this crisis is to convince two men that today is not a good idea.

"Mr. Kater, thank you for offering me a ride down to New York, but as you can see my father is here for a visit." When Jeremy looked confused by her formal greeting, Jeisa instantly felt sorry for keeping him in the dark about her father's visit. *I should have called him last night and told him that my father is here. But I didn't know what to say. Why do I always believe that if I pretend something is not happening, it will go away?*

Jeremy met her eyes for a minute and seemed to come to a decision. He looked past her. "Mr. Borreto, it's a pleasure to finally meet you." He held out his hand to her father. Her father shook his hand with what looked like a punishing grip that Jeremy smiled through.

"So, you're the man my daughter currently works for."

When Jeremy glanced at her over his shoulder, Jeisa pleaded with him silently to go along with it. Turning back to her father, he said, "Technically she works with me." Jeisa held her breath. "Corisi Enterprises hired her, but she's been helping me with a recent project."

"I see," her father said coldly. "And this project involves taking her to New York today?"

"Today isn't about work. It's Thanksgiving, a day when most Americans gather with family and friends."

"Will your family be there?"

"My mother will be. My father is no longer with us."

Jeisa's father ceased his interrogation long enough to say, "I'm sorry to hear that."

"Thank you."

Jeisa went to stand beside Jeremy. "My father's visit was a little unexpected." *Or I would have told you,* her tone implied. "I don't expect you to have room for him in your car."

Jeremy shrugged. "I came over in a limo and the helicopter seats six."

Hopefully not the *limo.* Jeisa remembered their last ride too vividly. She didn't think she could sit across from her father and not die of mortification if it was.

"Sounds like you live an expensive lifestyle," Romario said, his tone insinuating that it was one he didn't approve of.

Jeremy met the man's eyes. "Both are practical choices. One lets me get work done while I sit in traffic and the other will allow us to fly over the holiday highway congestion. We can be down in New York in a little over an hour."

Does Jeremy not see how badly this could go? "I don't think we should..."

Speaking over her as he often did, Romario said, "I hope my presence isn't an inconvenience."

Jeisa wanted to kick Jeremy when he replied, "Absolutely not, sir. I'm happy to meet you."

When Jeisa's father said nothing in response, Jeisa tried to bring the exchange to a conclusion. "Dad, now that you've met Mr. Kater, don't you think it's a better idea if we call off the trip? The Andrade family kindly invited me to join them for the day, but I didn't ask if I could bring a guest."

Romario directed his question at Jeremy. "What do you think, Mr. Kater? Will it be a problem?"

Back me up here, Jeremy. All you have to say is yes.

After a bit of a pause, Jeremy said, "The Andrade gathering is a huge event. I'm sure they would love to meet you. They adore Jeisa."

"It's settled then," her father said with finality.

Jeisa silently led the way out the door and into the hallway. The elevator ride was equally quiet and awkward. In the foyer, Jeremy shot Tim a thumbs-up as they passed. Jeisa heard her father make a guttural sound behind her and realized that she wasn't the only one who'd witnessed what Jeremy had done.

As Jeisa slid into the limo, she met Jeremy's eyes. He winked at her and smiled. For a fleeting moment she forgot to worry about what her father was thinking or how the day would unfold. Time was suspended, and all that mattered was Jeremy and the intimacy of their connection.

Jeremy asked her father, "Are you here on business or on vacation?"

"Neither," her father said curtly.

Jeremy studied her father like he was a puzzle to be solved. Jeisa wanted to warn him to leave it alone, but there was no way of doing that. And then a sudden thought came to her. She slid a hand into her purse and found her phone.

She typed, "He doesn't know we've dated."

Jeremy's phone beeped in his pocket. He said, "Excuse me," to her father and checked his phone.

"Something important?" her father asked.

"Hard to say," Jeremy replied as he texted back.

Jeisa's phone chirped to announce she had a new text. Her father glared at her. She smiled through her embarrassment. *I didn't think that one through very well. Shit.* She wanted to check her message, but didn't dare yet.

"So, what do you do for Corisi Enterprises?" her father asked.

"I'm sort of a technology consultant."

"That's not usually quite as lucrative as you seem to have found it."

"Dad," Jeisa cut in, "Mr. Kater works for several big companies."

"Amazing when you consider that he didn't go to college," her father spurred.

Jeisa turned on her father and demanded, "Did you already have him investigated?"

"I had to find out the truth somehow," her father said angrily. "You certainly weren't going to tell me."

"Why should I tell you anything? It's not like you're going to listen to me." She put her arms over her chest.

Jeremy intervened, "I'm sure your father just did it because he cares about you."

Romario grated, "This is none of your business."

Further discussion was delayed when the limousine pulled up in front of the Corisi main building. Jeremy stepped out of the limo first.

Alone for a moment with Jeisa, her father referred to the famous building. "Am I supposed to be impressed?" he asked sarcastically.

Jeisa exited the limo without answering him. She checked her phone. Jeremy had replied to her. "He will soon."

What does that mean? Hopefully the last exchange between her and her father had shown him why that wasn't a good idea.

They took the elevator to the top of the building without a word. When the doors opened at the roof, Jeisa stumbled in surprise. Jeremy took her elbow to steady her. She looked at him and then back at the scene before them.

White and red rose petals were scattered on a white carpet that led to a helicopter. A man in a tuxedo stood beside the helicopter with a tray that held two flutes of champagne. With leaden feet, Jeisa walked with Jeremy up to the aircraft and gasped when she saw that he had filled the interior with hundreds of white roses. She didn't know whether to laugh with joy or cry out in horror. She could only imagine what her father was thinking.

Jeremy referenced the tray of champagne and asked her father, "Would you..."

Jeisa's father emitted something akin to a growl, and Jeremy waved the tray away. "On the way back perhaps."

Jeisa almost giggled. Her father was quietly turning a deep shade of purple, but Jeremy was pretending not to notice.

Jeremy stepped inside the helicopter and moved flowers off an additional seat on the opposite side. Jeisa took one seat and her father took the seat next to her. Not giving away his thoughts, Jeremy took the seat across the small aisle from them.

Once they were airborne, Romario asked, "Do you give all of your coworkers this level of treatment?"

Jeremy looked her father in the eye. "Only the ones I love."

Jeisa's heart started to beat double time in her chest. *He does love me. How could I have been so stupid? I almost threw all of this away because I was scared.*

"Some things matter more than how you think you feel," her father said, killing her enjoyment of the moment.

Leave it to my father to even find fault in a declaration of love. Jeisa asked, "What's more important than love?"

Romario held Jeremy's eyes and said, "Integrity. Loyalty. Living a life you can be proud of."

"What are you saying, Dad?"

"We'll talk about it later."

Jeremy said, "I have nothing to hide from Jeisa. Mr. Borreto, you can say it now."

Romario leaned forward aggressively. "I don't like you, Jeremy. I don't like how you make your money, and I don't want you around my daughter after today."

Jeisa turned in her seat, her heart racing. "Dad..."

Jeremy also leaned forward and said, with some sarcasm, "I'm sorry you feel that way, sir. It's going to make holidays awkward."

"You little..." Her father started to rise from his seat.

Jeisa lost control and yelled, "Stop it. Both of you. Just stop it. Jeremy, I want to go home."

She'd expected him to signal the pilot, but instead he sat back, looking more determined than before. "No. I have something I want to show your father."

What? His affiliation with the Corisis? The Andrades? More of his not-so-subtle wit? Just like her father, he'd dismissed what she wanted because it didn't fit with his plan for the day. She'd always considered Jeremy the polar opposite of her father, but right now they looked like kindred souls.

"I hate both of you," she announced childishly and turned to look out the window.

"Jeisa—" Jeremy started to say something but changed his mind.

As usual, her father said nothing in response to her anger.

The rest of the flight was spent in a silent standoff that lasted until the helicopter landed on the Andrade's long driveway. Jeisa stepped out, followed by her father and then Jeremy.

Jeremy's mother rushed out to meet them with a camera.

Jeremy waved for her to put it away. "Not now, Mom."

His mother searched her son's face. "But I thought you said..."

He shook head dismissively. "I'll explain later."

Jeisa was too upset with both Jeremy and her father to care what Jeremy's mother was hoping to catch a picture of. She held it together long enough to say, "It's nice to see you, Mrs. Kater."

Therese Kater studied Jeisa's face with growing concern. "Is everything all right? Did something happen?"

Jeisa glared over her shoulder at her father and then shook her head. She tried to maintain her composure, but as tears threatened to spill, she blurted out, "I'm sorry, I can't..." She turned on her heel and rushed away before she made an even bigger fool of herself.

Mr. Borreto followed his daughter, leaving Jeremy in the uncomfortable situation of explaining the exchange to his mother. Therese broke the heavy silence first. She joked, "I take it you didn't propose."

Humor was what they both used when they were uncomfortable, and her use of it shifted his attention to her worried face. "It's fine, Mom. Her father doesn't like me, that's all."

Therese adjusted her son's tie. "He doesn't know you. When he does, he'll love you."

Jeremy laughed with some self-deprecation. "You always say that."

With a final tug on his tie, his mother asserted, "And I'm always right. I know you want to be like these people, Jeremy, but you already have something that money can't buy. You have a good heart. Jeisa is a lucky woman to have won it. Don't let anyone in there convince you otherwise." When he didn't say anything, Therese added, "Besides, I bought a new dress for today, so we can't leave now."

For the first time, Jeremy noted that his mother had put more effort than normal into her appearance. Not that she wasn't normally well dressed, it was simply that he was used to seeing her in her nursing uniform or in the casual clothing she wore around the house. As far as he could remember, this was the first time she'd ever worn a dress. On closer inspection, he guessed that she'd had her hair done for the day as well. He looked at the mansion behind her and back into his mother's uncertain eyes and felt suddenly guilty that he hadn't considered how intimidating the event might be for her. "They're just people, Mom. No different than you or me."

She clasped her hands nervously in front of her. "Marie introduced me to Katrine and Elise. They seem nice."

Jeremy put an arm around his mother's waist and guided her toward the house. "They are nice. And they're going to love you—even more once they know you better."

With a smile, his mother swatted at him. "You couldn't pick a less famous group to hang out with?" When Jeremy shrugged, Therese said slowly, "That helicopter of yours looks very expensive."

"It was."

Placing a hand on her son's cheek, Therese implored, "Tell me that you're not involved in anything dangerous."

From his earliest childhood, Jeremy could remember his mother stressing the importance of honesty. She'd never hidden a harsh truth from him, even when it may have been kinder if she had. "You know I hate to lie, Mom."

His mother's face crumpled a bit. "I don't know what I'd do if anything ever happened to you."

For the first time since he'd set himself on this course, he felt a real sense of shame. He'd never once considered how his business dealings would affect his mother. She'd already suffered one large loss. *After Tenin, I'm done. I already knew I'd have to be because of Jeisa, but now I know that I have more to lose than I thought.*

He reassured his mother the best he could. "Nothing is going to happen to me. I know what I'm doing. Now cheer up, Mom. It's Thanksgiving, and if anyone knows how to put on a feast, it's the Andrades."

CHAPTER *Eleven*

JEREMY AND HIS mother entered the large mansion and were instantly greeted by its owner, Alessandro Andrade, while his staff took their coats. Alessandro's wife, Elise, swept in to talk to Therese, which Jeremy had to admit was more than a small relief. Whatever Elise said to Therese elicited a shy laugh from that carried across the room and made Jeremy feel better about having brought her.

Out of earshot from the others, Alessandro clapped a hand on Jeremy's back. "We have been waiting for you. Is it true that we have another reason to celebrate today?"

How could he know?

Mom.

Jeremy shook his head, and Alessandro's smile fell away. Jeremy sought and found Jeisa looking at him from one of the adjoining rooms. As soon as their eyes met, she looked away.

Alessandro followed the direction of his gaze and referenced the man at Jeisa's side. "Is that her…?"

"Father?" Jeremy finished for him. "Yes, it is."

Alessandro gave Jeremy's shoulder a sympathetic squeeze. "Ah, how fate taunts the lovers. Did you know he was coming?"

Jeremy pocketed his hands and with some sarcasm said, "We wouldn't have flown down in a helicopter full of roses if I had."

After a hearty laugh, Alessandro asked, "So you didn't propose?"

"Not yet."

"Then there's still hope."

Jeremy looked back at Jeisa, who was introducing her father to Jake and Lil. He said, "I don't know. She said she hates me."

Alessandro moved his hands up and down like a balance scale. "Love and hate are close friends and are easily confused. Give me a woman who hates me over one who is indifferent to me any day. The sex is always better."

Jeremy's head snapped around. *Did he really just say that?*

Alessandro shrugged and smiled. "Don't tell my wife, but sometimes I get her angry just to spice it up." The older man dismissed Jeremy's surprised look. "You'll understand after you're married awhile." He tossed his chin at Romario and said, "Papa doesn't look very happy with you, my friend."

Jeremy didn't spare Jeisa's father a glance. "I don't care what he thinks of me."

Alessandro's voice deepened as he said, "Yes, you do. And so does Jeisa. You're a good man, Jeremy. I have no doubt you'll win him over as I did Elise's father. Show him that you will be good to his daughter and he'll overlook many things."

A weight lifted from Jeremy's chest. He and Alessandro had spoken at length during several past functions and Jeremy felt comfortable with him. He was exactly what he appeared to be: a self-made man who loved his family very much. Alessandro and his brother, Victor, shared an enjoyment of people that made everyone feel like a part of their family, regardless of the length of their acquaintance. Across the foyer, his mother was huddled with Elise and appeared to have discovered the same quality in her. It was good to see his mother laugh again, and he regretted not doing more to remove her worries earlier. *This is all going to work out.*

The absence of an older generation made Jeremy inquire, "Are you still close to Elise's father?"

A shadow passed over the older man's face. "He left us about eight years ago. A good reminder why not to keep a grudge, no? None of us are meant to be here forever. When you remember that, it's much easier to sort out the important from what should be forgotten. Jeisa's papa is here to protect his little girl. Respect that. It's his love for her that will outlive him, not whatever he says today."

Jeremy nodded. "You're a very wise man, you know that, Al?"

Alessandro's smile widened and he gave Jeremy's back a final pat. "I've always thought so, but don't tell Victor. He likes to think he's the smart one." After checking on the progress of the others, Alessandro said, "Most of the men are in the solarium and on the patio. Come, it looks like my brother is herding your future papa that way."

Jeremy hesitated. He wanted to say something to Jeisa, but didn't know where to begin.

Noting the direction of Jeremy's attention, Alessandro said, "Eat first, then talk to her. Everyone's temper is better on a full stomach."

Jeremy wasn't sure turkey would soften Jeisa's mood, but he wasn't about to ignore sage advice from a man with a happy marriage and a loving family. Evidence of his expertise on family matters was scattered throughout the house in the form of multiple generations.

Jeisa watched Victor Andrade lead her father away, leaving her with Victor's wife, Katrine, a tall Norwegian blonde who looked like she could still grace the cover of a fashion magazine. "Everyone will be thrilled that you've arrived, Jeisa," Katrine said. "Come, they're gathered in the kitchen."

The infamous Andrade kitchen. Jake's fiancée, Lil, had described it to her once, but it was larger than she'd imagined and a bit overwhelming at first. Everywhere Jeisa looked, the women were dressed in high-fashion gowns and enough diamonds to support a small nation. Her nude silk Carlos Miele spaghetti-strap gown was simple and fit in perfectly with what the other women had worn.

Through her time with Jeremy, Jeisa had gotten to know each of the women in the room. Alessandro's wife, Elise, was an elegantly dressed, petite, auburn-haired woman in her fifties who gracefully shared her role of hostess with her much taller and equally exquisitely dressed sister-in-law, Katrine. Although Alessandro and Elise owned the home, they lovingly shared it with Victor and Katrine when they visited. It was hard not to envy the closeness of the group.

Although the women had chosen the kitchen as a meeting area, it was obvious from the wine in their hands and their attire that their choice had nothing to do with cooking. One loud Frenchman was barking out orders to the kitchen staff as he orchestrated the countless dishes that were cooking on every heated surface.

Lil bounded forward in a deep-blue formfitting Mouret gown with her infant daughter, Colby—dressed in a complementary light-blue cotton dress and sweater—on her hip. Another woman might have handed her daughter off to a nanny, afraid that the young child might mar the perfection of her dress, but Lil looked unconcerned. "So, let's see it."

Her sister, Abby, was equally elegantly dressed in a melon-hued Oscar de la Renta strapless maternity dress with her hair swept up in a style that looked both effortless and modern at the same time. She rushed to her sister's side and said, "Lil, give her a minute to settle in."

Feeling like she'd walked onto a stage and forgotten her next line, Jeisa looked around the room and noted that all eyes were on her, waiting for her to say something. She directed her question to the most reliable source of unfiltered truth. "See what, Lil?"

Out of the corner of her eye, she saw Jeremy's mother shaking her head and waving for them to stop.

Lil looked down at Jeisa's left hand, then back to her face, and went red. "Ooh..."

Abby suddenly also looked quite uncomfortable. "Lil, didn't you want to change Colby before dinner? We should probably do it now."

Lil glared at her sister. "Come on, how was I supposed to know?"

Abby sighed. "I'm not saying it's your fault, I'm just..."

Jeisa's temper rose. "Will someone please tell me what is going on?"

Elise's daughter, Maddy, stepped into the group. Her playful manner made it impossible to do anything but smile when one saw her. She said, "Don't mind them, I'm sure they've been dipping into the cooking wine."

Therese said softly, "I am so sorry, Jeisa. I shouldn't have said anything. It's just that Jeremy was so excited and I was positive that we'd be greeting a newly engaged couple."

A growing understanding made the room spin. Jeisa held onto the back of one of the chairs. "A what?"

Lil spoke to the room in general, "I really don't think she knows."

In a softer tone, Abby suggested, "Maybe we should give Jeisa a minute alone with Therese."

No one moved.

Jeisa felt her face drain of color and her mouth dried. She searched the faces of the women around her and whispered, "Jeremy was going to ask me to marry him, wasn't he?"

His mother nodded.

Suddenly the helicopter of roses made sense. *Oh, my God. And I brought my father.* She started to laugh and cry at the same time.

Lil turned to Maddy and said, "Get her some of that wine you were joking about before she passes out."

Jeisa collapsed into the seat Katrine offered her, letting the events of the day run through her head again. What she'd thought had been part of a seduction scene had an entirely new meaning now that she knew what his real intention had been. The rose petals on the white carpet, the champagne—it all made sense now. "He was going to ask me to marry him."

Maddy handed her a glass of red wine. "This is my husband's own label. Careful, it has a kick."

Jeisa downed it in one gulp, barely tasting it. *All that planning to give me the perfect proposal and instead he gets grilled by my father and I tell him that I hate him. I don't hate him.* "I love him," she said aloud.

Lil laughed and bounced her baby. "We all pretty much guessed that part. What happened to the proposal?"

Abby cautioned, "Some things are none of our business, Lil."

Maddy chimed in with her opinion. "I have to agree with Lil on this one. I'm not going to be able to eat unless I know. I've got that nervous churning in my stomach again."

Elise hugged her daughter. "You're probably just pregnant again."

Maddy rolled her eyes. "I think I would know if I were pregnant." She looked up at the ceiling and started counting on her fingers. "Oh, my God, I could be. I thought you couldn't get pregnant while breast-feeding."

A quiet observer until then, Dominic's sister, Nicole Corisi, stepped forward and joked, "If you are, Maddy, I'm not going anywhere with you until the baby is born."

Jeisa looked questioningly at Nicole.

Lil explained, "Nicole delivered Maddy's son, Joseph, in a limo. I can't believe we never told you that story. That was back when Nicole pretended she was engaged to Stephan but they weren't even dating. He was so angry when he found out. It took them forever to figure out that they were meant for each other."

Nicole blushed. "I thought we were talking about Jeisa and Jeremy."

With that, everyone's attention turned back to Jeisa, who was feeling a bit sick from the wine she'd guzzled. "What can I say? He didn't ask me." She closed her eyes for an embarrassed moment and admitted, "Of course, he didn't know that my father would join us for the trip."

The ever-optimistic Maddy clapped her hands happily. "That's it, all we have to do is give the two of you a little time together and he'll pop the question."

Jeisa's eyes flew open and she admitted her mistake. She stood and hugged her arms around her waist. "I told him that I hate him."

Elise laughed and waved a hand in the air for emphasis. "I tell Alessandro that all the time. Sometimes that man knows just how to rile me. It means nothing."

Jeisa hedged, "I don't know..."

Jeremy's mother, Therese, said, "Maybe we shouldn't push..."

Abby nodded in agreement. "Jeisa, we're here for you. You can tell us to mind our own business and we will." She looked pointedly at Lil, who smiled back at her sister, promising nothing. "But if you want to marry him, you've got some of the finest matchmakers in the world right here. I can't figure out how they do it, but somehow the stars align and their crazy schemes work."

With a whoop of surprise, Lil grabbed her sister and hugged her. "Abby, that's the nicest thing you've ever said about my ideas."

Abby hugged her back, a rueful smile on her face. "I didn't say they weren't crazy, I just said they tend to work out."

Maddy snapped her fingers in the air. "I've got it. After dinner, Richard can ask Jeremy to come to the kitchen and we'll make sure no one but Jeisa is in here."

Her French husband walked up behind her, slid both of his arms around her waist, and nuzzled her neck. "Is that all I am to you? A patsy?"

Wrinkling her nose at Richard, Maddy teased, "You know you love it, Richard."

"I'll tell you what I love," he growled suggestively and whispered something into her ear that made her blush.

Maddy's smile held a cheeky promise. "Only if you get Jeremy in here after dinner."

Richard laughed, swatted his wife on the rump with a towel, and crossed back to where the staff was creating the holiday meal. He said, "I'll hold you to that."

Watching their open display of love left Jeisa yearning for that for herself. Could she and Jeremy get to that place?

Lil turned to Elise and asked, "Do you have candles? We can have the staff clean up early, dim the lights, and fill the kitchen with them to make it more romantic. This could work."

Practically dancing with excitement, Maddy declared, "Lil, you're a genius."

Abby shook her head and confided to Nicole, "Those two scare me when they're together."

Nicole laughed. "Twins separated at birth?"

Abby joked, "Thank God, because I wouldn't have survived raising both of them."

Therese touched Jeisa's arm. She wasn't laughing along with the other women. "Jeisa, don't feel pressured. This is a big decision and one that no one should rush into. I just want to tell you that I cannot imagine a better woman for Jeremy. I would love the honor of calling you my daughter." Tears began to rush down Jeisa's cheeks. Therese hugged her and chided, "Don't go crying now and messing up your makeup. I want pictures."

Jeisa straightened and wiped away her tears. She looked around the room and asked, "Where's Marie?"

Maddy pointed at the ceiling and said, "She took Joseph upstairs to put him down. I hope he doesn't spit up on her dress. She looks stunning."

Ha, I bet she wore the dress I sent her. The feeling of triumph was fleeting in the face of all the other emotions storming within Jeisa. "Does she know?" Jeisa asked.

Lil laughed and spun, eliciting giggles from her young daughter as she said, "Knowing Marie, she probably has your honeymoon planned out."

Maddy's mother piped in and took Jeisa's hand. "Speaking of honeymoons," Elise said, "sit down, Jeisa. We should talk."

Maddy gave a laughing groan. "Mom."

Grinning, Nicole asked, "Is this the bikini theory?"

Katrine shook her head and wagged a finger at the woman who would one day be her daughter-in-law. "No, your fiancé spilled the beans on that one."

Elise laughed. "I don't care if Alessandro knows the rules. It still works for us."

Maddy covered her ears at her mother's admission. "Please, no. You're scarring me."

Fascinated, Abby took a seat at the table and said, "I don't know the bikini theory."

Lil threw a napkin at her sister. "See what all that sophistication cheats you out of? Even I know the bikini story. I guess everyone figures I've done worse." She linked arms with Maddy and waved to Nicole to join them. "Let's escape while we can." To the young daughter on her hip she said, "Be grateful that you're too young for *the talk*."

Nicole smiled sympathetically at Jeisa as she fled. "Sorry, Jeisa. Sometimes it's every woman for herself. You'll know to run next time."

After the three young women left, Therese, Elise, Katrine, and Abby sat at the table with Jeisa. Elise jumped right in and asked, "How much did your mother talk to you about men?"

Jeisa's eyes rounded. "My mother passed away before she had a chance to."

Placing her hand over Jeisa's on the table, Elise said, "I'm so sorry to hear that, but don't worry, we'll fill you in."

Jeisa sank lower in her chair. "That won't be necessary. I figured it out on my own."

Victor's wife, Katrine, chuckled. "We're not talking about sex, honey. Well, not the act itself. A happy marriage is full of healthy sexuality. People confuse sexuality with the mechanics of the act itself. Good sex is like planting a garden in the spring. Do you put a seed in the ground and call that a garden? Would you expect to live happily off something you put so little effort into? Or would you tend that garden? Water it. Weed it. Watch it grow, knowing that the more you put into it, the more pleasure you get out of it. There are techniques you can use that will help you to maintain your garden, and so many of them should happen outside of the bedroom."

Jeisa looked helplessly at the kitchen's exit and then back around the table of women. *There is no escape for those who stayed, is there?*

Therese looked at the two older women with growing admiration. "What an incredibly healthy outlook on sexuality."

Under her breath Abby mumbled something and started to rise from her seat. "As a happily married woman, I should be exempt from this."

Jeisa grabbed her hand and pulled her back to a seated position. *Oh, no, if I'm staying, you're staying.* She said, "I bet it applies to all of us." Abby met her eyes with a smile that promised some future payback, but Jeisa didn't let go of her hand. There was no way she was going to sit through *the talk* alone.

Elise dove right in and started giving Jeisa relationship tips that no woman should hear in front of her future mother-in-law. When Jeisa thought it couldn't get more mortifying, Therese said, "That reminds me of what I used to do with my husband when we first married," and shared details that set Jeisa's cheeks ablaze.

Jeisa looked across the table and met Abby's eyes, and they both burst out laughing. In that place, with those women, Jeisa's heart filled with hope.

Jeremy is going to ask me to marry him.

Tonight.

In this very kitchen.

And she smiled.

CHAPTER *Twelve*

IN THE SOLARIUM of the Andrade home, Jeremy was finishing off a heated debate with Jake's parents, about their latest experiments with quantum computational operations and the feasibility of their success, when he noticed Jeisa's father nursing a drink and watching him. He could feel the man's dislike from across the room. He excused himself from the older couple and headed over to Romario. The man straightened as Jeremy's approach, and his eyes narrowed at Jeremy drew near.

With Alessandro's words echoing in his mind, Jeremy said, "I know we got off on the wrong foot, but I think you misunderstood what you saw earlier..."

"Don't waste my time with lies."

Jeremy stiffened. "I have no reason to lie. I simply want to explain..."

The older man's face tightened with anger. "Your intentions for my daughter were pathetically obvious. A young woman, alone in a foreign country. You thought she'd be easy to take advantage of."

"No, I'm serious about your daughter."

Romario leaned down aggressively. "Let's be clear about one thing. After today, you're never going to see her again, so I really don't care how you feel about her."

Jeremy fought down the anger that was building within him. This was Jeisa's father. Someone she loved even if she fought with him. If Alessandro could win over his wife's father and live to tell about it, then so could Jeremy. He swallowed his pride and said, "I intend to marry Jeisa. I'd like your blessing, but I don't need it." He took out the three diamond rings from his pocket, each over five carats but with different cuts. "One of these would have been on her finger if we'd taken that helicopter ride alone today."

Romario let out a harsh laugh. "You think I'd let her marry someone like you?"

A deep voice joined their conversation. Dominic chastised the diplomat. "Hey, ease up on the kid. He loves your daughter."

Romario spun on his heel and went nose to nose with the interloper. "Stay out of this, Corisi. It's none of your business."

Dominic snarled back, "You made it my business when you brought it here."

This wasn't how Jeremy envisioned winning Romario over. He said, "Dominic, I've got this."

Dominic persisted. "What makes you think Jeremy isn't good enough for your daughter?"

Romario gestured to Dominic. "Perhaps who he keeps company with."

"You don't know me," Dominic hissed.

"No, but I knew your father, and that was enough."

Dominic's fists clenched at his sides.

Stephan Andrade stepped into the conversation with his easy California smile. "Gentlemen, it looks like we're being called in for dinner." When none of the men responded, he directed his next comment to Jeisa's father. "Mr. Borreto, we made a place for you next to your daughter. I'm sure this discussion can wait until after dinner."

After a tense moment, Romario said, "I believe we all said what needed to be said."

Jeremy blocked Romario's way. "No, we didn't. I'm sorry you don't like me or my friends, but I will ask your daughter to marry me, and if she says yes there is nothing you can say or do that will stop us."

Tight-lipped, Romario said, "We'll see about that, won't we?"

Never one to back down from a challenge, Jeremy asserted, "I guess we will."

When Romario stepped away with Stephan, Jeremy let out a long, relieved breath. He met Dominic's eyes and said, "I'll win him over, just probably not tonight."

Dominic threw back his head and laughed. "I don't want to like you, but you are the craziest bastard I know." As they walked together toward the dining room, Dominic asked, "And why do you have three rings?"

Jeremy took out a green princess-cut diamond set in white gold. "This one reminded me of the outfit she wore the first time I met her." He held out a clear teardrop diamond, larger than the last. "A friend's wife told me that most women would love this one." The last ring he held out was twice the size of the others, a white cushion-cut surrounded by one-carat diamonds in a platinum setting. "The jeweler said that no woman could resist this one."

"Go with the green one and tell her why," Dominic suggested gruffly.

Jeremy put the other two in his pants pocket. "Thanks, Dom. You're really good at this relationship stuff."

Straight-faced, Dominic said, "Don't make me hit you." A hint of a smile curled one corner of his mouth.

Despite how it had worked out, Jeremy was grateful for what Dominic had attempted to do. "Thanks for what you said before… to Jeisa's father."

"Don't mention it," Dominic said. Then he frowned. "Seriously, don't tell anyone."

Jeremy merely smiled. *Your secret is safe with me.*

CHAPTER *Thirteen*

IN AN IMPRESSIVE display of hospitality, the Andrade Thanksgiving table sat thirty people, thirty-four if one counted the children in high chairs. Victor Andrade took his spot at the head of one end, flanked by his wife, Katrine, his son Stephan, his son's fiancée, Nicole, Dominic, and Abby. Alessandro Andrade, the owner of the home, sat at the other end with his wife, Elise, his daughter Maddy, her husband, Richard, and their infant son, Joseph. Jeisa took her place between a determined-looking Jeremy and her angry father.

Once everyone was seated, Victor Andrade stood and raised a glass to toast. "Thanksgiving is about gratitude and family. Our table grows every year, and I want to thank my brother for always graciously setting another place as it does." Across the room, Alessandro raised his glass to his older brother. "This has been quite a year for all of us, no? We have overcome our differences and grown stronger because of it. When I look around this table, I am reassured about the legacy I will leave behind. Life will throw you many challenges, but if you remember that this is what is important—your spouses, your children, your good friends—you will always find your way back to happiness."

In plain sight of everyone, Jeremy boldly took Jeisa's left hand in his. Jeisa turned to look at him and lost herself in the emotion she saw in his face. He mouthed, "I'm sorry."

She whispered back, "Me, too."

In an act driven by the emotion of the moment, Jeisa turned and put her right hand on her father's on the table. He looked down at her and some of the anger in his face lessened. He let out a long sigh as if releasing some tension. In a soft voice loud enough for only her father to hear, she said in Portuguese, "I know that you're angry with me, but try to enjoy today. These are my friends and this is the life I'm hoping to have."

Her father didn't say anything, but he rubbed his forehead in the way he often did when he was reconsidering his position on something.

Jeisa turned back to Jeremy and whispered, "I think he's starting to like you."

Jeremy coughed doubtfully. His response was more serious than she'd expected. "Maybe not yet, but he will."

As Victor Andrade's toast ended, Jeisa whispered to Jeremy again, "Did you see who they sat on his other side?"

Jeremy leaned back in his seat to see, then whispered back, "Your father had better behave."

Jeisa laughed into her hand. "He will." Watching her father bend his head to hear Marie better, Jeisa felt proud of the older woman. When she'd received a polite thank-you note for the dress, Jeisa had wondered if Marie would actually wear it. But there she was, looking elegantly sexy draped in the sleeveless, floor-length golden gown, dotted with silver appliqués, and a complementary sheer shawl.

And her father was hanging on her every word.

Jeremy interrupted her observation by asking, "Can we talk after dinner?"

With her heart fluttering in her chest, Jeisa asked, "So, you've made your decision?"

He leaned across to kiss her cheek. "There was nothing to decide, just foolishness to forget." He nuzzled her ear.

Jeisa's breath caught in her throat. She nodded.

He does love me.

Dominic growled into his wife's ear as he watched the couple across the table talking. "Look at him talking Marie's ear off. She can't wait for this meal to be over."

Eyes dancing with humor, Abby said, "I'm not positive that's what she's thinking."

"If he says one rude word to her, I'm throwing him out the front door."

Abby placed a soothing hand on Dominic's tense thigh. "He's a diplomat. I'm sure he knows how to behave himself at a social gathering."

Dominic glared at Romario. "You wouldn't think so if you'd heard him talking to Jeremy."

Abby rubbed her husband's thigh beneath the table until his attention refocused on her. "Tell me you didn't get involved in their family dispute."

Instantly attentive, Dominic lowered his head and whispered suggestively, "Move your hand a little higher and I'll tell you whatever you want to hear."

Abby slapped his stomach playfully. "I'm serious."

Dominic kissed his beautiful wife's neck, knowing there was no way to avoid her lecture but enjoying the delicious pink it brought to her cheeks. "So am I."

Despite the desire that lit her eyes, Abby chastised her husband playfully. "You are incorrigible."

He kissed her neck again, but also offered her what he knew she was waiting for. "I may have exchanged a few harsh words with Romario."

Abby's head cocked to the side in doubt. "May have?"

It was impossible to stay upset when his wife smiled at him that way. He conceded, "He doesn't think Jeremy is good enough for Jeisa."

Tongue-in-cheek, Abby asked, "Is any man good enough for a father?"

"Do not mock me, woman," he said, but there was no bite to his words.

Instead of continuing down the teasing thread, Abby took Dominic's hand and laid it on her small belly bump. "It couldn't have been easy for Jeisa's father to come here today. He doesn't know any of us, and from what I've heard, Jeisa wasn't entirely honest with him about what she'd been doing here in the States. He flew over here because he was worried about her and he met a suitor he'd previously never heard a word about. Can you blame him for being protective? How would you feel if Jeisa were our daughter?"

Dominic shook his head ruefully. "I'd want to kill the bastard."

"And?" Abby pushed.

With a groan, Dominic conceded, "And I might not want her to hang around with people who have been in the news for as many questionable reasons as we have been." He closed his eyes for a pained second. "Don't ask me to be nice to him. I'm only human."

Abby smiled up at her husband. "Do you know what I think?"

Looking down at his wife's beautiful, concerned face, Dominic said, "No, but I'm sure you'll tell me."

"You know that Jeremy looks up to you."

Dominic waved one hand in the air in frustrated emphasis. "He's just so… naive. He doesn't understand how the world works."

Tears of emotion filled Abby's eyes and she said huskily, "And you want to protect him. Oh, Dominic, you went through hell and it shaped how you see families. But this isn't the same, and Jeremy needs to work this out on his own. He'll be fine. He knows how to love through adversity. Romario is not like your father. It's too easy to judge him by what we see today, but he's trying to protect her. Today must be difficult for him. There is nothing worse than watching your child do the exact opposite of what you consider safe for them. It unhinges even the nicest person."

Dominic ran his hand lovingly over the nape of his wife's neck. "Is there anyone you hate?"

Her lips thinned. "Yes. The man who stole your childhood from you."

Dominic kissed Abby's forehead. For the millionth time since he'd met her, he wondered how he'd earned this second chance. Given the time, she might have redeemed even his father.

"Have I told you how much I love you?" He loved the way her eyes filled with tears again, but this time with happy emotion.

"Not since this morning," she said cheekily. As dessert was served, Abby said, "Jeremy does need you, but not as his defender. Your opinion matters to him. Show him that you respect his kind of strength, too."

Dominic looked across the table to where Jeremy was once again attempting to engage Jeisa's father in polite conversation and had to admit that Abby was right. Any other man would have gotten into a shouting match with Romario, but instead Jeremy had a stoically determined look on his face.

That kid doesn't give up.

CHAPTER *Fourteen*

AFTER DINNER, THE guests spilled out onto the patio and lawn. The sun, on this warmer-than-usual November day, was valiantly delivering its last hour of light, and some of the younger Andrades had shed their jackets and were tossing a football around in what looked like a lethargic attempt at the sport.

Although Jeisa had spoken to people throughout dinner, she couldn't remember a single conversation. All she could think about was what would happen when she and Jeremy were finally alone.

What if he doesn't ask me?

Of course he's going to. Why would he tell his mother if he wasn't serious?

Maybe my father scared him off.

She scanned the room for Jeremy and found him engaged in a conversation with Jake Walton and his parents. *He can handle my father.*

Maddy and Lil approached, and every muscle in Jeisa's stomach clenched in anticipation.

Lil's smile was infectious. "Are you ready?"

Maddy said, "We'd better hurry. We lit so many candles we may set off a fire alarm."

Jeisa was half-led, half-dragged to the kitchen by the two excited women. She caught her breath at the beauty of what they had done. Each table was covered with a white tablecloth and candles of all sizes scattered in every direction. In the fading light of the day, the large kitchen could have passed for a romantic restaurant. Jeisa hugged the two women who had scrambled to transform the space. "It's perfect," she said.

Maddy assessed their work with a critical eye. "It's not subtle, but he was going to ask you anyway—you're just giving him the perfect place to do it."

Lil confided, "Jake told me Jeremy bought three rings because he wanted to make sure you had one you loved." She sighed dreamily. "That's so romantic."

Or indecisive, Jeisa thought, then hated herself for thinking that.

Jeremy made his decision and it's me.

Maddy grabbed Lil by the hand. "We can't stay. I already told Richard to get Jeremy as soon as he saw us leave. He should be here any second."

They each hugged Jeisa one last time.

"Good luck," Maddy said.

"She won't need luck," Lil declared. "He loves her. We'll be toasting your engagement before dark."

Jeisa waved to them as they left her. She stood in the middle of the floor, her breath growing shorter as her excitement and nervousness grew.

And she waited.

Jeremy regretted mentioning his Tenin project in front of Jake. Although Jake's parents hadn't seemed fazed by his slip, Jake brought up the subject again as soon as they left the conversation.

"You're working a deal with Alvo? His time in power is coming to a fast end."

Jeremy dismissed his concern with a shrug. "Then I'll help the other side."

"You sound exactly like Dominic used to."

Jeremy puffed with pride. "Thank you."

Shaking his head in disgust, Jake said, "That wasn't a compliment."

Jeremy hid his confusion behind an accusation. "Who are you to judge my ethics?"

Calmly raising a placating hand, Jake said, "I'm not judging you. I'm cautioning you that you're going down a dark road."

A dark road you paved yourself. "It wasn't so bad when you and Dominic made your fortune doing something very similar."

Before Jake could answer, Dominic stepped into the conversation and said, "Jake, give me a minute with Jeremy."

After Jake was out of earshot, Jeremy said, "That guy is—"

Dominic cut him off. "Always disgustingly right when it comes to things like this." He put a hand on Jeremy's shoulder and cautioned, "Before you follow too closely in my footsteps, Jeremy, you need to know that even I don't want to be me."

In shock, Jeremy asked, "What is that supposed to mean?"

"I made my money by siding with whoever had the bigger wallet. I didn't care who got hurt as long as I won. But even when I thought that was how the world worked, I paid a price for that lifestyle. When money becomes an obsession, there is an emptiness that seeps into you like a poison. Nothing can fill it. Nothing I built or bought brought me happiness because I hated myself. I still do sometimes, even though Abby brings me comfort." There was such pain in Dominic's eyes that Jeremy didn't question his sincerity.

Not sure what to do with his idol's confession, Jeremy asked, "Why are you telling me this, Dom?"

"I can't undo what I've done, but you don't have to repeat my mistakes. Helping a dictator suppress his people will change you, but not in the way you seek. You are brilliant, Jeremy. Don't sell your soul to make your fortune."

Jeremy put his hands in the pockets of his trousers and rocked back on his heels. *It's too late.* "I can't back out of the deal now."

"If you don't, Jeremy, it will destroy everything you love."

The sadness in Dominic's eyes was testament to the truth in his words. It was also a sign that Jeremy was no longer an outsider. What do you say when your idol bares his scars as a warning to you? *Nothing.*

One of the house staff interrupted and said, “Excuse me, Mr. Kater?”

“Yes,” Jeremy said.

“There is someone in the foyer who would like to speak with you.”

Jeremy followed the uniformed man toward the main entrance. Richard met him halfway across the room and said, “Jeremy, can you come to the kitchen for a minute?”

Jeremy spoke while he kept walking. “I can’t right now, Richard.” He didn’t wait to hear the Frenchman’s answer. Whatever he needed, it could wait. Right now he had a pretty good idea who was waiting to speak with him, and the faster he addressed her concern and got her to leave the better.

Alethea was pacing the enormous marble foyer impatiently. The click of her black suede Rupert Sanderson pumps echoed through the empty space. She needed Jeremy to come with her so she’d worn a revealing cherry-red Versace gown to further entice him. She rushed forward when she saw Jeremy and said, “They wouldn’t let me in. Can you believe that? The one time I decide to announce myself and I’m not welcome.”

“What are you doing here, Alethea?” He didn’t sound happy to see her, nor did he exhibit any signs of being impressed by her attire. His lack of attention irritated her, but it also wasn’t worth wasting time on, considering the direness of the situation she and Jeremy had gotten themselves into.

“I’ve been calling you, but you’re not answering my calls or texts. I tried to reach you through the office and the receptionist said you were away. Did you get any of my messages?”

“I told you I’d call you back next week.” The same confidence that had impressed her the first time was now nothing more than an annoying speed bump.

Sorry to disturb your party with reality. "This can't wait until next week."

"It will have to. For once, you'll have to be patient."

Had she not heard his cold, dismissive tone with her own ears she wouldn't have believed him capable of it. Any other time, she would have gladly taken up the challenge, but her reason for crashing the Andrade celebration was serious. "This isn't about me. It's about our project in Tenin. We have people planted in the compound. Remember the ones you set up the communication network for?"

"Of course I remember."

"Well, someone has blocked me out of it. I can't contact our people."

Finally she had Jeremy's attention, even if he was giving it to her reluctantly. "I can look into it as early as tomorrow morning."

"We don't have the luxury of time, Jeremy. I have it from a good source that the next strike against Alvo is going to be a military one that wipes him out—and it's going to happen tomorrow. We have to get our people out of there and pull out of the deal. This is bigger than what I thought it was. We're in the middle of a war over there. We've got to warn Alvo, but first we've got to get our people out. Do you have your laptop with you? Can you work your magic from here?"

Jeremy rubbed his forehead in frustration. "I didn't bring it."

Alethea's jaw dropped. "You never go anywhere without it."

Jeremy said, "Today was different." He looked up at the ceiling as if he could see through it to what was upstairs. "The Andrades won't have a computer here with the ability to do what I need. If we're locked out, I might need to piggyback on a government server. I'm going to need either my stuff or… I could use what's at the New York Corisi building. I have access."

"Then let's do it."

"I have to tell Jeisa that I'm leaving."

"Your image consultant? Does she have you on a short leash?"

At least one part of Jeremy hadn't changed. He didn't hedge the truth. He said, "I love her, Alethea. Today I was going to propose to her."

Shit, we don't have time for this. In an instant she had an angle she could use. "Isn't she the daughter of a diplomat?"

Jeremy said, "Yes."

Alethea drove her point home. "Does she know that you're making your money by propping up a dictator?" When his face reddened, she said, "I'd say as little to her as possible about this while we try to get ourselves the hell out of this situation. You think her father is going to let his daughter marry you if Tenin becomes a massacre that has your name linked to it? It'll be all over the news—an American hacker involved in a foreign civil war. The press will crucify you and anyone associated with you."

As convincing as Alethea was, Jeremy knew what he had to do. He'd think of something, hopefully before he saw Jeisa, which would smooth the situation over. "I can't leave without saying something to her."

"Fine. Two minutes. Tell her whatever you need to, but don't tell her enough to jeopardize our people. This is bad, Jeremy. This is really bad. Do you have a car here?"

"I have a helicopter." *Full of fucking roses,* he thought with disgust.

"Great. We'll take that. Tell your girlfriend we'll be back before the party is over."

Jeremy nodded and walked away, his pace increasing as he searched the solarium for Jeisa. When he saw Lil, he asked her, "Have you seen Jeisa?"

Looking a bit confused, Lil glanced at the woman beside her as she answered, "Maddy and I left her in the kitchen about fifteen minutes ago."

Maddy scanned the room and asked, "Didn't Richard ask you to go to the kitchen?"

Frustration mounting, Jeremy grated, "I think so. I don't know. I couldn't go. Alethea is here and she needs me to do something. But I can't leave until I see Jeisa."

Lil's eyes widened. "Alethea is here?"

"Who's here?" Abby asked as she joined the group.

Lil groaned. "Alethea."

"Lil, tell me you didn't invite her..."

Jeremy cut in, "I'm going to the kitchen. Maybe Jeisa's still there."

With a wild wave of one hand, Maddy asked, "To tell her that you're leaving with Alethea? I don't think that's a good idea. She probably isn't there anymore. Right, Lil? Why don't you check the kitchen and I'll take Jeremy on the patio to see if she's out there."

"I'm on it," Lil said.

As Jeremy followed Maddy onto the patio, his mind was racing. He wanted to tell Jeisa everything. Hell, normally he would have taken her with him and even asked her for her opinion on how to resolve the situation. But Alethea was right. If there was a massacre in Tenin tomorrow, there would be an investigation, and his affiliation with Alvo would be in all the papers. For the first time since he'd charged forward into this endeavor, he had to face the fact that he may have gotten himself into a much more dangerous situation than he could handle.

A month ago, when he'd felt like he had nothing to lose, he was numb to the sting of fear. But now that he'd begun to imagine a life with Jeisa, one that included not only his family but hers… he could see the far-reaching consequences this could have. He might become a liability to Romario's political career, and the fallout of that would be he would lose Jeisa—even if she found a way to forgive him.

Unless I fix this.

Somehow.

Ten minutes dragged into fifteen. Some of the glow of anticipation faded from Jeisa's cheeks. How long do you wait for the man you love to come to you? How long do you stand there, torn between being the happiest you've ever been and giving in to the growing fear that you're making a fool of yourself?

He's not coming.

He changed his mind and can't face me to tell me.

No, if he doesn't love me, why would he tell my father that he does?

Just two more minutes.

Give him two more minutes.

But still, he didn't come.

How much of my life am I going to spend waiting for happiness to come to me? What had Marie said—you discover who you really are when you're willing to fight for what you want? I am going to go out there to find Jeremy and tell him that I am sorry.

I'm not going to hide anymore.

Jeisa took a deep breath and stepped out of the kitchen and into the hallway. Her step faltered when out of the corner of her eye she saw something that sent a cold chill down her back.

Although she'd never met her, there was no mistaking the impatient redhead pacing in the foyer of the Andrade home. Her desire to find Jeremy was forgotten as her feet carried her toward one of her greatest fears.

Alethea stopped and shook her head as Jeisa approached, looking at her as if she were an inconvenience.

Unable to help herself, Jeisa asked, "What are you doing here?"

"You must be Jeremy's little image consultant," Alethea said sarcastically.

The disappointment of waiting for a man who never came swirled and meshed with suspicion. "And you must be the woman who only comes to see him when she needs something."

Alethea rolled her eyes. "Don't go getting your panties in a wad. I wouldn't be here if it wasn't important. I'll have Jeremy back in a couple of hours."

Oh, no, you don't. You don't get to come here and ruin everything. He loves me, and all of the arrogance in the world isn't going to change that. Jeisa said the words she desperately wanted to believe. "He's not going to leave with you."

Alethea sighed impatiently. "I'll let him explain it to you."

Jeisa stepped closer, real panic making her heart race. "Why did you come here? Can't you let him be happy? Or are you afraid you'll lose your meal ticket? Everyone knows you built an entire career on his hacking skills, but he doesn't want you. He wants me. So whatever you ask him to do, he's not going to choose you."

Red spread over Alethea's face, and her claws came out as she snapped back, "The only reason you've had him at all is because I didn't want him until now. But I might just take him from you to prove that I can."

"That's enough," Abby's authoritative voice rang out across the foyer. The click of her heels echoed in the heavy silence that had enveloped the room. "Alethea, you need to leave."

When Alethea realized her comment had been witnessed by a growing crowd, she deflated a bit. "I don't know why I said that."

Abby stepped between Jeisa and Alethea. "You said it because you don't care who you hurt as long as you win. But this time you didn't check to see if you were alone."

Alethea looked around and sought the support of her best friend. "Lil, you know I didn't mean it. You heard what she said to me. I just lost my temper."

Near tears, Lil joined her sister and stood beside Jeisa in support. "You should go, Al. We'll talk later."

Jeremy came rushing into the foyer. "Jeisa, there you are!" He reached for her, but she stepped back.

Time froze and for a moment everyone else disappeared, leaving only Jeremy and a question that could not be denied. "Is it true, Jeremy? Are you leaving with her?"

Despite the audience of people, he kept his focus on her as he said, "Yes, but only for a couple of hours. I'll be right back."

Jeisa's stomach flipped painfully. "That's all I need to know." For a moment she thought she might pass out, and the voices around her grew faint and distant. Her greatest nightmare had become a reality—and a humiliatingly public one at that. "Go. Don't let me stop you."

He grabbed her hand. "Jeisa, if I could explain this to you I would. I swear I would."

She ripped her hand out of his and was instantly enveloped into the protective arms of her father, who said, "You little bastard. Get out before I wring your neck with my bare hands."

Stepping into the mix, Marie said, "Romario, there has to be a reason."

Above his daughter's head, Romario growled, "Do you have children?" Marie shook her head slowly, sadly, and took a step back. "If you did, you would understand why I don't care what his reasons are. I'm getting my daughter out of here and away from this toxic place."

Still in shock, Jeisa numbly let herself be led away by her father.

Dominic cursed and said, "I'm going to kill him."

Jake asked, "Which one?" Dominic glared at the departing Romario and Jake said, "I'm with you on that one."

In a few long strides, Dominic crossed the room to Marie's side and pulled her into his arms. For once the woman, who usually fussed when being touched, welcomed the embrace, knowing it meant Dominic loved her.

Abby stepped aggressively toward Alethea. "Are you finished here, or is there anyone else you'd like to upset before you go?"

A cold determination fell over Alethea's face. "Come on, Jeremy."

Therese clung to her son's forearm. "Don't go with her, Jeremy."

Jeremy looked around the room helplessly, gently removed his mother's hand, and straightened his shoulders. "I'll be back as soon as I can."

As they walked away, Jake hurried after them and said, "I sure hope whatever you're doing is worth it, Jeremy. Do you need help?"

Jeremy looked to Alethea, who vehemently shook her head. "No, this is something I have to do alone."

With that, Jeremy stepped outside with Alethea and motioned to the helicopter pilot to start up the engine. He gave him instructions to head to Corisi headquarters and helped Alethea into the main compartment. Once they were both settled into the flower-ridden seats and had left the ground, Alethea said, "You couldn't tell them, Jeremy."

"I don't want to talk about it." Jeremy turned away from her to watch the Andrade mansion quickly disappear behind them. Would Jeisa wait for him? For the first time since they'd met, he wasn't sure.

"We'll fix this." Alethea said. "You'll get a message to our people. We'll warn Alvo so he can live one more day, and then we'll pull out of this deal. No one needs to know what we've done if we cover our tracks well enough. Jeisa's angry with you now, but she'll forgive you."

"I hope you're right," Jeremy said tiredly, staring out the helicopter window.

During the silent ride into the city, Alethea had a lot of time to regret her impulsive words. Jeisa had been right in part. When Jeremy had announced his love for another woman, it had shaken her. Not because she loved Jeremy, but because she'd always assumed that he'd be there for her.

Selfishly. It hurt to admit that to herself.

Abby's harsh words hadn't hurt as much as the look in her best friend's eyes had. *Lil should have defended me. Who stood by her when she found out she was pregnant? Who risked everything to make sure Abby was safe when Dominic's motives had been questionable?*

I did that.

But sitting across from Jeremy, amid the evidence of his love for another woman, knowing that she might have ruined his chance with her, Alethea was struck by a real sense of shame that she had never felt before.

I used this man.

I took advantage of the feelings he once had for me.

I risked his life more than once without giving it a second thought.

What kind of person am I?

I could have reassured Jeisa. She could have come along.

But I didn't care about how this hurt him or her.

I wanted what I wanted.

Maybe I'm exactly the person Abby has always said I am.

Her voice husky with emotion, Alethea said, "I am so sorry, Jeremy." *Sorry for more than I could even begin to apologize for.*

He didn't acknowledge her words, and she didn't repeat them. She just let them hang in the thick, rose-scented air of a ride that would forever change how she saw herself.

Alone with her father in the library, Jeisa struggled to find her emotional footing within an embrace so tight she could barely breath. No matter how many times she ran the foyer scene over in her head, it felt surreal. Why would Jeremy go to so much trouble to convince her that he wanted her only to pick Alethea?

"Get your purse, Jeisa. We're leaving. I'll get a car to take us straight to the airport. We're going home."

"No." Jeisa pulled herself out of her father's arms. Her mind was still spinning with what had just happened, but she wasn't going to run back to Brazil.

"No?"

"I'm going back to Boston."

"I cannot allow—"

His words stung like a bucket of cold water to the face. Normally, this was where she'd retreat and despise him for not understanding her. *Never again.* "Dad, you're making things worse."

Unaccustomed to criticism from his daughter, Romario grew angry. "Worse? Worse than what I just witnessed? These people are not good for you."

The pain his words caused drove Jeisa to be honest. "And you think you're better? You just insulted a woman who has done nothing but help me since I came here. Marie didn't deserve what you said to her."

Romario looked away, his jaw tight with emotion. The sight of her proud father at a loss for words, even temporarily, touched Jeisa's heart. She'd created this situation—it was time for her to take responsibility and try to explain it to him. "I know you don't think I'm safe here. You think someone will try to hurt me, but these people are my friends. I did make the mistake of trusting someone I shouldn't have and you met him. Reese is an awful man who preys on women like me. Women who have been protected so much they are vulnerable. I don't want to be that person anymore, Dad."

Romario rubbed his temples. "I just wanted to keep you safe."

How can I make him understand? "I know, Dad, and that was okay when I was a little girl. But I'm a woman now. I can't live like that anymore. I want my own life."

With tormented eyes, Romario said, "I can't lose you, too."

Jeisa touched her father's cheek. Not since the day her mother died had she seen his eyes shine with unshed emotion. She was so used to seeing him as strong and inflexible that she often forgot he was also a man who had suffered a great loss. She wrapped her arms around his waist and just held him. When she lifted her head, she sniffed loudly and said, "You're not going to lose me, Dad."

He buried his chin in her hair and admitted, "I was scared when you stopped answering your phone. I thought something had happened to you. I wouldn't have been able to live with myself if it had." Jeisa hugged him tighter. "And then when I found out it was a lie… that you'd made up everything you'd told me for the past few months… I was angry."

"I know," Jeisa said. Seeing the events through his eyes filled her with both regret and a deeper understanding of how much her father loved her. "I was wrong. I should have told you as soon as I found out that Reese was a liar. I just didn't want you to—"

"Come here like I did."

Jeisa nodded. *Tell him. Tell him how you feel.* "I'm going to get hurt, Dad. I'm going to make mistakes. But you have to let me make them."

He gently pushed her back from him and asked, "Are you okay?"

In the past she would have lied and said she was. This time, Jeisa let out a long shaky breath and chose the truth. "With what happened with Jeremy?" He shook her head sadly. "I don't know, Dad. I keep going over the scene in my head and I don't understand it. That wasn't the Jeremy I know. He would never deliberately hurt me."

Romario tensed a bit. "You think he's in some sort of trouble?"

"I wish I knew," Jeisa said and turned to look out the window.

She was too emotionally spent to say more, or to care when she heard her father leave the room.

Only Abby's hand on his arm stopped Dominic from crossing the room and strangling the man who had, in one day, made his short list of those worth risking jail time to hurt.

Without so much as a glance at Dominic, Romario crossed directly to where Marie was standing. Abby stopped Dominic from intervening, softly saying, "Marie can handle this, Dom, and she knows she's not alone."

Romario stood before a tight-lipped Marie as everyone in the room collectively held their breath. "I didn't mean to lash out at you earlier."

Marie took a deep breath and chastised him softly, "It was rather cruel and poor manners for a man who should know better."

He inclined his head in concession to her point.

Relaxing a bit, Marie conceded, "However, I know you were concerned for your daughter and that can make a man say things he doesn't mean." Ignoring the fact that they'd become the center of attention, Marie asked, "How is Jeisa?"

Romario's jaw clenched. "Understandably upset."

Marie nodded. "My father loved to sail. He always said that children are like boats—they cannot reach their potential while tethered to the dock."

Looking less than pleased, Romario countered, "How very American of you. My family made their money from mining. I would say that when you have something as precious as a child, you must guard it as diligently as you would a diamond."

Marie raised her chin, looked him directly in the eye, and said, "You may have hoped for a diamond, but you birthed a boat. Denying it won't change the truth."

Romario straightened his shoulders and glared down at Marie. "Don't tell me how to raise my daughter."

Marie stepped closer, her hands going to her hips. "She's a grown woman. The raising part is finished. What she needs from you now is acceptance of who she is."

Romario growled down at her, "This is none of your business."

Marie held his eyes, her face flushed with emotion. “Yes, it is. I care about your daughter and her happiness. She loves you. I’d hate to see you lose her just because you’re too stubborn to hear what she’s trying to tell you.”

Jake murmured to Dominic, “You tell him, Marie.”

Dominic made a guttural sound in his chest.

Abby took her husband’s hand in hers. “I’ve never seen Marie look at a man like that before. I think she likes him.”

Dominic swore beneath his breath when Jake agreed.

“Does that mean we can’t punch him?” Jake asked blandly.

Dominic growled, “Not right this second.”

Abby leaned over and asked, “What are you two conspiring about?”

“Nothing,” Dominic said quickly. Too quickly. Abby eyed him suspiciously.

When Romario turned to Jake and Dominic, he spoke with the calm authority of a diplomat. “My daughter thinks Jeremy may be in some trouble. Do you know why he left with that woman?”

Dominic’s temper flared. “Hoping someone else will take him out so you don’t have to?”

Jake injected, “None of this makes sense unless Alethea told him something that he felt he couldn’t share with us.”

Jake’s mother stepped into the conversation and said, “Maybe something to do with his work in Tenin?”

“What would he be doing in that country?” Romario demanded. “They are verging on civil war.”

Ever the voice of reason, Jake suggested, “Whatever’s going on, I suggest we find out where he went.”

Dominic motioned for one of his security men to approach as he asked Jake, “Did you bring your helicopter?”

“Never leave home without it.”

Dominic conferred with his security for a moment, then said, “Let’s go. I think I know where he went.”

Jake’s parents joined them. “We’re coming, too.”

As Dominic started to refuse them, Jake's father said, "Jeremy has helped us more than anyone in our field. If the trouble he's in has anything to do with hacking, you're going to need us."

"They're right. We may need them," Jake added.

Romario flexed his shoulders decisively. "I'm also coming."

"No way in hell," Dominic countered.

Nose to nose with Dominic, Romario said, "My daughter loves that man. If there is the slimmest chance that he is not as bad as I think he is, I need to know. This involves my family. I'm going to either save him or kill him. Can you tell me that you'd do any differently?" When Dominic didn't waver, he added, "Besides, if this is a political issue, I may have some pull."

Dominic tensed. *God, I hate that man. I hate him even more when he's right.*

Victor Andrade put a hand on Dominic's shoulder and said, "Strength is also shown in restraint, friend. Take him with you."

Knowing that it's the right thing to do doesn't make the unpalatable more desirable. Dominic looked down into Abby's trusting eyes and swore beneath his breath in concession. "Is anyone else coming?"

"I'll stay here. Jeisa will need someone," Abby said.

Lil gave Jake a quick kiss on the lips. "Me, too."

Victor Andrade bowed out gracefully. "I can wait to hear how it turns out. I'm getting too old for all this."

Therese stepped forward and, with a hint of desperation in her voice, said, "Jeremy is a good boy. If he's in trouble, you've got to get him out of it."

Marie took the woman's hand in hers to comfort her. "If anyone can, it's these boys."

Abby met Dominic halfway for a lingering, parting kiss. "Be careful, Dom. You don't know what you're walking into. I know you have to go, but"—she stepped back and put a hand on her belly—"just remember all the reasons you have to come home."

He pulled his wife to him and gave her a long kiss that promised more than just his return. Marie cleared her throat behind him and said, “Enough of that, off you go.”

Dominic chuckled and reluctantly released his wife. “I’ll be back before you know it.”

Abby nodded and hugged herself.

With that, Dominic, Jake, Jake’s parents, and Romario—along with some of Dominic’s security—boarded Jake’s helicopter and headed after the elusive Jeremy.

CHAPTER *Fifteen*

A PERK OF being integral to fortifying Corisi Enterprises' technology infrastructure was that building security was no hassle for Jeremy. He simply showed his high-level badge, vouched for Alethea, and walked into an area of the building that very few ever saw. Behind the access-controlled security doors was a room filled with rows of black racks. The hum of fans and blinking of lights was familiar and calming to Jeremy. He and Alethea walked down one of the rows until he found the server he was looking for.

Alethea hadn't said much during their trip over and he was grateful for that. He didn't want to know if she had followed her usual behavior and made the situation worse rather than better. He was already having difficulty concentrating. He pulled a shelf out of the rack and flipped up a monitor. He took a seat in front of the console and started typing in codes.

Breaking through firewalls was something he normally did with ease. But Alethea was right—they'd been blocked out of the communication network he'd built. Someone had deliberately locked them out. He tried to gain access by using an SSH tunnel, but it failed. He tried again and, when that failed, he knew that whoever had locked him out had anticipated how he would try to break their codes.

This wasn't the Tenin government. This was personal.

Sliver.

He'd done something similar to his online nemesis a hundred times before—and laughed about it. But lives had never been on the line back then. Sliver had made a name for himself in the hacker community by hijacking the sites of major companies.

Although his real identity was a secret, many had felt his online presence had been felt in their wallets. In the past, when Jeremy had gotten a whiff of one of Sliver's planned stings, he'd locked him out just for fun. Sliver had threatened to retaliate, but Jeremy had always remained one step ahead of him.

Which was why some referred to Jeremy as a cyber-superhero.

And this was payback for that title.

What if I can't fix this? People are relying on me to save their lives.

I lose them. I lose Jeisa. Everything.

He couldn't shake the haunting image of Jeisa as she told him to go with Alethea. She hadn't looked as angry as she'd looked… defeated. Which didn't make much sense to Jeremy since he'd spent the day telling her he loved her. Why wouldn't she believe him? What happened to put that deep hurt in her eyes?

When he realized he'd stopped typing altogether, he swore. *This is too important for me to screw up. More important than Jeisa and me. There are people depending on me to save them. Focus. Fucking focus.*

He paused to send a plea out to the heavens. *Let me figure out this one issue and I will change my ways. I swear it.*

When his next attempt failed, he slammed his hand down on the table near the keyboard. "I can't break through," he said in frustration.

Alethea paced behind him. "Keep trying."

He tried another code. Tried another access point. Each attempt had been anticipated and blocked.

"You've never met a code you couldn't break. Don't give up." Alethea's words of encouragement left him cold.

Jeremy shook his head. Even when he tried to clear his thoughts of the dire situation he and Alethea had placed people in, his mind kept racing. Images of Jeisa, of her father, of his mother with that stupid camera waiting to take photos of what should have been one of the best moments of his life.

But I screwed it up.

I screwed everything up.

Jeisa is never going to forgive me.

Not when she sees what I've done—not when this all explodes and hits the news.

She and her father will run as fast and as far as they can from me, and who could blame them?

He had stopped typing again when a message popped up on the screen in front of him. An instant message sent via a site he'd been trying to gain access through. It read, "Ready to give up? ~ S"

He typed back, "This isn't a game, Sliver. There are lives at stake here."

"Then you must really want to access this network."

Noticing Jeremy's online conversation, Althea asked, "Who is that?"

"It's Sliver. Remember the guy Stephan hired to plant a virus in Dominic's server? I guess he's still upset that I stopped him."

"Shit. What does he want?"

"Revenge… and to be known as the best."

Alethea said, "Maybe we can use that."

Jeremy thought about it, looked at the ceiling for a moment, then typed, "Let me back in and I'll never mess with you online again."

"You really are desperate," Sliver answered. After a moment Sliver wrote again, "Give me the access codes to Dominic's server and I'll give you your network back."

What does he want with Dominic? This wasn't how Sliver normally operated. This felt personal. Jeremy stalled. "What makes you think I have them?"

"You wrote them."

Shit.

He looked over his shoulder at Alethea. "He says he'll give me the codes if I give him access to Dominic's server. I can't betray Dominic, but I can't let our people die in Tenin, either."

Behind him, Jake's father, Jim, said, "When forced to choose between two impossible scenarios, the solution is often a third and more creative option."

Jeremy spun in his chair. The previously empty room was filling with almost everyone he'd hoped to keep this a secret from, along with what appeared to be a private swat team that was stationing itself throughout the room. Only Jeisa was missing. In her place, her stone-faced father stood in judgment.

Jake flanked Jeremy's right side and said, "We can't help you unless you tell us what exactly you've gotten yourself into."

Alethea moved back as both of Jake's parents stepped forward to hover over Jeremy. Hope surged through Jeremy. With the two infamous Waltons and their genius son on his side, they had to be able to beat Sliver. It wasn't easy to admit the scope of his mistake to them, but it was necessary. "I went to Tenin for the fast money. Alethea worked on propping up their facility security. I took care of the software side. We planted people on the inside to keep us informed of changes, but Alethea heard chatter of a military strike as early as tomorrow." He looked at Jeisa's father and said, "My name is all over this if it goes bad. We'd hoped to send word to warn our people to get out before informing Alvo of the attack. I didn't consider how the fallout of this situation could affect anyone else. I just saw easy money. Now I'm locked out of the communication network and I can't break Sliver's codes."

Jake pulled a chair from a neighboring station and took a seat beside Jeremy. "Are we talking about the same hacker that Stephan used? What does he want?"

Jeremy looked over his shoulder and met Dominic's eyes. "He wants access to Corisi Enterprises' server."

Judy, Jake's mother, asked, "Stephan wouldn't have hired him again, would he? He seems like such a nice boy."

Dominic's face whitened with anger, but his voice was deadly calm when he spoke. "If he's smart, he had nothing to do with this."

Jeremy quickly interjected his gut feeling on the matter. "Dom, I've known Sliver a long time. Well, not personally, but via our online clashes. He doesn't normally take it this far. At first I thought it was about our history, but this is his second swipe at you and he's escalating with each attack. You may know him. Is there anyone else who would want to sabotage you?" Jake and Dominic shared a look across the room. *Right. Stupid question.* "I don't know for sure, but this feels more like a vendetta than one of his stunts."

Dominic moved closer until he stood right behind Jeremy's chair. "There is only one way to deal with a cowardly enemy. Lure him out and crush him."

Jake agreed. "Sliver's strength is his anonymity."

As Jeremy switched his goal from code breaking, inspiration hit. Jake's mother read as he typed and exclaimed, "Oh, that's good."

Jake scanned the screen. "That'll definitely stop him in his tracks."

"What are you doing?" Alethea asked in a rush.

Jeremy typed even as he answered. "I'm giving him access—but it's limited. As soon as he tries to use it we'll trace him back to his hole, then light up the Internet with his identity and location. I don't care how many dummy IP addresses he uses, we'll find him, and then so will everyone else."

Jake turned to Dominic and explained, "It'll be like handing someone a loaded gun with blanks that has a deadly backfire. It won't hurt him unless he uses it."

Alethea strode back and forth behind the huddled team. "But then how are we going to get the network codes?"

Jeremy paused. *Tough question.* "I'll make one contingent on the other—like a choreographed hand-off."

Alethea shook her head. "You need a decoy. He'll expect you to try to stop him. Put a weak code in the forefront. Let him break through that and think he's smarter than you. Use his ego against him. Then threaten to link him to the Tenin disaster so he'll want that crisis averted. You have to give him a reason to want to save our people. He'll do it if he thinks it takes away your trump card."

Jake put a hand on Jeremy's shoulder in support. "That's a sound strategy."

"Of course it is," Alethea said impatiently. "My people are in there. This has to work."

"Don't use the standard encryption methods," Jake's father advised. "They will be too easy for him. He'll know what you're doing. He needs the challenge of breaking a 256-bit cypher. It still won't take him long, but if he's as ego driven as you say he is, he'll think he's outsmarted you. Send him the authentication information for Dom's server. Once he's in, push the 256 encrypted module to him. Let him execute it. Inside of that, hide your call-home code in a far more vigorous protocol. We've been working on a new type of file encryption that is as strong as 1028-bit military grade encryption but doesn't show any signs of actually being encoded. He won't know you are executing a Trojan attack. In that file, your code will then call back to us over variable proxy servers, distributing the information over https and SSH tunnels while maintaining the encryption. Once it gets back here, we'll be able to use our decrypter and establish full control over his system. It will take him decades to break it, if he ever does."

"What will stop him from using another computer?" Dominic asked abruptly.

Everything, Jeremy thought. "Sliver built a life online. We're about to block him out of all of it."

Romario stepped forward and asked, "And then expose him?"

Now they're getting the idea. "By the time we're done with him, there won't be a place he can hide online… possibly not on this planet, either. We'll have his real name and access to everything connected to him."

Judy shook her head sadly. "It's a shame that someone as gifted as he seems to have ended up on such a dark road."

Her husband, Jim, agreed and added, "That's why science is best kept isolated from society. Too many temptations."

"Wait a minute. Jake, are your parents *the* Waltons?" Romario's level of surprise was almost amusing.

Jake conceded dryly, "That is our surname."

As the full magnitude of whom he was standing beside sunk in, Romario asked the computer icons, "What are you doing here?"

Judy answered him. "We came to have a holiday with our son, but these boys are always into some trouble." She looked down at Jeremy and said, "Jeremy is one of the greatest minds of his generation. He just hasn't found his niche yet. When he gets serious, he's going to change the world."

"We tried to tell Jake that pursuing money instead of research was a waste of his potential, too, but you know kids." Jim shook his head at the loss.

Despite the banter going on behind him, Jeremy completed the task the Waltons had outlined. "It's done. I used all of your ideas. It looks like he's going to take the bait."

"Now what?" Dominic demanded.

"Now we wait," Jeremy answered. "If he believed what I said about Tenin he'll open the network, because he won't want us to have that leverage over him."

Alethea tried to access her network via her phone a moment later and exclaimed, "I'm in. I just sent a message warning them to get out. I'll give them an hour and then I'll warn Alvo. You did it, Jeremy."

Not this time. "No, it wasn't me who figured this out."

Jake patted his shoulder. "No one makes it very far alone, Jeremy. It's the network you build offline that ensures success online."

Jeremy met Dominic's eyes and said, "Like a family."

"Don't push it," Dominic said curtly, but the corners of his mouth twitched with a suppressed smile. In a flash, he was serious again. "How long will it take to expose this bastard?"

Jeremy nodded toward the console. "It depends how fast he breaks through the Trojan code and how eager he is to take you down."

Through gritted teeth, Dominic said, "I want his name as soon as you have it."

Jake offered a calmer plan. "Dom, you won't need to go after this guy. He has compiled quite a list of enemies himself. Once his identity is known, he won't last long."

Undeterred, Dominic asserted, "I still want to know who he is."

In the uncomfortable silence that followed, Jeremy chanced a look at Romario. "I know what you must think of me."

"Do you?" Romario asked blandly.

"I really messed up. I got involved in something that was way out of my league."

Instead of agreeing, Romario asked, "Why didn't you tell Jeisa about any of this? And if you had all of these people as a resource, why didn't you ask them for help?"

With an awkward shrug, Jeremy admitted, "That was my mistake. I didn't want to endanger anyone else. If this had gone public, it would have been a reputation-destroyer. I didn't want to take anyone down with me." He held the older man's eyes and said, "I didn't tell Jeisa for the same reason I didn't want you to know. I wanted you to respect me. I've made some big mistakes with my life lately, and with your daughter, but I do love her."

Romario folded his arms across his chest. "I believe you, but I doubt it'll be enough."

It has to be. I didn't come this far to give up now. "I know she's upset with me, but hopefully she'll listen to why I had to leave the party. We were okay at dinner."

After an audible intake of breath, Jake asked, "So you don't know about the kitchen scenario?"

Jeremy shook his head in confusion. "The kitchen?" He vaguely remembered Richard asking him to go there. "Lil said something about Jeisa being in the kitchen, but why is that important?"

"Lil told me that the women had filled the kitchen with candles to give you a place to propose. She was waiting for you in there." Jake's words sliced through Jeremy's confusion with painful precision.

Jeremy sat down with a thud. "Oh, my God. And I didn't show up." *What have I done?*

From the back of the room, Alethea's next words added to Jeremy's nightmare. "And I did."

A silence hung heavy in the room.

Intent on clearing her name, Alethea continued to speak. "No wonder she wasn't happy to see me." She looked at Dominic, whose displeasure was evident on his face. "I didn't know how serious Jeremy and Jeisa were. I certainly didn't know they were getting engaged. I said something stupid when she goaded me, but I wouldn't have if I had known any of this." She looked at Jeremy. "You have to believe that."

Still digesting the enormity of how he had hurt Jeisa, Jeremy asked, "What did you say?"

Chin held high, Alethea didn't shrink from her mistake. "I told her that I could have you if I wanted you."

Now Jeisa's sad question made sense to him. She had been asking him to make his choice. Jeremy's face drained of color. "And then I left with you."

Alethea nodded.

Jeisa thinks I chose Alethea. Acid churned in his stomach as he remembered how she'd accepted his decision and turned to her father for comfort. He directed his next words to both the woman he'd once considered a friend and to the father of a woman he might have lost forever. "I would have never left her standing there if I had known that."

Alethea shrunk a bit beneath his accusation and her own guilt. "I know."

Not good enough. Jeremy rubbed his forehead angrily and demanded, "Why would you say that, Al? Why would you stand by and watch me hurt a woman you know I love?"

Alethea's shoulders came up a bit helplessly, as even she could not defend her actions. "I don't know."

Romario intervened and sought answers to his own questions. "So you didn't know anything about what had gone on?"

Jeremy shook his head sadly. "I had no idea. I thought the worst part of the day was that you didn't like me."

"That's the least of your problems," Romario answered.

Jeremy stood. *What if this is how it ends? What if this is the price I must pay for having believed there would be no consequences for my actions? Jeisa is a good person. Maybe she deserves better than me.* "I see that now. She's never going to forgive me."

Jake's mother comforted him in the only way she knew how. "'Never' is an unquantifiable and unrealistic amount of time."

Dominic turned to Jake and tried to lighten the mood with humor. "I see how you became the man you are."

"Let's remain focused on Jeremy," Jake said, but the dry humor in his tone sounded forced.

I refuse to accept this. There must be something I haven't thought of—Dominic. "What would you do?" Jeremy asked the man he still admired greatly.

Before Dominic answered, Jake said, "He'd call Marie."

"I don't call her about everything," Dominic denied hotly.

Romario looked at Dominic in surprise. "You take relationship advice from your assistant?"

Dominic stood straighter and snarled, "I'm looking for a reason to hit you. Don't give me one."

Instead of backing down as many men would have, Romario straightened to his full height and looked down his nose at the younger man, who was just a hint shorter than he was. Dominic was in his prime, but Romario had aged well, and Jeremy wasn't sure which man would come out the winner if they came to blows. In a soft but deadly tone, Romario issued an offer. "Maybe you should take your best shot and see if you live."

In an attempt to diffuse the situation, Jake joked to Jeremy, "See why Dominic didn't have to pay for boxing lessons? People volunteer to hit him."

"That's not even funny," Dominic said dryly, and the tension of the moment fell away.

Jake shrugged, unperturbed by his friend's correction. "Humor is a matter of perspective."

"I don't know if I approve of you spending so much time around Dominic if this is his approach to conflict resolution." Judy's comment drew a chuckle from several of the men, including some of the security team, who quite wisely became stone-faced again beneath Dominic's glare.

With a bit of red highlighting his cheeks, Jake said, "Mom, do you have to talk to me like I'm twelve?" His plea elicited several coughs as those around him held their laughter in.

Jim attempted to defend his son. "He's right, Judy. Jake is perfectly capable of choosing his own friends. If he wants to surround himself with those who are less intellectually challenging, that's his business."

Jeremy burst out laughing and didn't stop even when Dominic's jaw started to clench. It was simply too tempting to resist saying, "I don't know, Dom, I think they just called you stupid." He gave his idol a supportive smack on the back.

Jake's father quickly backpedaled. "Oh, no, no. I didn't mean that. Dominic has a different type of intelligence."

"I'd stop while you're ahead," Romario interjected with a chuckle.

Dominic growled, "Unless you're also sporting an IQ of 180, they don't think much more of you than they do of me."

"I'm going to go now. Jake, tell Lil to call me." Alethea stood at the door and said, "Jeremy, I know I said this before, but I want you to know how sorry I am. If you need me to say something to Jeisa..."

Too little, too late. Jeremy wasn't one to hold grudges. He knew life was too short for that, but he'd wasted too many years believing Alethea cared about him to forgive her for this. With the clarity of hindsight, he saw the reality of what they'd had. She'd used him. *And I let her. I thought her love of danger was exciting and cool. Now I see that it has cost her more than it ever brought her, and I hope she sees that one day and finds happiness. I'm going to do everything I can to ensure I fix this and regain my own.* "You've said enough. Good-bye, Alethea."

Alethea left quietly.

Breaking the quiet after her departure, Jake joked, "Seriously, should we call Marie?"

Raising his hands in a sign to override Jake's suggestion, Dominic said, "No, we've got this. I may not be a member of the Mensa club here, but I understand how the female mind works."

"Oh, boy, here it comes," Jake said with a growing smile. Jeremy loved watching the two men rib each other. They often sounded more like bickering brothers than business partners.

"When you mess up as badly as you have, Jeremy, you've got to come back with something equally amazing for your apology," Dominic explained, not bothering to acknowledge Jake's joke.

"The parsimony of his solution is almost elegant," Judy said enthusiastically.

Her husband continued her observation. "Like the Occam's razor principal, there is value in the simplest form."

Looking a bit irritated, Dominic turned to Jake and asked, "Did they just insult me again?"

Jake's laugh boomed. "No, that was a compliment of sorts."

Jeremy chimed in with the Waltons and said, "A stochastic process really, because although the initial condition is known, there is some indeterminacy on how it will evolve." Jake's parents beamed in agreement. Jeremy smiled and continued, "Although, I do have an idea." He looked at Jeisa's father and announced, "I know what your daughter cares about, and if my idea works we could both be back in her good graces."

"Does it involve computers?" Romario asked doubtfully.

"Not at all."

"Then tell me about this plan."

Back at the Andrade home in the gallery off the foyer, laughter and family banter still rang out loudly, grating on the nerves of a shell-shocked Jeisa. Victor Andrade had graciously offered to fly her home, but she'd called a limo service instead and retreated to a corner of the mansion to wait for her ride.

She looked around the room and fought her inclination to run from the concern she saw on the faces of her friends. It had been a long day, one that had drained her of a desire to talk to anyone. *I just want to go home... wherever that is.*

"Are you sure you don't want to wait for Jeremy to return?" Lil asked, wringing her hands.

Jeisa let her tired expression be her answer. A part of her would always be grateful to the women around her. They'd stayed with her even after she'd told them that she'd rather be alone. She remembered her mother doing the same when she'd been very young, and their persistence touched her heart. It's easy to find a friend to laugh with. It's harder to find one to cry with. Harder still to find one who knows you need them even as you try to push them away.

Abby motioned to the door with one hand. "We can ride back with you, if you need the company."

"No, I'm okay." The lie caught in her throat, revealing how very far she was from that state.

Jeremy's mother stepped forward, looking like she wanted to throw her arms around Jeisa and hug her to her chest. Thankfully, she didn't. Jeisa wasn't sure how much longer she'd be able to fight back the tears as it was. Therese said, "I feel awful about how today turned out for you. I know it won't make you feel much better, but I don't think Jeremy knew that you were waiting for him in the kitchen."

Jeisa felt sorry for the woman who was torn between her love for her son and concern for the woman he'd hurt. *She would have made a wonderful mother-in-law,* Jeisa thought, and then wanted to kick herself for that unnecessary reminder of what she'd lost.

Marie took one of Jeisa's hands in hers. "He doesn't love her. He loves you."

A tear ran down Jeisa's cheek. Her strong façade felt so brittle that she feared one wrong word would have her bawling in the arms of one of these women. *And what would that do? Just give me another reason to be embarrassed today. No, it's better to remain angry.* "Then why did he leave with her?"

"Jeremy may have an explanation," Abby said tentatively.

Jeisa wiped her cheek and straightened her shoulders. "I'm sorry. I know you're all trying to help, but I really don't care what his reasons were. I will never forget how it felt to stand there, waiting for him to come to me, and then watch him choose her."

"Yeah, that was awful," Lil agreed wholeheartedly.

"Lil," Marie cautioned.

"Sorry," Lil said. "I'm just acknowledging that I wouldn't want to hear his excuses, either."

"You're not helping," Abby said softly, giving Lil a look that would have silenced many but had never succeeded in curbing her sister's tongue.

"No, the one who didn't help was Alethea," Marie said with some disgust.

"I don't know why Al did that. It's not like her," Lil protested passionately.

Abby's normally sweet expression twisted a bit with a long-festering anger. "Don't. Don't defend her. That was classic Alethea."

Lil threw her hands up in frustration. "That's not true. I can't defend her this time, but that doesn't mean I love her less. She has been there for me every time I needed her, and that means more to me than one mistake. She was wrong today, but she's not a bad person."

"We may have to agree to disagree on that point," Jeisa said quietly. On more than one occasion Lil had told her that Abby needed to let go of the past and forgive Alethea. Lil could be quite persuasive, and Jeisa had sided with Lil. Until today, when Alethea had proven to be exactly what Abby had accused her of being.

Jeremy's mother asked, "What do you want us to tell Jeremy when he gets back?"

Jeisa took a deep breath. *He made his choice. There is nothing to say.* "Tell him that I need time to heal from today. I may feel differently in a week or a month, but for now—I don't ever want to see him again. Tell him if he really is sorry, he should give me time. I need..."

In a voice that was suddenly authoritative instead of consoling, Marie said, "You need a change of scenery. I'll call the Watts Institute of Technology. I have connections there. They were interested in hearing from you. You should head out there and see how you'd fit into their team." Her smile was gentle as she teased, "And leave the ice cream in Boston."

Quickly blinking away a wave of fresh tears, Jeisa threw her arms around Marie, feeling a bit ridiculous as she did. She pulled back and said, "I know that I have nothing to complain about. My life is wonderful. You all have been so kind to me. I do need to be working on something like the water project so I can remember what is really important. There are people who are living in a state of suffering every day. By comparison, my problems are ridiculous."

"California sounds like a good choice for you," Abby said, "but give yourself permission to be sad about what happened today. You're right, we're incredibly fortunate and we should remember that every day of our lives, but that doesn't mean that we don't hurt." Abby gave Jeisa a warm hug. "You're not alone. Nicole and Stephan spend half their time in California. Maddy has been trying to convince Richard to open a restaurant out there. All of us are only a phone call away."

Lil held her hand up to her ear like a phone and said, "If you need to go out, get drunk and stupid to forget about all this..." Her offer came to a slow halt beneath the disapproving glare of the equivalent of three mothers. She dropped her hand and changed her speech on the fly. "Don't. Because drinking is bad."

Abby covered her face with her hand and laughed.

Marie shook her head and hugged Lil. She said, "You must have been hell on wheels in your teens."

Abby groaned, but her next words held both humor and love. "You have no idea."

Their banter brought a reluctant smile to Jeisa's lips. "I am going to miss you all."

The housekeeper entered and announced the arrival of Jeisa's car. Therese asked, "So, you're going to San Francisco?"

Jeisa nodded. "Yes." She looked around at the supportive women surrounding her and vowed, "But I'll keep in touch."

After one final hug for each woman, Jeisa headed down the stairs and into the limo that promised to take her far away from what had been a very bad day.

CHAPTER *Sixteen*

A WEEK LATER, Jeisa was back in her Boston apartment, packing her things in cardboard boxes. It had taken a few days of reassuring him, but her father had finally flown back to Brazil. He promised to call her weekly instead of daily, so they were making progress. Per her request, they hadn't spoken of Jeremy—not once.

It was a blanket rule she'd issued to everyone. *Do not mention his name or that day. Just let me heal.*

The only painful reminders that remained were the messages Jeremy periodically left on her cell phone requesting that she call him. But she couldn't. Not yet. She was still as angry with herself as she was with him. *What sane woman sleeps with a man who clearly loves someone else? A desperate one.*

And that's not me.

Not anymore.

He was damn lucky to have a woman like me care about him at all. Unlike Alethea, I wanted him just the way he was.

Alethea. It was hard not to be intimidated by a woman who looked and acted like she belonged in a James Bond movie. Of course Alethea had won. She'd fought, rather viciously, for what she'd wanted.

And I didn't fight at all.

As usual.

Well, that's not entirely true, I fought for this. Jeisa kicked one of the already packed cardboard boxes—and immediately regretted it, as pain shot through her foot. With renewed resolve, she told herself, "This is a fresh start. No more lies. No more excuses. No more men. From now on, it's just me and the work I can do on the water project."

If all went well, Monday would find her in her new office on the WIT campus, helping the GWP raise funds to start on production. There was enough work to keep her busy—hopefully so busy that she could forget how sad she was.

She jumped when the phone rang. Either it was Jeremy, in which case she didn't want to answer, or it was someone else and she didn't have the energy for small talk. She checked her caller ID.

Alethea?

Don't answer it.

I can't not answer it. I want to know what she has to say.

No, I don't.

Yes, I do.

Jeisa answered her phone in a higher pitch than she would have liked. "Hello?"

The line was quiet for a moment and then Alethea said, "Jeisa, I know I'm probably the last person you want to speak to but..."

But you want to gloat? You want to tell me how wonderful things are now that you have Jeremy? Or worse, pretend you care that you hurt me?

"You are," Jeisa said coldly.

Alethea started over. "I want to apologize for what I said to you at the Andrades'."

"Why apologize? You got what you wanted."

Alethea was quiet for a moment. Then she said, "I'm not with Jeremy. I never have been and I never will be. I said something stupid because I was frustrated that he wanted to see you before we left and angry about what you said to me." When Jeisa said nothing, Alethea added, "He never cared about me the way he cares about you."

Hurt and anger surged through Jeisa. She didn't want to hear about Jeremy at all, and certainly not from this woman in particular. "It doesn't really matter if you're still with him or not. He chose you that day."

"No, he went with me because he wanted to protect you from what we had done and I told him that involving you would endanger you."

No. No. No. Don't waver. It'll only hurt longer if you do. Jeisa let out a shaky breath. "Why should I believe you?"

There was a surprising humility in Alethea's answer. "Jeremy and I were friends of a sort. Well, he was a friend to me. I wasn't much of a friend to him. It took seeing him hurting over losing you to understand how selfish I've been. He is a good man and he deserves someone better than me… someone like you."

Jeisa cleared her throat of the emotion clogging it. "I've been naive, but I'm not stupid. You don't do anything unless there is something in it for you. I won't let you use me to fix the situation you created when you showed up at the Andrades'. So, thank you for the apology, but you'll have to find another way to redemption." With quiet force, Jeisa clicked her phone off.

As tension throbbed through her body, Jeisa sat heavily on a pile of boxes behind her. *What if Alethea was telling the truth?*

What if they aren't together?

What if he does love me?

Did he really leave that day because he wanted to protect me?

She ran the scenes through her head over and over again. Once she put aside the overwhelming humiliation of the day, she wasn't sure what to think.

How would the day have ended if my father hadn't shown up? If I hadn't lied about where I worked? If I had stood up for what I wanted? If I hadn't forgotten to turn on my phone after our trip? If I had called Jeremy to warn him about my father's visit? If I had trusted him? The list of "if" questions was infinite.

The alternate scenarios were not as significant as what had actually happened. *I didn't warn him. I didn't trust him. I didn't believe that he loved me. Where does that leave us?*

Shattered and irreparable.

Jeremy paced in what would soon no longer be his office in the New York Corisi building. He'd already cleared out his Boston office. Seventeen days, nine hours, and forty-three minutes since he had left Jeisa standing in the foyer of the Andrade home, and she still wasn't answering his phone calls. Luckily, her father was.

"Alô?" Jeremy said in what he hoped was a Brazilian accent.

Romario answered him gruffly in English. "Yes?"

"*Como vai, gatinha*?" Jeremy asked cheerfully.

With an impatient growl, Romario said, "I'm not a kitten and I'm about to walk into a meeting. What do you need?"

Jeremy put Romario on speakerphone so he could search his phone for some phrases he'd been noting since he decided to learn Portuguese for Jeisa. "Shit, sorry. I must have looked at the wrong list this morning. How do you say future father-in-law in Portuguese?"

"Let's not rush your bilingualism, or your relationship with my daughter. Is there something you need right this moment?"

Jeremy heard but was not deterred by Romario's curt tone. "I wanted you to know that everything is in place at WIT. I've instructed the project leader to keep it a secret until I get there. I fly out tonight, but I'll try to see her tomorrow."

"You told me this yesterday," Romario reminded him none too gently.

"Yes, but you said you would talk to Jeisa today and I wanted to ask—"

With a sigh, Romario said a bit more kindly, "No, she didn't mention you, Jeremy."

Jeremy sat down heavily in the chair behind his desk. "I love your daughter and I will win her back."

"I don't doubt how you feel, Jeremy, since you've proclaimed it every day since I returned to Brazil. Keep in mind, however, that if she tells me she doesn't want to see you after tomorrow and you persist, I will have to return, hunt you down, and ensure that no one ever hears from you again."

Jeremy paused at the threat. He wasn't sure if Romario was serious or not, but he decided to reassure him anyway. "That won't be necessary because this is going to work. I know I can get her to forgive me."

"I hope so, because she cares about you. That's the only reason I'm going along with this at all. She is where she said she wanted to be, working on what she said she wanted to do, but she still sounds sad."

"That will change tomorrow. We'll even name our first son after you," Jeremy jokingly promised. When Romario made a bit of a hissing sound, Jeremy amended quickly, "Once we are married, of course."

"Good-bye," Romario said. However, instead of hanging up as he normally did, he added, "Be good to my daughter, Jeremy."

The softly voiced request took Jeremy by surprise and spoke volumes of Romario's love for his daughter. That he trusted Jeremy with her heart was a humbling honor, and one that Jeremy took seriously. "I will," he swore. "I'll tell you how it goes." As he said the words, he imagined how he hoped the day would end and rushed to correct himself. "Not right away, and not everything. Just what is appropriate to tell you. Not that anything inappropriate will happen."

With a pained groan, Romario said, "Perhaps you should let her tell me. Good luck."

A few minutes later, Jeremy was still sitting in his chair staring at the ceiling as he replayed their conversation in his head. *I called Jeisa's father a kitten.*

He covered his face with one hand.

I should probably keep my apology to Jeisa strictly in English.

Sitting forward, Jeremy took the three ring boxes out of his pocket. What had seemed like a good idea a few weeks ago now felt foolish. He didn't need three engagement rings to win Jeisa's heart, and he was no longer confused about which one she would want.

The six-carat diamond the jeweler had suggested now seemed gaudy compared to the other two. Jeisa dressed nicely, but she didn't flaunt her wealth. She wouldn't want to wear it, especially not when she worked on charity projects. The clear diamond Tim's wife had picked out was classically beautiful, but any woman would love it and any man might have purchased it. It didn't speak to the specific beauty of who Jeisa was. The green princess-cut diamond contained a hint of blue in it, which Jeremy had read was rare because the circumstances required to turn a blue diamond green were nearly impossible. The presence of boron with a low level of nitrogen produced a blue diamond, while radiation made a diamond become green just beyond the surface. To him, Jeisa was a blue-green diamond: beautiful on the surface, complex and precious because of her core.

He was looking at the chosen engagement ring when Dominic and Jake entered his office. Dominic sat on the chair in front of his desk and Jake took the seat across from him.

"So, this is it. Your last day here," Dominic said in a drawn-out way that Jeremy took as evidence that he wished it weren't.

"You can still call me to troubleshoot for you, though," Jeremy offered sincerely. His place was in California with Jeisa, but he would miss these men. It may have taken him a while to earn their respect, but he valued it even more because it had not been given freely.

Jake made a generous offer of his own. "If it doesn't turn out the way you planned, you can come back."

Jeremy's lips thinned with determination. "Failure is not an option."

Dominic beamed with pride as if Jeremy had hit his first home run. "That's the spirit. Don't take no for an answer."

Ever the voice of reason, Jake shook his head and countered, "Unless she says no, and then that's your answer. Consider the possibility that she is ignoring your phone calls because she really doesn't want to talk to you."

"Jake, were you born a killjoy or did boarding school do that to you?" Dominic asked sarcastically.

"I'm sorry if I would rather not have to recommend a good lawyer to him because he took your advice too literally."

Fully enjoying the tennis-like banter, Jeremy sat back in his chair and smiled.

Dominic clarified his suggestion with a heavy layer of irony in his voice. "Jeremy, don't attack the poor girl. Clear enough?"

"But kidnapping is acceptable?" Jeremy couldn't help but refer to the controversial way Dominic had wooed his wife.

Although his lids lowered in response, a small smile tugged at Dominic's lips. He shook his head with humor.

"I'll stick to my original plan," Jeremy reassured Jake.

"How are you getting out there?" Jake asked, returning to a less volatile topic.

"Marie said she'd find something for me. I sent back the jet I leased and it's really too far for the helicopter." He'd miss Marie, too. In a short time, she'd made him wonder how he'd gotten along without her. It was no wonder that the two men before him were so loyal to her. She was the glue that held them together.

Dominic interrupted his thoughts with an uncharacteristic offer. "I have an extra private plane I don't use often. You can borrow it if you'd like. It's very nice. I only buy the best."

I know. Heat filled Jeremy's face as he remembered how intimately acquainted he and Jeisa already were with that plane. "I'm okay with whatever Marie found for me." Time for a subject change. "Word on the street is that Sliver went underground after his identity was exposed. His real name is Stanley Parker. No wonder he went by Sliver online. It's hard to fear a Stanley. 'Run, Stanley is coming!' See, no one would care." While Jake and Dominic chuckled at his joke, Jeremy moved on to a more serious subject. “Don’t trust him to stay gone, though. Sliver is more dangerous now than he was before. He has nothing to lose and all the time in the world to plan his revenge. And he will try to pay us back for outing him. I feel awful about involving you with him at all.”

Instantly, Dominic’s humor dissipated. For a moment he was the man his enemies feared, ruthless and coiled to strike. “You didn’t. Stephan did that.”

Jake continued in a rational tone meant to calm his friend. “We have people tracking Sliver. We’ll know instantly if he attempts anything again.”

“I hope so.” Jeremy wished he were as certain.

“So, you enrolled at WIT?” Jake asked in another attempt to redirect the conversation away from the unpleasant.

Jeremy smiled. “Yes. You’d be surprised how quickly they can process paperwork when you give their school a substantial donation.”

“I’m sure.”

Dominic stretched his arms out and referenced the building around him. “You can walk away from all of this? Your potential annual income, even if you kept to just the safer domestic projects, would have brought in more than many CEOs make.”

For Jeisa, I can. My transformation is still in progress, but this time I just might have it right. “I’ll still juggle some freelance work to keep my hand in it, but the whole Tenin thing taught me something—I have a lot to learn before I play on the global level again. For now, I am going to study ethics and international relations.” He leaned forward in his seat and said, “Dom, you were right. I was on the wrong path.”

“I believe I said that first,” Jake stated, claiming his due credit.

“But you’re not his hero.” Dominic patted his pride-puffed chest. “I’m the one he looks up to.”

A thought struck Jeremy and he shared it spontaneously. “I know who you two remind me of—Alessandro and Victor.”

Jake frowned. "He just called us old."

Waving his hands, Jeremy laughed and rushed to clarify, "No, I mean it. Victor makes all the speeches, but Alessandro always has his back. You're like Batman and Robin, but less ambiguously oriented."

Dominic stood up abruptly. "I won't ask what that means because I don't want to have to hurt you."

Jake also stood and, in a dry tone, joked, "I should explain it to you, Dom, if only because he made me Robin in that analogy."

Marie walked into the room just as the joke began to sour. "There you all are. Jeremy, I sent your itinerary to your phone. Did you check it?"

Jeremy stood and gratefully looked down at his phone. "Cool, a Citation X. Those jets can go seven hundred miles an hour. Where did you find it?"

Dominic grumbled under his breath. It was often wiser not to ask him to repeat himself. His expression made his choice of expletives easy enough to guess.

Jeremy decided to focus on the positive and said, "Thanks, Dom. I didn't realize which plane you were offering me. I'd love to try that one out."

"My generosity amazes even me sometimes," Dominic said and looked pointedly at Marie, who didn't seem bothered by his comment.

"A man only runs off after the woman of his dreams once in his life—he should do it in style." She smiled her approval at Jeremy.

Not ready to accept what he was beginning to see might be the tip of a much greater iceberg of generosity, Dominic grumbled, "Do you lend anything else out of mine, Marie?"

Her cheeks grew a bit rosy as she retorted smartly, "Only when I want to."

Jake's laugh boomed through the office and down the hall.

Looking every bit the innocent, gentle woman she pretended to be, Marie sweetly added, "Why have so many toys if you're not going to share them?"

Ruffling her composure was almost as much fun as needling Dominic. With what he hoped was just as innocent of an expression, Jeremy suggested, "You should use one of them to fly over to see Jeisa's father."

Pink spread down Marie's neck at the thought. For a moment, she looked at a loss for what to say, which only made the situation that much more amusing. Finally, she smoothed her already perfectly groomed hair and said, "Why would I do that?"

I really shouldn't tease her, but maybe even she needs a little shake-up now and then. As far as Jeremy had heard, Marie hadn't dated since her husband had passed away years ago. She deserved as much happiness in her own life as she helped others find in theirs. And really, she could do worse than Romario. Like Dominic, his growl was worse than his bite. "He asks about you sometimes."

"Does he?" Marie asked, trying—but not succeeding—to sound disinterested.

Aha! She does like him. "Yes, I talk to him daily and he's mentioned you at least five times."

Oblivious to the undercurrent of the conversation, Dominic focused on what he found amusing. "You talk to Romario daily? He must love that."

Marie chastised Dominic in the motherly way she often did. "Don't be cruel, Dominic. You know Jeremy really wants Jeisa's father to like him."

Dominic shrugged like the petulant son he became when she corrected him. "Cruel? Two minutes ago he questioned my orientation."

"No one likes a tattletale," Marie said with a *tsk, tsk,* then winked, and all three men broke into laughter. She walked over to Jeremy and fixed his tie, clearing her throat as she did. "We're going to miss you."

He hugged her, knowing that even though she wasn't a demonstrative person, she glowed in the face of affection from those she cared about. "California is not that far away. We'll fly back to see you guys as often as we can."

Flushed but smiling, Marie stepped back and nodded her approval. "I can't believe how much you've changed since we first met."

Jeremy blushed beneath her attention.

Marie brushed a speck of lint off Jeremy's shoulder. "Just remember that a woman in love doesn't care which plane you show up in or how much you spent on your suit." Marie rested her hand over Jeremy's heart and said, "Jeisa loves the good man that we all know you are. All you have to do to win her back is be that man."

"Don't worry, I have a plan," he assured her.

Marie dropped her hand and stepped back but held his eyes. "I hope this plan involves telling her that you love her and that you're sorry." She looked at the other two men in the room and advised, "If anything goes wrong, call me before them."

Dominic covered his heart as he feigned injury. "That hurts, Marie."

Jeremy took her hand in his for a moment and voiced something he'd meant to say a long time ago. "I will always be grateful to you, Marie. You were kind to me when everyone else saw me as a joke."

Her eyes misted with emotion and she gave his hand a supportive squeeze. "You were never a joke, Jeremy. You were a hero in a bad suit."

Jake shuddered. "A very bad suit." His well-timed humor lightened the mood.

All three men smiled at the memory of what felt like another lifetime. Jeremy returned to his desk and took out a paper. He handed it to Jake. "I wrote this résumé for a friend of mine. I won't have a business capable of employing him for a while, but I was hoping you could find him a good paying position within Corisi Enterprises."

Jake read over the résumé quickly, flipped it over, and then looked at Jeremy with some confusion. "This is quite a résumé. All it says is that he has been a doorman for the past ten years."

Jeremy nodded. "Yes, as far as I know that's all he's done."

"And you want him to work as a security man here?" Jake asked.

"No, I'd like to see him in an office position with a good salary." *What is good fortune if you don't share it with the people who supported you along the way?*

"Doing what exactly?" Jake's tone did little to conceal his thoughts on the matter.

Don't worry, Tim. No one believed in me, either. "I don't know, but I'm sure he can learn fast. He's a smart man."

Jake shook his head and patiently explained, "Business doesn't work that way, Jeremy. He has to have some kind of skill for me to recommend him to one of our departments—"

"Do you owe this man something?" Dominic cut through Jake's brush-off.

"Just gratitude. I'd like to see something good happen for him."

Ever the voice of reason, Jake asked, "Have you even asked him? He may not want—"

Dominic spoke over him again, "Send him to me. I'll find something for him."

Yes! "Thanks, Dom."

Dominic swaggered over to his business partner and slapped him on the back. "That's why *I'm* Batman."

Jake rolled his eyes and appealed to the powers above for help, then laughed. Jeremy joined in, followed by Marie and Dominic.

Marie turned her attention to Jake and asked, "Jake, how is the wedding coming along? I thought you were shooting for a winter wedding, but now it looks like you're waiting for spring. Should I give Lil a call? Are you having trouble finding locations?"

Dominic motioned toward the door. "Come on, Jeremy. It looks like they're going to be awhile."

As they walked out the door together, Jeremy was struck by how much had changed between them over the past few weeks. He turned to Dominic and said, "Thank you for helping me break ties with Tenin, and for everything else. Every last one of our people made it home safely. I don't know if that would have happened without your help."

Dominic nodded slowly. He wasn't a man who accepted gratitude, and Jeremy guessed it was because it was still a novel experience for him. On his journey to find himself, Jeremy had learned that he wasn't alone on that quest. Even his idol had lost and fought his way back, a fact that made Jeremy admire him more instead of less. The people around Dominic didn't share much about his private life, but the old newspaper articles Jeremy found online described a painful childhood that Jeremy couldn't even imagine. His own experience had been one filled with sorrow instead of violence. Still, he sensed a need in the man. The same part of him that had cared for his own father for so long reached out and offered comfort to a man who, if asked, would have denied needing it. "I know you're not that much older than I am, but I have to say something. I used to imagine what my father would be like if he hadn't been so ill. I'd like to think he would have been like you."

Dominic's jaw clenched and he looked away. "I hope to God I do better than mine did." Once again, Jeremy was given a glimpse of the tortured man beneath the tough façade. Then Dominic said, "Get out of here, Jeremy, I've got phone calls to make."

As Dominic walked away, Jeremy said, "You're going to be an amazing father, Dom."

Dominic didn't stop, but Jeremy knew he'd heard him, and that was enough.

CHAPTER *Seventeen*

DUE TO THE upcoming winter holiday, the campus was unusually empty when Jeisa arrived at WIT, and that had worked out well for her. With most of the student body gone, she was able to meet with the project head several times. She'd rented a small condo in a quiet area a short way from the university and had spent her evenings furnishing the modest one bedroom.

It was impossible not to wonder how Jeremy was, or feel some sadness at the realization that things were truly over between them. His frequent attempts to call her had dwindled to once a day and then had finally stopped altogether.

Things happen for the best, isn't that what everyone says?

Maybe I needed to have my heart broken to find myself.

Jeisa went into the main building that housed the GWP and used her access code to enter the administrative offices beside the lab. She hadn't expected an office of her own. Most of the people in the department were given a corner of the large central office—some even shared desks. Perhaps they thought being the daughter of a well-known politician made her a valuable member of the team. Still, it was a bit of a surprise, considering the honesty she'd exhibited during her interview regarding her lack of real experience.

All in all, everyone had been very nice—a little odd at times, but nice. The spike-haired blonde grad student who had adored Jeremy during their first visit sighed dramatically each time she saw Jeisa. On Jeisa's second day in the department, she dropped by her office and asked, "What is it like to be you?"

Not quite sure what the woman was asking her, Jeisa had referenced the room around her and said, "I am grateful for the chance I've been given, and I intend to work my tail off to show everyone that I deserve it."

The woman had looked up at the sky, shook her head, said something beneath her breath, then left.

Jeisa unlocked the door to her office now and smiled when she saw the fruit basket on her desk. She walked over and reread the card. "Please join us for dinner this weekend. We'll send a car. Nicole and Stephan."

Gifts had arrived daily and had become somewhat of a joke in the office. Abby had sent a care package full of office supplies—everything from personalized stationary to a very practical stapler. Every corner of her office was full of flowers from the Andrades, chocolates from Maddy, and cards from both her American and Brazilian friends. The overwhelming support she'd received was humbling and made her a little ashamed that she hadn't trusted them to support her dream.

Even her father had changed his stance. He'd sent her a ridiculously expensive leather chair to put behind her desk. She wanted to say, "I'm working, not dying." But she didn't.

I don't need sympathy, I need a kick in the ass.

She looked out the window of her office and watched a couple walk by, hand in hand, laughing about some secret joke. She wanted to open the window and warn them to savor every second of it in case it didn't last.

Marie had said you find yourself when you fight for something that's important to you. Do you lose yourself when you don't? WIT was everything she'd dreamed it would be, but being there hadn't made her as happy as she'd thought it would.

Because when it mattered, I ran.

The view from her office window blurred as Jeisa turned her thoughts inward. She found herself back in the Andrades', waiting for Jeremy to come. The kitchen scene faded as she remembered how his helicopter had looked overflowing with roses. *If I had been braver, he would have proposed. If I had waited for him to return to me that night, we might still be together.*

But I was hurt.

And angry.

And afraid—too afraid to risk opening my heart up again to the kind of pain I felt when he left with Alethea.

Jeisa took out her cell phone and called her father. In Portuguese she said, "Dad, are you busy?"

"Jeisa? What's wrong?" he sounded concerned, and she instantly felt guilty that she never called him. Instead of telling her father what she needed from him, she'd always avoided confronting him. She was beginning to see a pattern in her behavior, and it wasn't one she liked.

"I'm fine, Dad. If you have a minute, I want to ask your opinion on something."

She heard her father tell his secretary to hold his calls and then close the door to his office. "Talk to me, Jeisa. You know I'll help you with whatever this is."

Jeisa's eyes filled with tears. She choked out a question she'd been asking herself too often recently. "Do you think I'm a coward?"

With a voice deep with emotion, her father said, "Oh, baby."

Sniffing, Jeisa persisted. "No, I'm serious. I lie when I don't want to upset someone. I run away from what I don't want to face. What if that is who I am? How do I stop? What do I do?"

Her father didn't say anything at first, then he cleared his throat and said, "Only you know the answers to those questions, but my daughter is not a coward. My daughter left home to follow her dreams and she is making a difference in the world. She is a brave and beautiful young woman. Part of growing up, Jeisa, is taking responsibility for the role you play in your own mistakes and your own destiny. Maybe you weren't ready to do that before, but you're ready now. Things get better when you make them better."

Wiping away one stray tear, Jeisa said with growing resolve, "I will, Dad. I really will." *No more excuses. No more wasting time trying to figure out who was wrong or why I've made the mistakes I have. You're right, the only way things can get better is if I take responsibility for my happiness. Maybe it's too late for Jeremy to forgive me. Maybe I've doubted him right out of loving me, but he deserves to hear my apology. Our love deserves a chance and I'm going to give it one. I won't hide behind anger or fear anymore. I am going to be the kind of brave that Jeremy has always been, and if we are meant to be, he'll forgive me.*

After a brief pause she said, "I have next week off for winter break. Would you want to meet me in Boston?"

"Boston?" her father asked quickly.

"I've decided to fly back there, Dad." As Jeisa said the words, she became more and more sure it was the right thing to do. *What's stopping me from flying out tonight? Nothing.* She said, "I will find Jeremy and apologize to him. I need to make things right between us. I won't jeopardize what I have here, but I've let my fears keep us apart for too long. I love him, Dad, and if he still loves me I'm going to marry him."

Jeisa's father made a gurgling sound. "Don't leave California just yet."

What is he not telling me? "I thought you liked Jeremy."

With a groan, Romario said, "I do, but you have a surprise coming and you have to be in California to receive it."

A surprise? This is about more furniture? "Dad, I told you I don't need anything else."

"Just promise me you won't leave until tomorrow night." The strength of his request dissolved Jeisa's remaining protests. Waiting wouldn't be easy, but her father had never asked for something like this, so she agreed.

"Okay, I'll book a flight for the next day and I'll call you when I get the package."

Romario answered vaguely, "Call me when you get a chance. No rush."

"I will." Just before she hung up she said, "I love you, Dad."

"I love you, too, baby," Romario said and hung up.

The blonde grad student came barreling down the hallway. "Jeisa, looks like you have another delivery."

Already?

Before she'd gathered her thoughts on the matter, four older men dressed in white shirts, white pants, and red striped vests walked into her office. Behind them, the skeleton crew of the department gathered. One of singers introduced themselves as WIT's a cappella group. They hummed to harmonize and began to sing:

Jeisa, Jeisa, here you are
Wish you hadn't moved so far
Don't be sad, you're not alone
We're just as close as your phone
Hope you like your new job there
Call me if you want a beer
Abby said you'd hate this attention
So if she calls please don't mention
Jeisa, Jeisa, don't be blue
Hope you laughed
We love you
From Lil and Jake

Happy tears gathered in Jeisa's eyes. Never in her life had she imagined that so many wonderful, caring people would surround her.

One of the singers awkwardly asked, "Should we sing it again or just go?"

Jeisa smiled through her tears and reached into her purse, handed one of them a generous tip and said, "No, thank you. You were great, though."

The blonde grad student lingered after the others had left. Jeisa struggled to remember her name and hated that she'd wasted so much time mourning what she'd lost instead of appreciating the good that had entered her life.

The woman said, "You must miss your old friends very much."

And the name came to her finally. "I do, Geneva. I do."

The woman appeared to waver between retreating without saying more, as she normally did, and continuing the conversation. "We all left something behind to be here, but it's an important project."

Her words touched Jeisa even more because of how uncomfortable the woman looked as she voiced them. Geneva was putting her own discomfort aside in an attempt to cheer Jeisa. And it worked. "It is, isn't it? The water project could impact a third of the world's population."

"And you're part of this now. You're part of the solution," Geneva said with quiet sincerity.

Jeisa raised her chin as the words filled her with pride. "I am, aren't I? I will make a difference here." Deciding to share more of herself, Jeisa added, "I'll be returning to Boston soon, but I'll be back just after the holidays. I'd love to go out for coffee with you when I return."

The woman smiled. "I'd like that. Are you going back to Boston to celebrate Christmas with your family?"

Jeisa turned and looked out the window again. "No, I'm going back to do something I should have done weeks ago. I had the perfect man and I let my fear come between us. He was kind. Smart. Funny. Hot as hell, but didn't know it..." She stopped when she realized how her description had teetered on too personal.

"Hot as hell, huh? I like that."

Jeisa whipped around when she heard Jeremy's voice behind her. "What are you doing here?" She looked around and noted that the others had left and they were alone.

He closed the door behind him and crossed the room slowly toward her. "I am far from perfect, though. And not nearly as smart as I thought I was, because I hurt you and I never meant to." He ran his hands down her arms and took both of her hands in his.

Sheer surprise held Jeisa immobile.

He came!

Jeremy pulled her closer, bringing her body flush against his and tucking her hands behind her back. His warm breath fanned her cheek, sending a tingle of awareness through her. "I was wrong," he said as his held her against him, his eyes burning with a mix of desire and emotion. "Wrong not to see what we had. Wrong to allow you to believe I was choosing between two women, because from the moment you kissed me, it was all about you—just you." He released her hands and raised one of his to caress her cheek. "I had to help Alethea that night at the Andrades', but if I had known what she'd said to you, I would have brought you with us. I thought I was protecting you."

With a shudder, Jeisa said, "I should have given you a chance to explain. I should have trusted you."

Jeremy's eyes darkened with pain. "I didn't give you a reason to. It's a good thing you didn't answer my phone calls, Jeisa, because you gave me time to process what I'd done. These past few months were all about me. What I wanted. What I needed. I didn't stop to ask you what you wanted."

"I'm not sure I could have told you if you had. I'm only now sorting it out."

"Let's figure it out together then." Her heart soared at his suggestion. Could he really forgive her this easily?

Even as Jeisa's heart began to speed up with excitement, she attempted to tamp down her emotions long enough to ask, "What are you saying?"

"I've enrolled at WIT as a full-time student."

Did that mean...?

She didn't dare allow herself to believe he was saying what she hoped he was saying. "Why?"

"I want to be with you." He pulled her gently against him again, this time resting his hands lightly on her hips. His head bent and his lips explained what he struggled to find the words to express. She hesitated for only the slightest second before her arms wound around his neck and she lost herself in his kiss.

When he broke off, they were both flushed, and their ragged breathing was the only sound in the otherwise quiet office. "We don't have to rush. We can start over and date if you'd like."

Her body was alive and yearning for him. She rubbed herself against him and loved how instantly he was hard and ready for her.

With eyes ablaze with hunger for her, he amended huskily, "Or we can take up where we left off."

Even as she began to drown in the delight of his nearness, she asked, "Did you really enroll here just to be with me?"

He reached around to unbutton the top of her blouse and said, "Yes and no." His hand stilled. "In my rush to make money, I made some bad choices. The night I left you, it was because I had gotten myself involved in a situation that promised to be profitable because it was so dangerous. Before you, I didn't care if anything happened to me. I felt like I had nothing to lose. But you changed all of that. I couldn't let you and your father pay the price for a mistake I had made. I see now that I have a lot to learn."

"Oh, Jeremy. I didn't know."

"I should have explained it to you."

Jeisa remembered the state she'd been in that night and admitted, "All I could see that night was that my greatest fear was coming true."

He reached down and took both of her hands in his. "I had no idea you were waiting for me in the kitchen. If I had known that, nothing could have stopped me from going to you."

"I believe you," she whispered. "I had just decided today to come find you and apologize."

"You did nothing wrong," Jeremy said passionately, but Jeisa disagreed.

"I did everything wrong. You never lied to me, Jeremy. You were honest every step of the way, and I should have believed you when you said that you loved me. I was scared. I'm not scared anymore."

"Good," he whispered against her lips. "But you can stay angry with me a bit longer if you'd like. I've heard that makeup sex is fantastic." The twinkle in his eyes was irresistible. Their lips met in a hungry expression of what they could no longer deny.

He swung her up into his arms and crossed the room to the couch, a sexy smile on his face. Returning her to her feet, he made quick haste of her skirt's button and zipper. It slid to the floor at her feet. She stepped out of her shoes and kicked the clothing aside. Without taking his eyes off her, he loosened and removed his tie. They continued to strip off their clothes, one by one, until they were both nude and his need for her was erect and pulsing between them.

He kissed his way across her cheek, down her neck, and cupped both of her breasts in his hands, taking a moment to appreciate them before circling one of her puckered nipples with his hot tongue. He stopped briefly to blow on it before shifting his attention to the other one. When Jeisa was gasping with pleasure at the creative ways his finger and tongue were working together to increase her excitement, Jeremy paused and said, "I've been reading about how to do this better. Information drives ingenuity," he said and bent to kiss her neck again.

Jeisa's head fell back and she moaned with elation, "I'm not complaining."

The door of her office opened and a flash of a female head poked in, quickly followed by a familiar squeak of a voice that said, "Oh, my God, I'm sorry! I wanted to make sure you were okay." The door slammed shut. Before either Jeisa or Jeremy could react, the door opened again slightly, a hand came around to the handle, locked it, then slammed the door again.

"I like the people you work with," Jeremy remarked with some humor.

Laughing half out of mortification and half out of the sheer joy of being in Jeremy's arms, Jeisa replied, "I do, too."

Now, where were we?

Later, wrapped in Jeremy's jacket and tucked against his side, Jeisa was jerked back from near sleep when Jeremy exclaimed, "Shit, I forgot to ask you to marry me."

Jeisa smiled against his chest. "You scripted this?" She knew he only did that now when he was nervous, and that made her love him even more.

He smiled a bit ruefully. "I didn't want to forget anything, but you were so beautiful that I forgot everything."

You could forgive a man anything with that excuse. She propped herself up on her elbow and kissed him lightly. "Not everything."

A slight flush spread across his cheeks. He reached behind her and felt around the pockets of his jacket until he found what he was looking for. He laid it on his chest in front of her and said, "Jeisa Borreto, I love you and I intend to marry you. Today, tomorrow, or however long it takes for you to be ready." He tapped the ring box with one of his fingers. "You don't have to open this right now. You can think about it if you—"

She stopped his words with a kiss, one that held all the heat of their prior union but also something much more significant: her answer. She whispered it against his lips as she broke off the kiss. "Yes, Jeremy. Yes. Yes. Yes."

His grin could not have been broader as he smiled up at her. "It'll be good, Jeisa. You'll see. You'll be the big director of grants and production and I'll get the degree my mother always told me I should."

She paused and cocked her head to one side. "That's not my title. I'm really a glorified intern supporting the fundraising department."

"Not since the Borreto/Kater donation moved up the production timetable and opened a new position. Or was it the Kater/Borreto donation? I suppose it doesn't matter."

Jeisa stilled his hand with hers. "You made a donation to the university?"

"Yes, and your father matched it."

Because when it's right, you don't have to choose.

"When did you speak to my father?"

"Every day. He didn't like me at first, but I wanted him to know how serious I was about you. I told him how much this project means to you and he believed me. I hope I was right because he might have used your inheritance. You may be poor now, so it looks like you're stuck with me." Suddenly serious, he put a hand under her chin and raised her face to look into his. "I want forever with you. I've seen the kind of love that endures even when intimacy is no longer possible, and I want that." When she couldn't think of what to say, he blushed and quickly added, "I want this, too. I just mean..." He looked down as he searched for how else to say it.

With tears in her eyes, Jeisa raised a hand to caress his cheek as she spoke. "I know exactly what you mean, and I want that, too."

With a little maneuvering, he opened the small box and slid the ring on her left hand. She held her hand out in front of her and admired the unusual stone.

Jeremy said, "It's a blue-green diamond. Incredibly rare. A nearly impossible set of circumstances needs to occur at just the right time for it to form. When I saw it, I thought of you and the dress you wore the first day we met. We were nearly impossible, you and I, but it looks like nature had other plans for us. I cannot imagine my life without you in it."

Jeisa took his face in her hands, grateful and humbled by his love, but no longer afraid. "You'll never have to because I'm not going anywhere." A sudden thought hit her and she said, "I did tell my father that I was going to Boston and asked him to meet me there."

Jeremy's eyebrows shot up. "What did he say?"

Their earlier conversation came back to her, but now in a whole new light. She said, "He told me to stay here another day because he'd sent me a surprise. That little liar. He knew you were coming here, didn't he?"

Smiling, Jeremy said, "Absolutely."

She shook her head in amazement. "I can't believe he didn't tell me." She slapped a hand on Jeremy's chest. "He does like you."

With an adorable shrug of his shoulders, Jeremy said, "What's not to like? He knows how much I love his daughter."

"My father has never approved of any of the men I've dated. Honestly, he intimidated most of them. He doesn't scare you at all, does he?"

With a jokingly pained expression, he admitted, "Sure, he may have threatened to wipe me off the face of the planet if I hurt you, but isn't that what fathers say to prospective sons-in-law?"

Jeisa didn't doubt for a second that her father would learn to love Jeremy as much as she did. Well, maybe not quite as much, but Jeremy had a way of winning over even the most reluctant. Her father didn't stand a chance. "Christmas is next week. Could we invite him to come for a visit? We could ask your mother, too."

"I'll make sure his limo is full of white roses," Jeremy said without missing a beat.

Jeisa laughed. "You're so bad! Only you would consider teasing my father. Are you afraid of anything?"

He tightened his embrace in response, rubbing his chin on her forehead. "Yes. You terrify me. I had my life meticulously planned before I met you. I thought I knew exactly what I wanted. You changed all that. I'm really good at what I do, but you made me ask myself if it was important. And if it isn't, what am I supposed to be doing? I'm hoping that taking classes here will help me figure that out."

Jeisa laid her head on his chest and simply absorbed the magnitude of what he was sharing. She often thought she was the only one who struggled with finding her path. It touched her that Jeremy not only asked himself the same questions, but that he shared that side of himself freely with her. "Will you miss the hacking?"

Jeremy rubbed her back absently. "I'll still take freelance jobs now and then, but I'll choose them more carefully. I've already made more money than I could even begin to know how to spend. The work I did for Rachid and Zhang was quite lucrative. Nothing attracts new clients like a royal referral."

Lifting her head, Jeisa spoke the truth that was welling within her heart. "I don't care about the money, Jeremy."

He reached up and tucked a stray curl behind her ear. "Because I'm so hot?"

Jeisa pushed his side playfully. "You weren't supposed to hear that."

He kissed her nose gently. "You should say it proudly since I'm your creation."

With a shake of her head, Jeisa said, "All I did was add a little frosting to an already delicious cake."

He nuzzled his face in her neck and growled, "I like the way you describe me." He licked her skin, sending waves of hot pleasure through her. "And speaking of delicious..." He rolled over so he was on top of her and his hands warmed the places his lips would soon touch.

CHAPTER *Eighteen*

IN LATE MARCH, at the top of a long gated driveway, a driver held the door of Jeisa and Jeremy's limo open. Jeisa didn't move. Jeremy took her hand in his. "What is it, Jeisa?"

Just outside the tinted back window, the Andrade home loomed before them—both a welcome sight and a reminder of how close she had come to losing him. It wasn't their first time back there, and Jeisa couldn't imagine being happier than she was. She and Jeremy had moved into a large apartment closer to the WIT campus, where they had spent the last several months building a life together and sharing it with the new friends they'd made through the water project. She felt guilty to have hesitated at all in the face of memories from a day that no longer mattered. She looked up into the concerned eyes of her fiancé. "Do you ever think about how close we came to losing each other?"

"No," Jeremy answered easily as he pulled her into his arms and kissed her forehead. "Remember my first boxing lesson?"

Jeisa laughed even though her emotions were high. "How could I forget?"

"I don't let myself think about what could go wrong. There is too much in life that can. All I thought about that day was what I wanted and what was standing between me and getting it. And then I did the only thing I could do—I stood my ground." He kissed her lightly and said, "I may have modified my path, but not my methods. There is nothing in the past or in the future that could change how I feel about you."

Jeisa threw her arms around his neck and gave him a kiss that showed him exactly how much his words had moved her.

She would have never guessed by their awkward first meeting that she would learn so much from him. *Problems are best resolved when faced full-on. Run toward what you want, not away from what you're afraid of. And stand your ground.*

When she broke off the kiss, his cheeks were flushed and his eyes burned with desire for her. "You know, we could leave our gift with the doorman and come back later."

With a chuckle, Jeisa eased off him and said, "No, Abby would never forgive me for missing her baby shower, and she's gotten more emotional as her due date gets closer."

Jeremy stepped out of the limo and took her hand to help her out. "Which means that Dominic is going to be a wreck today."

Jeisa warned, "If you tease him, don't complain if you come home with a black eye."

"Don't worry. I'm younger, faster, and I've learned how to bob and weave like a professional."

Their eyes met and they broke into laughter. They were still laughing when the door opened and Alessandro greeted them both with a bear hug. He stood back and gave them an approving once-over. "Young love is a beautiful thing, no?"

His wife Elise rushed forward and greeted them both with a kiss on each cheek. "Alessandro, can't you say hello without mauling the guests?"

With a shrug that said his wife's comment didn't bother him at all, Alessandro said, "These two aren't guests anymore, they're family."

Elise linked arms with Jeisa and led her into the party. "You'll have to pardon my husband, he is getting sentimental in his old age. Come on, there is so much to talk about before Abby arrives. Everyone else is in the kitchen already."

Surrendering to being led away, Jeisa looked over her shoulder to Jeremy, knowing that she likely wouldn't see him again until the party officially began. He winked at her as if he'd been thinking the same thing.

Nicole greeted her with a warm hug as soon as Jeisa entered the kitchen. "Did you and Jeremy just get in?"

Jeisa eased out of the light sweater she'd worn over her boldly flowered dress. "Yes, we flew in about an hour ago on a commuter flight. With all the work we're doing to purify water, it's hard to justify the pollution of flying a plane back and forth just for us."

"Now you sound like Stephan," Nicole said with a smile. "We flew in yesterday on an airline for the same reason. Don't get him started about diminishing fossil fuels."

Lil bounded forward and hugged Jeisa. "You two are very admirable, but don't you miss the privacy?" When no one said anything, Lil wiggled her eyebrows and said, "Come on, I can't be the only member of the mile high club here."

Nicole and Jeisa blushed. Maddy roared with laughter. Elise motioned to Stephan's mother across the room and said, "Oh, honey, we founded that club."

Tears of laughter were smearing the women's mascara when Princess Zhang from Najriad entered the kitchen. "I see nothing has changed here since I've been gone."

Lil bolted to her side. "Zhang!" and threw her arms around her friend. "You came!"

Returning Lil's embrace for a moment before easing out of it, Zhang said, "I wouldn't have missed this for anything."

With an impish smile, Lil asked, "Zhang, tell me something. Did you fly over on a public or private airplane?"

"Private, of course," Zhang said, and the women burst into laughter again. "I've always preferred privacy and now I'm married to a sheikh." The more she spoke, the more the women laughed. "Is our desire to fly on our own plane really that amusing?"

Wiping her cheeks, Stephan's mother, Katrine, said, "Only after Lil has been oversharing about why she prefers to fly that way."

A slight red flush tinted Zhang's cheeks, but she said proudly, "I'm sure I would have agreed with her reasoning."

Everyone burst into laughter again.

"Oh no, what did I miss?" a very pregnant Abby asked from the doorway.

Elise rushed forward to greet her. "Alessandro was supposed to tell me when you arrived. I would have met you at the door."

Abby happily received her double-cheeked kisses. "With all the fun you ladies are having, he may have tried to call down, but don't worry, I'm fine."

Lil gave her sister a huge hug. "Did you see who came?"

Abby exchanged a light hug with the princess. "Thank you, Zhang, I appreciate you coming all this way for the party. I know it's a long flight."

Zhang smiled and stepped back. "A very long flight. Thank goodness."

Lil laughed so hard she was gasping for air as she said, "Oh, my God, stop, my face is starting to hurt."

Abby looked around the room for help. "I don't get it."

Nicole greeted Abby with a kiss to the cheek and said, "We'll explain later, although I suspect that you're also a member."

Abby turned to another source for information. "What are they talking about?"

Jeisa wasn't sure where to begin. Instead she joined in the fun and said, "We borrowed one of Dominic's planes, so I have to agree with Nicole. He has beds everywhere."

Abby blushed and chided the women around her even as she began to smile. "I can't leave you guys unsupervised for two minutes..."

Her sister teased her a bit more. "Don't even pretend you haven't gone there with Dominic. I'll be surprised if you don't name your baby after one of his planes."

That had Abby laughing out loud until she stopped and held her side. "Don't make me laugh. I've been having Braxton Hicks contractions for the past week and they are only getting worse."

Suddenly serious, Nicole looked at one of the new mothers in the room and asked, "Maddy, wasn't that what you said you were having the day I delivered your baby in my limo?"

Abby rushed to reassure her. "Don't worry, I've been to the doctor, these are not real contractions. Well, they feel real, but I'm not in labor. I have two more weeks before I'm even at my due date and first-time mothers often go past that date."

Nicole paled. "All of that sounds painfully familiar."

Abby moved over to sit in a chair Katrine held out to her and said, "I'm not even having contractions right now, it's just that it seems like anything can set them off lately. I shouldn't have brought it up."

Not looking particularly reassured, Nicole waved her hand in the direction of Abby's stomach. "I want to make it clear that delivering a baby was a beautiful, once-in-a-lifetime experience for me and I want to keep it that way—as just that one time."

"Why don't we change the subject before I start getting nervous?" Abby suggested. "Jeisa, I didn't see Jeremy out there, did he come with you?"

Zhang answered instead. "Rachid asked about him when we arrived. I believe Alessandro said he'd stepped into the library to talk to someone."

Lil and Abby's eyes met. "It's not Alethea," Lil blurted then instantly looked contrite. "Oh, my God, Jeisa, I didn't mean to say her name."

All eyes turned to Jeisa, who smiled because she realized that Jeremy was right—there was nothing in the past or the future that could threaten their love. "You can say her name, Lil. She's your friend. I should have trusted Jeremy that day. It would have saved me a lot of heartache. I'm not about to make that mistake again."

Lil wrinkled her nose at Abby. "See, I told you it wouldn't be a problem anymore. Does that mean I can invite—"

"No," Abby said in a tone that implied that was the end of that particular discussion.

Marie walked in with Colby, Lil's little girl, who high-stepped proudly as she clung to both of Marie's hands for support. "It looks like almost everyone is here. How is our mommy holding up?"

Abby pushed herself awkwardly to her feet. "Ready to get this over with."

Lil bent to rest one knee on the floor so her daughter, Colby, could take a few independent steps into her arms. She hugged her daughter to her even as she spoke to her sister above her head. "Oh, come on, Abby. This is going to be great. Imagine the presents you're going to get."

Abby braced her back with one hand. "Really, there was no need to register for anything. We have more than we need. In fact, I asked for donations to the maternity ward of the hospital in lieu of presents."

Colby raised her hands greedily in the direction of a woman who had never been comfortable with children, but who now also dropped down onto her knees to greet the child. "Ni Ni!" Nicole didn't seem to mind how her drool-covered little hands wrinkled her silk blouse. She stood and twirled with the girl on her hip and after they both came to a laughing stop, she said, "Stephan and I gave a donation, but we couldn't help ourselves—we also bought you a present."

Marie added, "By the look of the growing pile of gifts out on the patio, I'd say that everyone did the same."

"Did you finally tell Dominic the sex?" Nicole asked her sister-in-law.

Abby rolled her eyes skyward. "I wanted to keep it a secret until the end, but that man is unshakeable when it comes to anything related to the health of this baby. He's already hired a bodyguard for her. Can you imagine—she's not even here yet and she has her own security."

With a smile of approval, Marie said, "You know he does it out of love."

Abby laid a hand on top of her rounded stomach. "I don't even want to think about what he's going to be like in the delivery room."

Lil wrapped an arm around her sister and rubbed her belly playfully, earning a not-so-playful swat from Abby, which only amused Lil more. "That's why you invited me to join you. I'll handle him."

Nicole turned to Jeisa and in a stage whisper said, "Now that is something I'd pay to see."

Me, too, Jeisa thought. "If she's smart, she'll have Jake as backup."

From a corner of the kitchen, Maddy's husband piped in. "My money is on Lil."

Maddy turned with her young son in her arms and admonished him playfully. "Richard, what did I tell you about listening in?"

His wide grin was unabashedly unapologetic. "You can punish me later."

Marie shook her head while the other women gave in to laughter. "In my day we weren't quite as open as this new generation is."

Elise and Katrine exchanged a look and then Elise asked, "Aren't you our age?"

Marie looked a bit flustered at the question. With her chin held high she said, "Yes."

As Jeisa looked on with sympathy, she noticed the beautiful dress Marie had chosen to wear. It was one she'd sent her months ago as a thank-you. The dark-blue fitted top took years off her age, as did the additional makeup she'd chosen. *Marie, you sly dog.* "Not too old to have caught my father's eye. You were the reason he agreed to come here for Christmas last year. He still asks about you."

Marie flushed a bright red but said nothing.

Lil interjected her own brand of wisdom. "At your age you probably shouldn't make him wait too long. The life expectancy of men is shorter than it is for women. However, thanks to Viagra, at least you know everything will still function."

Abby clapped a hand on her forehead. "Lil!"

"What?" Lil asked, unperturbed. "Do you think Marie is too old to want a piece of that Brazilian stud?"

Jeisa choked on bubbling laughter as she imagined her father's reaction if he'd overheard this conversation. *Brazilian stud. You go, Dad.*

Maddy clasped her hands together in excitement. "I've never tried my matchmaking skills on an older couple. This could be fun."

Despite the futility of it, Abby cautioned, "Or, it could be none of our business."

Lil's and Maddy's eyes met and they dismissed Abby's advice in unison. "Nah, Marie, you'll thank us."

Marie cleared her throat and said, "Enough of this foolishness. We have guests arriving and presents to open." With that, she led the way to the doorway.

Jeisa spoke softly so the departing Marie wouldn't hear. "We should invite my father to your wedding, Lil."

Maddy bounced her son gleefully on her hip. "That's perfect. He'll be irresistible in a tux."

Lil danced with excitement beside her. "We can figure out a way to give them some time alone—and let nature take its course."

"Speaking of nature, I have to pee again," Abby said as she retreated. "So, you ladies can plot away and I will waddle back to meet you on the patio."

Being summoned to the Andrade library to speak with Dominic and Jake gave Jeremy a moment of apprehension. He ran through a quick list of what might have gone wrong that would have necessitated the privacy they'd requested. Had Sliver broken through? Had he been naive to believe a dictator like Alvo would let him live if he backed out of their negotiations?

If something bad had happened, it hadn't stopped Jake or Dominic from enjoying Alessandro's 1939 Macallan scotch and his Nicaraguan cigars. Still, these men might face the apocalypse with the same nonchalance, so Jeremy felt compelled to ask, "Is something wrong? What happened?"

Dominic let out a puff of smoke and asked, "Does something have to be wrong?"

No, but I don't normally get invited unless something is, Jeremy thought, but instead asked with some sarcasm, "Oh, so you missed me? I just saw you at Christmas."

Dominic flicked his cigar ashes in a tray and motioned to the empty chair across from him. "Have a seat."

Jake poured a third glass of scotch and handed it to Jeremy. "We want to talk to you about something."

Jeremy took the open seat and the drink. "I don't need any more advice. Jeisa and I are fine."

Dominic rolled his eyes at the ceiling, but looked amused.

Jake puffed on his own cigar before saying, "We don't have a lot of time before the women come looking for us. Jeremy, we have a business proposition to discuss with you."

Tempting as the idea was, Jeremy had set his course and would not be led easily from it. "I haven't finished my first ethics course. I need some time before I attempt to play at your level again."

Dominic flicked the ashes of his cigar into the tray on the table beside him. "I have a master's degree in business. Those ethics courses never helped me."

Jake choked on the sip he'd been taking, then parried, "They might have if you had taken fewer hits on the rugby field."

Dominic glared at his best friend for a moment before turning his attention back to Jeremy. "I respect that you want a formal education, but don't underestimate your natural talent. I doubt anyone at WIT can do what you can."

Jake added to Dominic's opening. "It's time for us to branch into a new field of technology. In the past we've worked mainly on designing infrastructures and software integration. We've recently come into possession of a prototype for something we think you'd be interested in helping us develop."

Jeremy took his first sip of scotch and gasped as the liquid burned every internal surface it touched. He coughed until his eyes watered, then replaced the glass and ignored the amused expressions on the other two men's faces. When he could speak again, he said, "I've never created anything. My skill is breaking into what others have."

"You don't give yourself enough credit," Jake said. He handed him a tablet that displayed the specs for the project he was asking Jeremy to consider. "Take a minute to look over our design before you make your decision."

As Jeremy studied the plans, his jaw dropped. "Do you know what this would mean to the gaming world? We could finally be inside the game. No more keyboards, joysticks, or visual cueing. This would be full immersion. The virtual reality of science fiction. A program that learns to read your body language better than a person can. Is it possible? That many biosensors would require massive processing power. Right now you'd need a server the size of a farm in Kansas."

Jake sat back in his seat and said, "Obviously there are issues with the current silicone chip sets available. However, my parents have made headway with increased processing power using biologically based architectures. We're not there yet, but we're close. Dominic has connections to someone who is developing a generation S quantum computing system for a university. The government just cut his funding, so he's ripe to join us. We need someone who can design the codes to support the bioinformatics sensor interfaces."

Dominic stubbed out his cigar and asked impatiently, "So, are you in?"

Jeremy handed the tablet back to Jake and stalled. "It's a tempting project, but I can't leave WIT. I've made a home in California and promises to Jeisa. I want to finish my education."

Jake didn't appear surprised by Jeremy's hesitation. "We can work around your classes and your location."

"I appreciate the job offer, but..."

Sitting forward in his chair, Dominic said, "Don't consider this a job, consider it a partnership. It would be an offshoot of Corisi Enterprises, but independently owned. California is the perfect place to base this entertainment-focused company. We'll even relocate Tim. We haven't found his niche yet. So far, he's really good at standing at his office door and talking to people."

With an amused look, Jake placed the blame for that where he thought it belonged. "He may still be shell-shocked from the way you hired him. Not everyone gets your humor, Dom."

Jeremy chuckled. "It was hilarious, but, yeah, Tim was scared when four guys pulled up in a black Suburban and took him to the Corisi building. He says he likes his job, but I don't know if he'd tell us if he didn't."

The widening smile on Dominic's face revealed how amused he still was by the way he'd hired Jeremy's friend. "Abby didn't like it, but it was worth it."

Jake shook his head, but it was clear that he'd given up on this particular subject. Looking back and forth between two of the most powerful men on the planet, Jeremy finally understood that they respected the parts of him that hadn't changed at all. Their acceptance of him had nothing to do with the clothing he wore or how much he could bench-press. They valued his intelligence and his honesty. Eventually, they might even get his dry humor.

Working with them could be an unbelievable opportunity. Jeisa had found her passion at WIT. Could this be the second chance he'd asked for? And if it was, was he ready for it? The lesson he'd learned in Tenin was still fresh in his mind. It was with true humility that he admitted to himself that he still had a lot to learn. "I don't know anything about running a company."

Dominic shrugged and nodded toward Jake. "Never stopped me. Jake handles the legal side. This is about trailblazing and that's a strength of mine."

In complete agreement, Jake said, "You wouldn't be in this alone. And it would be a legitimate income—for all of us."

That idea seemed to please Dominic most of all. He said, "Abby will be happy. And when she is, I am."

With a laugh, Jeremy asked Jake, "What does a happy Dominic look like?"

Jake joined him in ribbing their moody friend. "Mostly the same, but with less swearing."

There was one final area of concern that Jeremy felt needed to be voiced, and it could easily be a deal-breaker for these men. "I'm not hurting for money, but I did just take a huge hit by donating to WIT. I won't be able to match your investment."

Dominic smiled and said, "Jake will lend you the money."

Following his friend's offer with one of his own, Jake added a bit gleefully, "And Dominic will give you his Citation X to expedite your bicoastal travel."

Although their tone was teasing, Jeremy knew their offers were sincere. He asked, "Why would you do that?"

Suddenly serious, Jake said, "My parents weren't kidding when they said that you are one of the greatest minds of your generation. We want you on our team."

As Jake's words sunk in, Jeremy knew he would never forget that day. No longer the bumbling basement genius they tolerated and mocked, he was one of them.

"Okay, I'm in." After a moment Jeremy asked, "What's the name of this new company?"

Once again sipping his scotch, Dominic replied, "We're tossing around ideas. We've considered CWK for Corisi, Walton, and Kater Enterprises."

An idea tickled at Jeremy and he blurted out, "We'd be like Batman, Batman, and Robin."

Shaking his head, Dominic corrected him. "There is only one Batman."

Jake threw both hands up in the air in mock frustration and asked, "Why am I still Robin?"

"I don't care what we name it or what you call me, this is going to be awesome," Jeremy said with confidence.

I can't wait to tell Jeisa.

Maybe she'll let me start wearing my Superman boxers again.

When the baby shower presents were opened and family and friends had once again scattered throughout the Andrade house in chatty pockets, Jeremy sought out Jeisa. He quietly walked up behind her, slid his arms around her from behind, and kissed her cheek. She leaned back into his embrace and smiled, content within his arms.

Peering up at him, she asked, "Is everything okay? How did your talk go?"

"Fine. Better than fine." Being so close to Jeisa was sending zings of desire through him. There would be plenty of time later to tell her about how he was soon going to be able to fund any and all humanitarian projects she found interest in. For now, all he cared about was how she fit perfectly against him and how her breath quickened along with his, evidence that she was experiencing a similar reaction to their nearness.

She asked huskily, "Are you ready to go home?"

His breath tickled her ear and he whispered, "I'm already there."

EPILOGUE

BEFORE LEAVING THE Andrades' home, Lil slipped into the hallway to call her best friend. Alethea had texted her early that morning, but with everything that had gone on she hadn't had the time to do more than respond that she'd call her later. It couldn't have been an easy day for Al knowing that Lil was at another family function where she wasn't welcome. Still, Alethea had sent a beautiful nanny-cam teddy bear that Abby had graciously opened and would surely send a thank-you card for.

It would take time, but the rift between Abby and Alethea could be mended. Lil was certain of it.

"Al?"

Her friend sounded relieved to hear from her. "Lil, I'm glad you called. I figured you might be too busy today."

Lil smiled sadly. It broke her heart that two of the women she loved most in the world could not stand to be in the same room. "I'll always make time for you. Abby liked your present."

"I'm glad."

Lil didn't like the tone in her friend's voice. She knew it too well. "Your text was vague this morning. Is everything okay?"

"Lil, I have to tell you something but I don't want you to get upset."

Lil felt her blood pressure rise. "So say it fast."

"It's just a feeling I have."

Lil shook her head vehemently. "No, Al. Don't do this. You're already on everyone's shit list here. Jake and I are planning our wedding for early May and you promised me that you'd try to get along with Abby until then. She's going to be my matron of honor. How are you going to be one of my bridesmaids if the two of you aren't talking? I'm working on her. She's softening toward you. This is not the time for one of your conspiracy theories."

Alethea said more passionately, "They aren't theories. They are hunches based on the data I collect from a large number of sources. And I'm always right."

"Do you remember thinking Jake was a criminal and Abby was in danger?"

"I might have had details of the scenario wrong, but Jake was in trouble, as was Dominic. Do I get any credit for being part of the reason they still have a company?"

Lil checked around the room to make sure she was still alone. "You would, Al, if you toned it down a bit. Just lay low for a while. Let them get over what happened at Thanksgiving. Smile when you see them. You know, normal stuff."

In a tone that revealed she disagreed, Alethea said, "So, you want me to pretend that I don't know something even though it endangers the people I care about?"

Lil looked at the ceiling.

Shit. Shit. Shit.

Lil asked even though she didn't want to hear the answer, "How reliable is your information this time?"

Alethea continued, "I've heard it from several sources. I would handle it myself if I could, but I can't. I'm going to need your help."

Oh, my God, I can't believe I'm even considering this. I have Jake. I've made up with Abby. Everything is going so well. All I have to do is not mess it up.

Shit.

Lil shook her head, waved her phone at the sky in anger and then in resignation said, "You'd better be right, Al."

Ominously, Alethea answered, "No, I'd better be wrong..."

Can't wait to read the next book in the Legacy Collection?

Go to RuthCardello.com and add your email to the mailing list.

We'll send you an email as soon as
Breaching the Billionaire
is released!

Made in the USA
Middletown, DE
06 January 2023